Harder than Words

A Montgomery Ink Novel

CARRIE ANN RYAN

Dedication

To the Sprinting Skype Ladies. Thank you for being there when I needed you. Always.

Acknowledgments

With every book, my world of help expands yet the crew that I run to when I need them tightens. This book wasn't easy to write, but none of them are these days. Luc and Meghan took me to an emotional place I wasn't ready for, but I know it was needed. So here are a few people who have helped along the way.

Thank you Charity Hendry for keeping me sane when I ended up doing forty things and once and unable to remember what book I was writing, let alone how many bookmarks I needed for a table. And thank you Mr. Hendry for answering all my questions about being an electrician. Luc's job came from Charity wanting to see a version of her HEA in a book and you helped me so much. I think we were both nervous so I hope I did Luc justice for you!

Thank you Kennedy for dealing with my doom every day. No really, I think the mix of coffee, deadlines, and a new kitten have made our writing times a little more adventurous. Thank you for pushing me and keeping me on target, even when I'd rather be resting my wrists and finding a new book to read.

Thank you Dr Hubby for knowing that some weekends I'm locked away in my office. I'm trying to do better. I promise.

Thank you my Sprinting Skype Ladies, Kennedy Layne, Shayla Black, Lexi Blake, Julie Kenner, Carly Phillips, Jenna Jacob, Stacey Kennedy, and Angel Payne. Y'all push me every day even if sometimes we're not all on at the same time. I would never be able to work as hard as I do without you. You bring a motivation and a sense levity when the words get too hard and my characters only want to fight with me...and each other.

And again, thank you readers, for going on this journey with me. I am so blessed that you have embraced the Montgomery Ink series as much as you have. I hope you love Luc and Meghan's story.

Harder than Words

Meghan Montgomery-Warren thought she knew what love was when she'd married young and had two children. After years of being emotionally beaten down, her husband has finally left her and now she's forced to find her way once again. Somehow she needs to find the person she used to be and figure that the strength she'd thought she'd lost was always there.

Luc Dodd left Denver and his best friend Meghan when he was forced to watch her walk down the aisle with another man. He might have only been her best friend, but he held his true emotions close to the vest. Now he's back in town and in Meghan's life. Only he needs to decide if that's enough for him...and her.

Their journey from friends to lovers is a slow burn of seduction and pain. When Meghan's past comes back to haunt them both, the two of them will have to stand closer together or be torn apart by their own misgivings forever.

CHAPTER ONE

*N*ine Years Ago
If today didn't kill him, the thought of what would happen later that night would. Luc Dodd ran a hand over his face, wishing he'd been smart enough to down that shot of single malt whiskey the father of the bride had offered him a couple hours before. Instead, he'd waved it off, wanting a clear and collected head when the deed was done.

Not one of the most logical things Luc had ever done in his life.

For a normal person, watching his best friend get married would be one of the best days of his life. For Luc, not so much.

Today royally sucked.

He rolled his shoulders back, the ache down his spine clinging. He hadn't slept for shit the night before, but he'd expected nothing less. It wasn't as if he spent the evening with the groom making sure the guy was ready to be married or even helping with any of the setup. No, he wasn't friends with the man and, honestly, never planned on trying to be.

Not anymore.

The bride? He wanted to be there for her no matter what. He'd promised her he'd always be there and always help her follow the path she'd been destined for. Only he didn't know what that was anymore. It had forked in a new direction he wasn't sure he could follow with her.

It seemed he wasn't going to be able to live up to his promises.

Not that Meghan knew that presently.

No, that bomb would drop when she came back from her honeymoon.

Damn. Her fucking *honeymoon*.

His best friend was getting married to a man Luc didn't know much about, and what he did know he hated. As much as he tried to jump on board with the whole damn thing, he hadn't been able to.

Not when he loved Meghan with all his heart.

Fuck. He let out a breath and paced the hallway. He needed to get his head out of his ass and back squarely on his shoulders. He'd paste a smile on his face and fake it through the ceremony and the reception. Then he'd jump on his bike and head out because he wasn't sure he'd be able to make it if he had to see her day in and day out in her new life.

That didn't make him much of a friend. In fact, that made him a shitty one. He was pretty sure she'd never forgive him for leaving, but he also figured it would be for the best. He didn't want her to see the man he'd become once he was forced to watch her grow and intertwine her life with a man who wasn't him.

Jealousy wasn't becoming, but it was the only thing he had left.

That and the memories of what he'd had with her.

He'd take those, and he'd leave. She'd be better off without him and his moods.

It wasn't as if she didn't have seven siblings and countless cousins to rely on anyway. Luc wasn't family. He wasn't her fiancé. He wasn't good for her.

And as soon as she said her vows, he'd put the last nail in the coffin of what they once were and never see her again. His stomach rolled, and the lead weight grew heavier. That weight had been there since the moment Meghan showed him her shiny ring while crying happily in his arms. He didn't want to do this, didn't want to see the lace and silk with roses and baby's breath. He didn't want to watch her walk down the aisle with her hand tucked inside her father's elbow. He didn't want to stand on the sidelines at the reception while those who were actually part of the wedding gave toasts and celebrated the union of a man and a woman who couldn't be more different from one another.

Well, in that, he was wrong. He and Meghan were the ones so opposite even their friendship didn't make sense.

Meghan and Richard made more sense.

And if he kept telling himself that, then maybe one day he'd believe it.

He was only a guest at the wedding, not a groomsman or even an usher, though Meghan had done her best to try and get him to be a freaking bridesmaid. He grinned in spite of himself at the memory of her begging him to stand at her side. She'd promised him he wouldn't have to wear a dress and heels, though her sister, Maya, pointed out that his legs would look damn fine in heels. Maya scared the shit out of him sometimes, but he wasn't about to admit that out loud.

He did agree to stand as her man of honor because he couldn't help but say yes when Meghan blinked her big eyes up at him and smiled. He would walk with Meghan's sisters, Maya and Miranda, down the aisle and stand in a row up front, and make damn sure his best friend was happy.

Of course, the groom nixed the whole idea as soon as he could. Oh, he wasn't rude about it. Richard was smart when it came to Meghan's feelings, but he'd pressed ever so slightly about appearances and his family. Ironic that the bastard would be so concerned with clean lines and perfection considering the fact that most of Meghan's family members were tattooed and pierced. Luc could at least hide most of his ink under a shirt—not so for many of the other Montgomerys.

Meghan conceded defeat and didn't ask Luc to be on Richard's side since her groom had his roles already handed out.

So Luc would sit in a pew in the back of the church and nod along, and watch his best friend slip through his fingers.

He hated the fact that he couldn't be happy for her.

But most of all, he hated himself for loving a woman who would never love him.

In his early twenties, he should have been sowing his oats or some shit like Meghan's brothers and cousins had done, but he'd fallen in love with his best friend in high school and was too chickenshit to tell her.

It was his fault he was in this situation, so he would just have to deal with it.

Fuck.

Again.

"Luc? What the hell are you doing pacing the halls? Get in here. We need you."

His head snapped up at Maya's words, and he couldn't help smiling. Her black and hot pink hair was in some kind of complicated updo, but with the vibrant colors, it made her look just punk enough to still be Maya. Meghan had gone with a soft dove gray with a subtle pink outline for her wedding's color scheme, and the look on Maya worked for her. He was sure that the other Montgomery sister, Miranda, would look just as good. As soon as he thought of her, Miranda stuck her head out the door and smiled.

"Oh good, Luc. You're here. Meghan wants to see you." She opened the door a bit wider, and Luc shook his head.

"It's bad luck to see the bride before the wedding." And if he saw her so close, he wasn't sure he'd be able to leave when he had to—either then or later.

Maya raised her pierced brow at him, and he held back a curse. That damn woman could always see through his bullshit. Meghan usually could as well, although she'd been blissfully oblivious to his feelings for her.

"That's for the groom, silly," Miranda said, rolling her eyes. She was still a teenager, so he was surprised she didn't huff when she said it. There were so many freaking Montgomerys that they ran the gamut on ages.

Luc cleared his throat. "Damn. Who knew?"

"Everyone," Maya said dryly. "Now get your ass in here because Meghan wants to see you before the wedding. This way I don't have to go hunt you down."

"Tactful as ever, Maya," Miranda remarked sweetly, then reached out and gripped Luc's arm. "Come on." With surprising strength, she pulled him into the bridal suite and closed the door behind her.

And he found himself alone in the room with Meghan after the others had scurried away.

He couldn't find the words to scold Maya. Not when he'd just swallowed his tongue at the sight before him.

Holy Mother of God, she was captivating.

Breathtaking.

Gorgeous.

Fucking sexy as hell.

Every word that described the picture she made slammed into his brain then fluttered away, leaving him at a loss for words.

"Well?" she asked, her voice low and husky. Or maybe that was just his hearing because she was usually a little more crisp and to the point. "What do you think? I trust you to tell me if I look like a hag or something. You're my best friend."

The dress molded her body and flared out at her hips and knees slightly. The lace looked antique over a more golden white than a bright white. He wasn't a tattoo artist or good with colors, so he couldn't tell what the true difference was, but he knew it made her pale skin glisten in the light. She'd opted not to go sleeveless since her breasts were too big for that kind of dress. The lace-capped sleeves were so delicate he wasn't sure how they were holding up the dress, but he didn't care. The fact that she felt free to tell him that even now told him she thought of him only as her friend, but right then, he pushed that thought out of his head.

Her hair had been pulled back in soft curls that bunched at the base of her neck with flowers tucked here and there. She'd chosen delicate jewelry that paled in comparison to the brightness of her eyes and the width of her smile.

Damn it to hell, she was *happy*.

6

Happy to marry a guy he hated.

Happy to marry a guy who wasn't him.

He swallowed hard and smiled back. It wasn't her fault, he reminded himself. He'd never stepped up to the plate, and now he had to deal with the fact that he'd never have the woman he wanted.

This was *his* doing.

His shortcoming.

"Luc?" A hint of uncertainty layered her voice.

He shook his head and winced. He was totally botching this. "Meghan, you look utterly breathtaking." He spoke softly, his voice low, deep. "I don't think I've ever seen you look so beautiful." Her eyes brightened, and he grinned. "Well, maybe that one time when you were covered in mud, grass, and who knows what else after the mud run, but I'll let you take this one as the top runner. It *is* your wedding day, after all."

She let out a laugh then rolled her eyes. "Jerk. You had me worried for a moment. Come over here and help me make sure my lace is right in the back, okay? The girls left me, and I'm freaking nervous."

He didn't want to step closer to her because, if he did, he'd be able to touch her, scent her, and he'd never let her go. He wasn't sure he was strong enough to resist that.

He stepped closer anyway.

When he reached her, she tilted her head up at him, a single tear rolling down her cheek. His chest ached, and he reached up to brush it away with his thumb. The image of his dark skin against the creamy paleness of hers made his cock twitch and his heart thud, but he pushed that away.

"What's wrong, angel eyes?" He kept his hand on her cheek, his thumb running along the silk of her skin.

She licked her lips, and his eyes followed the motion. He swallowed hard, forcing himself not to move, not to breathe, not to think too hard.

"I'm getting married today," she whispered.

He tried to smile but knew he failed. "I got that from the dress and the fact that I'm wearing this monkey suit."

"I'm happy," she said softly, her gaze on his.

"Are you telling me that or yourself?" he asked before he could stop himself.

She tilted her head, her cheek pressing into his palm. "Both of us," she said firmly. "Thank you for being here, Luc. I know you couldn't be part of the wedding, but I'm grateful you're here."

"I wouldn't be anywhere else." With that, he leaned down and brushed his lips against hers. It was just a moment, nothing more than a whisper between friends. They'd done it countless times before during special circumstances, but he knew this would be the last.

Not only because he was leaving, but also because he couldn't stand by and watch her move on anymore.

From the look in Meghan's eyes when he pulled back, she knew it too.

She would soon be Mrs. Richard Warren. A wife. A partner.

Not his.

"I wish you all the best, Meghan Montgomery. I want you to be happy, loved, cherished, and the center of his universe. I love you, Meghan. You'll always be my angel eyes. No matter what."

She swallowed hard and gave him a searching look, her eyes glittering with tears. "I love you, too, Luc."

"Good luck today, Meghan. Good luck with everything." With that, he kissed her cheek then moved away.

He turned his back on her, unable to look at her any longer and not tell her everything in his heart. He was too late. Too fucking late.

He left the bridal suite just as Maya and Miranda stormed in, a blur of silk and lace.

"See you soon, Luc!" Miranda called as he made his way down the hallway.

He sucked in a breath and tried to calm his heart down. He could make it through the ceremony, make it through the reception...right?

He let out a breath and moved out of the way as a flower girl did tumbles down the hallway, a harried-looking mother following her. The woman gave Luc an apologetic look then ran after her daughter.

He heard the music starting up in the distance and felt the tension in the air rising. His stomach clenched, and he fisted his hands at his sides. He didn't think he had the strength to endure the sight of her promising herself to another man.

He was a coward. A useless, fucking coward who needed to find the man he would be without Meghan Montgomery by his side and in his life.

Knowing he was about to do something she would never forgive him for, he stepped outside the church. The sun beat down on his face as if casually judging him for breaking a promise and his soul.

He jumped on the back of his bike and slid his helmet on. Meghan was strong, so fucking strong; she'd be fine without him. She had Richard to lean on and a family that would never let her fall. If he stayed, he'd only regret who he'd become. Instead, he kick-started his bike and gunned it out of the parking lot.

Meghan Montgomery wasn't his anymore.

She never had been.

Present Day
There had to be a better way to deal with files and estimates other than wanting to burn them in a fire of glory and pain.

At least that's what Luc figured when he stopped himself from slamming his head against the desk. He knew for a fact that wasn't true. He'd been the journeyman electrician for Montgomery Inc. for over a year now, and he felt like all he did was paperwork. Estimates, bids and proposals were the bane of his existence. It didn't matter that he knew his shit inside and out. It still sucked. The family-owned business was the most efficient one he'd ever worked for, and their administrative assistant, Tabby, did most of the work with her scarily organized methods, but he felt the need to complain about it anyway.

When he'd come back to Denver after almost a decade away, he never thought Storm and Wes Montgomery would hire him on without even looking at his resume. Yeah, Luc had worked for them before and grew up learning the trade. He was over at the Montgomery house more than his own most weeks, but still… He'd left everyone without a word, and they welcomed him back with open arms.

Well, that wasn't strictly true. At the time, he'd told Harry Montgomery, the Montgomery siblings' father and owner of the company, he'd be leaving, but that was it. He swore Harry to strict secrecy, even though he knew it had hurt the older man to keep it from his daughter. But if Luc thought about it too hard, he'd recognize the fact that nothing got past Harry, and there was a reason the man let Luc go without a word.

But, again, Luc wasn't going to think about that.

It had been too fucking long, and he was no longer the lost boy who wanted the girl he could never have. He'd lived his life and seen the world to become the man he was today.

A man who wanted to scream at the numbers on the screen.

He'd rather be working with his hands than doing this number shit, but being an adult meant he had to be accountable and actually do his job.

Fun times.

"Are you still threatening to slam your head into the screen rather than actually finish up the work?" Wes, his boss and friend, said as he walked up to Luc's desk.

Wes, like the rest of the Montgomerys, had dark brown hair, strong features, and bright blue eyes. He wasn't as built as some of the others, not even his twin, Storm, but he was still pretty big. Luc had a couple inches on the man, but it didn't feel like that much when he was surrounded by the whole Montgomery crew.

"I hate doing this." Luc pushed his chair back so he could stretch his legs. "I have everything input and triple-checked, but I still have to freaking organize it and make sure I'm not fucking up. I hate working with estimates."

Wes shook his head. "Then don't. You did the part you needed to do. Let me or Tabby work on the other parts. I'd rather you get out to the project house and work on the system than sit here and let your eyes dry out because you're not blinking."

Luc ran a hand over his face then blinked a few times. Huh. He guessed his eyes *were* drying out. Who knew? "It's not your job to take care of my work, Wes."

"Actually, you're doing *our* work," Wes countered. "We're a team, and you did your part. I know you want to be able to handle everything, but the number parts aren't your job. You did most of the estimates already, and now you're just nitpicking. You've put in everything you can, so now, let's work on the projections and everything else that comes with them."

And this was why Luc didn't want to own his own business. Yeah, he could do it all if he had to. He'd even been forced to do it a couple times when he preferred working as an electrician and not on payroll. He'd rather fix the problems he could handle rather than make more for himself by worrying about those details that were out of his control.

"You're working too hard on things you can delegate. Let us help."

"But I should be able to do it all." Luc was annoyed with himself for some reason.

"You can, but you don't have to. That's the whole point of delegating."

"Funny words coming from your mouth, bro," Storm said as he came up from behind his twin.

They were fraternal twins, so they didn't look too much alike, other than clearly being siblings. Storm liked to dress down all the time; Wes dressed in slacks and pressed shirts while he was in the office and not on a project site.

"I delegate," Wes said. His friend was lying. But Luc wasn't one to talk then, so he didn't point it out.

"We all kind of suck at it," Decker said. Decker was Miranda Montgomery's husband and their lead contractor. "But still, stop doing everything and try to work less than sixty hours a week. It's okay to actually have a life."

Luc frowned. "I have a life outside Montgomery Inc."

"Do you?" Decker asked, and Luc just glared.

As much as he liked working with his friends, sometimes it sucked that they knew so much about him. Or at least were learning about the man he was now.

There was only one person who knew more about who he was.

"What are all of you gathered around for?"

And there she was.

Luc looked over at the front door of the building as Meghan Montgomery-Warren came in, her face freckled with dirt and her jeans caked with mud. As she was the Montgomery Inc. landscape architect, so the mud overlay wasn't an unusual occurrence. Still, every time he saw her, he got what felt like a kick to the solar plexus. After all these years, he figured he'd be over her by now, but nope. He still thought she was fucking gorgeous.

Her long chestnut hair fell over her shoulders in waves as she took it out of her ponytail. Her high cheekbones had become more prominent over the years as she'd grown out of her youth. Her bright blue eyes weren't as carefree anymore—the darkness of divorce and the pain of her life since he'd left taking hold—but damn, she was still beautiful. She'd lost weight when she was married and was just now starting to gain it back. But because she worked her ass off—more than any of the men around his desk, including himself—she was still too thin for his liking.

"We're just trying to convince Luc to not work so hard," Wes said as he grinned at his sister. "Though since you're here, we'll yell at you, too. Why the hell are you covered in mud?"

Luc held back a groan when Meghan narrowed her eyes at her brother. "Excuse me? I'm working for a living. It gets messy. I can't help it if you love your pressed linen to the point of obsession."

Luc snorted a laugh, as did the other guys, but Wes just grinned. "I look good, and you know it. Anyway, you were supposed to be back from your job site an hour ago. What happened?"

Meghan shrugged. "Had an issue with one of the burlap-wrapped trees. Little bastard didn't want to go in the hole."

"Probably should have used more lube," Storm said with a straight face, and Luc closed his eyes.

Nope. Not going there.

Meghan clucked her tongue, but when he opened his eyes again, she was smiling. "I walked right into that one. Anyway, I need to go pick up the kids and head to the parents'. You guys coming to dinner?"

"Yep," the three others said.

Meghan turned to Luc then and, for the first time that day, met his gaze. They'd seen and talked to one another often in the past year she'd been divorced and he'd been back. He even held her that one time she'd needed it. But they'd never be the friends they once were.

He'd broken that.

"What about you, Luc? You coming?"

He shook his head, regret in his heart. "I'm having dinner with my own folks tonight. But have fun."

She smiled then, the light in her eyes reminding him of a better time. "Have fun."

"Always," he said softly then cleared his throat. "Okay, then. If I don't need to work on this paperwork, I'm heading out."

He said his goodbyes and made his way out to his truck, determined not to stare too long at the woman who had once been the best, and most painful, part of his life.

He couldn't help but stare at her.

But he didn't love her. Not anymore. The man he used to be loved the woman she had been long ago. He didn't know this Meghan, and that was on purpose. The distance between them was calculated and necessary.

He'd left Denver and the life he'd created for the woman in front of him once before, and he wasn't about to do it again. Staying away and being the man he was now, and letting her find the woman she wanted to be, was the only way he could survive.

Even if it hurt like hell.

CHAPTER TWO

M eghan Montgomery-Warren wasn't going to freak out.
She wasn't.

Okay, so she might, but she'd bury it where she'd buried every other freakout over the past twelve months and ignore it. Because ignoring her problems and worries was better than having to deal with him.

She winced.

That might have been one of the most idiotic things she'd thought about in a good long while.

Good job, Meghan.

Her kids were getting out of school, and her babysitter was sick. Her last job had been a pain in the ass since the old man who owned the house hated anyone without a dick. Her ex had called but hadn't left a message, scaring the shit out of her. Her dad's new test results after his latest treatment would be released tonight. Her truck hadn't started on the first try that morning. And her stomach ached something fierce since she'd forgotten to eat lunch.

This was just a normal day in the grand scheme of things.

So she'd worry about the stresses of her daily life once she was home and behind the closed door of her bedroom. That way, she could deal with it all alone and not in front of her clients, family, or children.

That was much better than giving herself an ulcer.

The sun beat down on her skin, and she took off her baseball cap, fanning herself with the brim. It was freaking October in Colorado, and she was sweating outside from the lingering heat of summer. It should have at least been raining or maybe snowing. Though with Denver's weather, it might do that later in the day. Colorado was the shining example of needing to dress in layers. One minute it would be freezing, the next too warm, and after that, she'd be trying to cover her newly planted designs so they didn't get drenched in the downpour, and all in one day.

This time of year was usually the worst for her job until the winter came full-on, but she was almost done with her last big project for the year. Once she finished this for her last client, she'd be able to break for the winter and work on the planning and other stages for her clients. Mother Nature was the one in charge of her job, and she'd learned that the hard way years ago.

Marie Montgomery loved the land and had held this exact job as part of Montgomery Inc. when the company first opened. Meghan was an infant then. She'd grown up watching her mother work. Marie worked in the trenches and lifted more than she should have for her body weight to provide for her eight children. Meghan was now doing that and felt freaking exhausted—plus she had only two kids, not eight. Honestly, Meghan wasn't sure how her mother had done it. Sure, her mom had her dad, and the two of them were a powerhouse couple, but that still put the math in Meghan's favor.

17

She never did like math much.

Now she was rambling, and she had things to do other than think about how much harder her parents had it and the fact she was lacking.

Richard had told her that enough to last a lifetime.

Meghan pinched the bridge of her nose. Why the hell had she thought about her ex-husband? She wanted nothing to do with him or his goddamn emotional kinks, but apparently, he was going to haunt her beyond their marriage. He'd beat her down emotionally, told her she wasn't good enough, pulled her away from all her friends and family, and had somehow convinced her that it was all her fault in the first place.

"Everything okay, Meghan?"

She turned on her heel at the sound of Luc's voice and stumbled over her own feet. She reached out and tried to grab her truck's side mirror and missed.

Oh, hell.

She did her best to brace herself for the fall to the parking lot asphalt, but just when she figured she'd hit, strong arms wrapped around her waist. Luc's heart beat against her ear, and his muscled chest should have felt hard and unyielding against her cheek. Instead, it was warm and...inviting?

No. That couldn't be right.

She must be lacking oxygen from preparing to fall. Luc's hands moved down to her hips, and she placed her hands on his chest—was he always so built?

Okay, enough of this.

"Uh, thanks for saving me from making an ass out of myself," she said then blushed. "Okay, so I *still* made an ass out of myself, but at least I'm not bleeding."

Luc smiled down at her. "I'm used to women dropping at my feet. No worries."

Considering how hot he'd always been, and the fact that he was one gorgeous specimen of a man now, she figured he was probably not exaggerating in the slightest. His dark skin was flawless over hard muscles, and his face held strong features. His jaw was strong, and every once in a while, he let his beard grow out just enough that it left a nice shadow. He kept his midnight black hair cut close to his head, and sometimes he even shaved it. At least he did when he was younger. She hadn't seen him shave it in the year since he'd been back.

His honey-colored eyes bored into her, and she pushed at his chest so she could stand away from him. Easier to collect herself when she wasn't draped over the man like some weak-kneed southern belle.

"Well, thank you for catching me."

"Why did you swoon?" He smiled as he said it, so she knew he was teasing her, but she still narrowed her eyes.

"Swoon? I don't swoon. I tripped over my own feet, but I didn't swoon."

He held up his hands in mock surrender. "Whatever you say, angel eyes."

She froze for a moment at the nickname.

Angel eyes.

Hell, he hadn't called her that since before he left town without a word.

Since her wedding day.

She wasn't sure how she felt about him calling her that now. While they had been closer than close before, they weren't those people anymore. Life had changed them both, and if she was honest with herself, she wasn't sure she could ever forgive him for leaving her when he did.

She never blamed him for leaving her in the situation she'd put herself in with Richard and everything that came with that, but she couldn't get the idea out of her head that he'd walked away so easily.

Meghan cleared her throat and pushed those thoughts away. "Well, thank you anyway."

"You're welcome. Now what's wrong?"

She shook her head. "Nothing."

"You were focused on something before I walked up, so what is it?"

She raised a brow at him. "It's not work-related, so don't worry about it." She held back a wince at the snap in her words.

"Are we really only allowed to talk about work things, Meghan?" he asked, his voice soft.

She sucked on both lips and sighed. "I don't know, Luc. But right now, I need to go pick up my kids and then deal with a few invoices. I'm not in the mood to live in the past right now."

"You let me hold you when I came back, Meghan," he reminded her. "You let me be in your life and your kids' lives when Miranda and Decker were going through their shit. But since then, we haven't talked other than at work or in passing."

She was weak and broken when he came back, and she'd fallen into old patterns. Patterns she forced herself to take a clear look at so she'd be able to fix herself. She refused to be the woman she'd once been, but it was damn hard to remember to be strong every moment of every day.

You're nothing.

She pushed that memory away and raised her chin at Luc.

"I can't talk about this right now. I need to go. Thank you again for not letting me fall."

She turned away and climbed into her aging truck, praying it would turn over so she wouldn't have to embarrass herself again by asking for a jump.

"This isn't over, Meghan," Luc said from the side her truck, his voice firm, before she closed the door.

She didn't answer, not knowing what she would say if she did. She'd made so many mistakes before, and she vowed she wouldn't do it again. Her kids came before anything, and if she spent time wondering how she let the man who had once been her best friend back into her life after he abandoned her, she'd mess it all up. She refused to be that weak, refused to be that woman.

She wouldn't do that again.

Not when Cliff and Sasha needed her more than anything.

Thankfully, her truck started without a problem, and she left Luc standing in the parking lot. At one time, she might have wished to be able to go back and make sure the man she once knew was still inside the man he was today, but she couldn't do that. Not anymore.

She didn't want him to see the woman she'd become.

She'd once been strong, independent. She laughed and chose her own destiny. She'd married young—too young to know better and see the slithering snake lurking beneath the charming veneer waiting to strike.

Even after a year of being on her own with her children, she still wasn't sure who she was, and she hated that. All that mattered, however, were her children. They had a roof over their heads and food in their bellies. As long as they had that, she knew she wasn't failing completely as a single mother.

Although, if she thought about it too hard, she'd been a single mother for far longer than a year.

21

Richard had never liked their children. They hadn't been Warren enough for him. They'd been a means to an end, a way to fill up his quota of the perfect family life. All they needed then was a dog—one he hated—for his life to be complete. He hadn't liked the fur that came with the perfect family puppy, but Boomer was just as much a part of their family as anything.

Only Richard wasn't anymore.

And if she truly thought about that, she was happy.

She was.

She didn't love the man. Didn't want him in her life. Didn't like the person he'd molded her into.

He'd left on his own terms. She didn't have a say. She *never* had a say. She'd *never* spoken her mind.

She'd let him live her life.

And when he left, he'd convinced her she was the reason.

She'd failed him.

She'd failed *them*.

God, it hurt to think about that.

Why was she still allowing him to fill her thoughts? Why was she still thinking this way? She knew he wasn't good for her when she was married to him. But she thought that, as long as she didn't rock the boat, he wouldn't leave and she wouldn't fail in her marriage.

Her head ached, and she did her best to push those thoughts from her mind once more. She needed to be positive and happy now when she picked the children up at school.

By the time she made it through mid-afternoon traffic to the kids' elementary school, the bell had rung and kids were scattered around the building, either going to the busses or to the line of cars waiting for pickup.

She pulled up into the line and craned her neck to watch for her babies. At eight and four, both of her children were in all-day classes. Cliff was in classes full-time, and four-year-old Sasha was also in all-day classes. This cut down on childcare costs, and Meghan suspected Sasha was clever enough to have somehow figured this out.

When she spotted them walking toward her hand-in-hand under the teacher's aide's watchful eyes, she got out of her truck and opened the extended cab's doors so she could buckle her babies in. She used to have the mini-van and everything that came with being a stay-at-home mom, but when she was forced to go back to work, she traded it in for her used truck. Her brothers had offered to buy her a new one since it was for the company as well, but she declined. She was starting from the ground up with them, and at a lower wage, because she wanted—no, *needed*—to prove to herself and to them that she was worth the job they'd given her. She didn't want to go through life on the Montgomery name alone.

The fact that Montgomery was no longer her only last name made her even more determined to succeed on her own.

"Mommy! Mommy! I got a gold star on my color sheet! See? I colored in the lines and everything!"

Sasha spoke a mile a minute, and Meghan couldn't help but smile at her baby girl. Both her kids had the Montgomery looks, which bothered Richard to no end. He'd wanted little Richard replicas, not Montgomerys. Her babies had dark brown hair and vivid blue eyes with long lashes. Seriously, her children were freaking gorgeous, and she wasn't just saying that because she was their mother.

She kissed Sasha's cheek and picked her up to put her in her booster. "You did? I'm so proud of you, honey. We'll put your sheet right on the refrigerator when we get home so we can all see the gold star. Do you want to take it with you to Grandma and Grandpa's tonight when we go over there for dinner?"

Sasha clapped her hands together and smiled, sticking her tongue against her front tooth so it wiggled. Meghan did her best not to shudder. She'd never done well when Cliff lost his teeth, and now Sasha was about to lose hers, too. Meghan could deal with all forms of gross and normal things that came with having babies, but loose teeth wigged her out. She couldn't help it. It was just one of those things.

"Coloring is for babies," Cliff mumbled as he got into his booster.

"I'm not a baby. You are."

Meghan closed her eyes for a moment then made sure Cliff was buckled in tight. Someone honked behind her, and she held back a curse.

"Cliff, stop calling your sister a baby," she said sternly then closed the back cab door before jumping in the front seat and buckling herself in.

"But she *is* a baby," Cliff sneered.

Meghan pulled out of the pickup line and let out a breath. "That's one, Cliff. Don't do it again."

He muttered under his breath then folded his arms over his chest and stared out the window. Meghan wanted to scream or cry or do *something*. Her baby boy had never been this way before the divorce. He'd been sweet and loving, so polite and caring.

Then they'd been forced to move out of the home he'd lived in his entire life when Richard left them. Them. Not just her. She remembered that each time she thought of the look on Richard's face when he found her wanting and had packed up and left, leaving a last barb or two on the way out the door.

Now she and the children lived in a small home that she rented rather than owned as she saved every last cent so she could provide a better life for them. Richard paid child support, but it was never enough. And he was always just late enough with the payments that he wouldn't get in trouble, but it was a way to rub her face in the fact that she still relied on him.

Oh, she could have asked for money from any one of her siblings or her parents. They would bend over backward for her without asking for anything in return, but she couldn't do it. As long as her babies had a roof over their heads and food in their bellies, they would be fine. She would be the one to make sure they were healthy and safe because, if she had to rely on anyone else, she might end up the way she was right after Richard left. She'd been a shadow of herself, a broken women who stayed silent, broke down when she couldn't figure out what she needed to do, and felt useless. She promised herself she would never be that way again.

She wasn't that person anymore.

Of course, she didn't know who she was now, and that was part of the problem.

Sasha chattered animatedly in the backseat, and Meghan answered when she needed to, but in all honesty, her little girl just wanted her to listen and nod along. Meghan didn't mind because at least Sasha was still the same bright-eyed baby girl she was before. Cliff was the one who had changed, and she didn't know what she'd done wrong. She didn't know how to fix it. But she had to because she couldn't continue like this with her son acting out, and when he wasn't doing that, he wasn't speaking to her.

She knew it was, in part, because he hadn't seen his father in months. Meghan had full custody, but Richard had partial visitation on certain weekends and holidays. Only the man had canceled the last few times due to work or whatever petty excuse he could invent to get out of seeing his kids. He couldn't use them for his image at work, so he wouldn't use them at all.

It killed Meghan that he was an absentee dad, and she couldn't be both the father and the mother. There was only so much she could do, and she knew her father and brothers did their best to fill that void.

It would never be enough though, and she had a feeling Cliff knew it.

She also knew that Cliff blamed her for the divorce.

From his attitude, there could be no other explanation. And sometimes, when she wasn't thinking clearly, she catalogued her failures in her relationship with her ex-husband and what she could have done to be a better wife and woman.

If she hadn't been so cold in bed, he wouldn't have left her.

If she hadn't wanted to see her family so much, he wouldn't have left her.

If she hadn't put her foot down to keep Boomer, he wouldn't have left her.

If she hadn't burned the meals one too many times, he wouldn't have left her.

If she hadn't been Meghan Montgomery, he wouldn't have left her.

"Mommy? Are we going to Grandma and Grandpa's now?"

Meghan once again blinked away her thoughts of inadequacy and looked in the rearview mirror at Sasha.

"That's the plan. We're having dinner over there tonight, and then we'll go home afterward and put your work on the fridge. Sound good?"

"Yay!"

Sasha clapped again, and Meghan couldn't help but smile at her daughter's enthusiasm about something as mundane as going to dinner at the Montgomerys'. But as long as Sasha was happy, that was a win. She gave a quick glance in the mirror at Cliff who still looked out the window, a frown on his face. He wasn't pouting, but he wasn't happy, either. If she could just figure out how he ticked, she could help, and if she kept telling herself that, maybe she'd start to believe it.

She pulled up to her parents' place, the home she'd grown up in, and turned off her truck. Before she got out, she sat for a moment and took in the house and grounds. She loved it so freaking much. With so many siblings, she'd always had to share a room, but her mom and dad had done their best with additions to the home and good planning, so she'd never felt blocked in. Her father and brothers were contractors, so they knew how to make a house livable for so many people at once. Her mother knew how to make a house a home.

Meghan had been so lucky growing up the way she did. Her goal was to make sure Cliff and Sasha got the same things and were as well adjusted as the rest of the Montgomerys.

Considering the members of her family were all inked, pierced, and a tad crazy, that wasn't asking for much.

"Mommy? Are we going in?"

Meghan shook her head quickly at Sasha's words then jumped out of the truck. She wasn't that tall, only five foot seven, so she was always jumping in and out of her truck. By the time the kids were unlatched and had their feet firmly placed on the ground, her mother stood on the porch, a big smile on her face and her arms open wide. Sasha immediately ran to her grandmother and babbled as Marie covered her in kisses and snuggles. Cliff held back, quiet but still near enough that Meghan's mother could reach out and pull him close.

That was one thing Meghan loved about her parents. No matter what mood her kids were in, her parents always had the ability to make her kids feel loved and snuggled. In fact, Meghan could use a few snuggles herself at the moment, but first, she needed to get the bags out of the car and say hello.

It didn't escape her notice that her father hadn't met them at the front door. Since his cancer diagnosis over a year before, he'd been venturing out of his chair and comfort zone less and less. The chemo had been hard on him, and each time they thought he was headed into remission, he'd take a downward turn.

It scared the hell out of her that her tough-as-nails, bigger-than-life father was a shadow of himself, even with a smile on his face and a gleam in his eyes. She prayed the test results they got tonight or later this week would be better than what they had been.

Meghan couldn't lose her father.

Her children couldn't lose their grandfather.

Her mother couldn't lose her husband.

This world couldn't lose Harry Montgomery.

She shook off her melancholy and walked up to her mom, and kissed her on the cheek. "Hello, Mom."

"Hello, Meghan, darling. Head on in and drop off their stuff. I'm going to go make sure the cookies taste right. What do you say, kids, do you want to help?"

Meghan rolled her eyes. "Cookies before dinner? Really?"

Marie just grinned. "It's an after-school snack, and I'm the grandmother. I have to spoil. You know that." She patted Meghan's cheek with a slender, strong hand. "Only one cookie and carrot sticks on the side, baby girl. You know me better than that."

She did and shook her head anyway. "Have fun, and Sasha has something to show you."

Her mother smiled wide and hurried off to follow the kids into the kitchen. Meghan closed the door behind her and made her way into the living room, where she knew her dad would be.

He looked smaller than he had the previous week.

Or maybe that was just her imagination. His eyes were closed, and she was afraid she'd wake him, but he smiled as she walked in.

"The kids just said hello."

"Hi, Daddy," she whispered then kissed his temple. She straightened the blanket on his lap and sat down on the love seat beside his chair.

"You never call me Daddy. What's wrong, honey?"

She shook her head then leaned over so her head rested on his chair. "Nothing." *Everything.* "I'm just glad I'm here. With you. I could use you and Mom." More than she wanted to admit.

Her dad reached out and clasped her hand. "We're here for you, Meghan. No matter what."

She blinked back tears and prayed he was right. There was only so much she could bear, and if she lost her father on top of it all, she'd break.

She was Meghan Montgomery-Warren. Mother. Daughter. Ex-Wife. Woman.

CHAPTER THREE

"You've been back for a year, but I haven't heard you speak about a woman. Is there something wrong with you? Are you hiding someone? Tell me everything."

Luc gave his sister Tessa a dry look then took a sip of his only beer for the evening.

Dinners at his parents' home were a weekly event. Getting grilled from his eldest sister Tessa was one as well. The former was something he'd actually missed when he was living outside of Denver and hadn't had the chance to visit as much as he would've liked. The latter, not so much.

Not that he'd ever tell Tessa that, considering the fact that she'd never leave him alone if he did.

Not that she left him alone much anyway.

He ran a hand over his face but didn't answer her. He knew he should probably give in and let her win since she'd pester him until she got every ounce of information out of him, but he wasn't in the mood. It wasn't as though he had a woman anyway.

He'd had a few relationships, some even slightly serious over the past few years on the road, but he'd never introduced them to his family. In fact, the last woman he'd brought home was Meghan, but that didn't count, as he and she had never dated.

Fuck, he sounded like some lovesick loser with his mind in the past rather than on the future he could have now. He'd had the whole world in front of him, walked its roads and followed its paths, only to come back home again.

"Come on, Luc, what are you keeping so secret? We're family. You're supposed to tell us everything. And by everything, I do mean *everything*."

"For the love of God, Tessa, leave your brother alone." Maggie Dodd, his mother and now savior, walked into the living room. His mother might have been edging on the other side of sixty, but he thought she could pass for forty, easy. Her cocoa skin had a dusting of lines that came from smiling and raising four children. She was still as strong as she'd been the day he was born, maybe even stronger.

As the youngest of four and the only boy, he knew he'd been a little spoiled, but Maggie never let it get out of control. She and his father, Marcus, had raised him and his sisters with an iron fist and warm hugs.

For that reason, they reminded him of the Montgomerys. In fact, he'd grown up thinking of his family as a smaller version of the other crew. His mother had commented more than once on the strength of Marie Montgomery for raising eight, rather than four. Luc wasn't sure how either woman had done it, but he counted himself lucky to have been raised with the people he called family—Dodd and Montgomery.

Well, maybe not lucky every day since he still had to deal with his eldest sister, Tessa. The woman was only a few years older than he and sometimes tried to hold the maternal edge where he'd never felt it necessary.

"Why should I leave him alone?" Tessa snapped. "He was gone for years because of *that woman,* and now he's back and still alone." She faced Luc and narrowed her eyes. "She might be divorced, but she didn't want you then, and she's not going to want you now."

He took a deep breath, ignoring the voice in his head telling him that Tessa was right. He didn't want Meghan, not like he once had, so it didn't work. However, his sister needed to get a fucking clue.

"I love you like a sister, Tessa."

"I *am* your sister."

"And because of that, I'm not going to beat your ass for talking the way you do about my friend." He held up his hand when she opened her mouth to speak. "No. I don't want to hear it. Mom would be sad if I bruised you because you're acting like a bitch."

"You've never raised your hand toward any of your sisters, boy, so don't start thinking you will now," Maggie said from behind him, but he heard the smile in her voice.

That much was true. No matter how much his three older sisters smothered him, annoyed him, and hurt him when they hadn't thought better of it, he'd never fought back. There were other ways to get even with sisters. He wasn't too old to put a frog in Tessa's bed.

Later. When she wasn't expecting it.

He held back a smile at the thought of her scream.

Oh, yes, he would have fun with that. For now, though, Tessa needed to get her act together

"Leave Meghan alone, Tessa," he said, his voice deep and calmer than he'd thought possible. "I don't know what your problem is with her, but I work with her family, and I'm still friends with the lot of them. I know you think it was her fault that I left Denver, but you know what? I'm back. Yeah, I left, but it wasn't like I lost touch with all of you. Not all families live in the same city all their lives. I'm allowed to travel and see other parts of the world."

Denver would always be home though, not that he'd mention that fact in front of Tessa. He was trying to make a point, after all.

Tessa crossed her arms in front of her chest. "I don't like her, Luc. And I probably never will. She strung you along for years and always thought she was better than you."

"Now you're just fucking lying, Tessa."

"Stop it. Both of you." Maggie pulled Luc back and shook her head. "I'm not going to listen to this fight again. Luc is back. Meghan is a mother of two, working her ass off. I will never blame her for my son leaving, Tessa. He was an adult. You need to get over it. My baby is back again."

Tessa shook her head and walked out of the room. Luc sighed and leaned against his mother but didn't put his full weight on her.

"I don't know where I went wrong with that one," Maggie whispered. "Not that I don't love her dearly, but sometimes that girl thinks that the sun doesn't shine bright enough on sunny days."

"That's just Tessa, Mom. I'm not too worried."

Tessa might annoy the hell out of him sometimes, and she held grudges for far longer than she needed to, but she was also his sister. She fought for him and wanted him to have the best in life. He couldn't fault her for her wishes, only the way she went about getting them sometimes.

Maggie reached up and patted his cheek. "That's my baby. Now come help me set the table and call your father for dinner. I want to hear all about how working with Montgomery Inc. is going." Her eyes filled, and he wanted to curse. "I'm so happy you're back, baby boy. So happy."

His heart ached, but he buried the pain. He knew he'd hurt his family by leaving, but he hadn't had a choice. It would have been harder to stay and watch the one person who could cause him pain like he'd been sliced by a blade be happy with someone else. He'd needed to find out who he was without Meghan Montgomery by his side.

He'd done that and more, but she'd always hold a special place in his heart.

Only it wasn't where she'd been before, and he was okay with that. Finally.

Luc shook away those thoughts and did as his mother asked. The past was the past, and there was no point trying to relive it.

His other sisters, Jillian and Christina, sat with their father in the dining room, rolling their eyes at one of his stories. Marcus Dodd was a big man, even bigger than Luc, and that was saying something. His father had gone gray at the temples but still had a full head of dark hair that matched Luc's. In fact, Marcus was just an older copy of Luc.

Considering his father had aged well, Luc didn't have a problem with that. The glimpse of his future was pretty fucking good.

Luc might not have had everything he'd wanted when he was younger, but he wasn't left wanting. He had a family, a job he loved, and was finally home after having been away too long.

Things were good.

And if he kept telling himself that, one day he might believe it.

The next morning, he dragged himself out of bed, his alarm clock sounding like it was one of Satan's bells. It wasn't that he wasn't a morning person. It was more because whoever had invented early rising needed to be shot and quartered. Naked and with only one eye open, he shuffled toward the coffee pot. He pressed the button and sniffed as the sweet elixir filled the cup he'd left underneath the funnel the night before. He knew himself well enough that he couldn't be counted on to find the cup without coffee in his system first. He'd brewed enough coffee on his counter rather than in a cup to learn that lesson the hard way.

As soon as the coffee finished brewing, he grabbed hold of the mug for dear life and shuffled to the bathroom. The first cup would help him jump in the shower, and the second would help him get ready for the drive to work.

By the time he was drinking cup three from his travel mug on the road to the office, he would be ready to face other people.

Luc was the journeyman electrician for Montgomery Inc. Montgomery Inc. was larger than it had been a decade ago, but it was still relatively small, which led to a more hands-on experience for Storm and Wes, who ran the company. Storm was the lead architect, meaning, with every rehab or new project that started from the ground up, the man had his hands in every slice of the pie. It was his vision that the rest of the crew made into reality. Wes was the numbers man as well as the one who organized their lives with permits and schedules, and was the very heartbeat of the company.

Decker, the man who had grown up with the Montgomerys and was now engaged to Wes and

Storm's younger sister, Miranda, was the lead contractor and site manager. His job was to take what Wes and Storm came up with and make it into a home or an inn or whatever their project was for the month. The three of them worked so cohesively that there had been a scare when Decker almost quit when things got rocky with Miranda in the early stages of their relationship.

Each of them picked up tool belts and built their dreams with their bare hands. And he counted his blessings that they'd taken him into that work family. He brought the rehabs up to code and started the new places with Decker, hand-in-hand. Each house or building took months of planning and then more months of work, but when the job was complete, it was worth the grueling hours and back pain. His job was to ensure that whoever lived in that building could live a safe life by just flipping a light switch. Having something esthetically pleasing as well as functional was just part of the job. He couldn't count the number of times he had to switch out wires or boxes because the previous electrician had been a fucking idiot when it came to practicalities like putting the light switch in an easily accessible place.

He pulled up to the building, shut off his truck, and pounded back the last of his coffee. His mother would probably freak out over the amount of caffeine he drank throughout the day, but what his mother didn't know...

Well, actually, she probably *did* know. She seemed to know everything.

Scary thought.

He grabbed his things and headed into the office, his stomach growling. He probably should have eaten something, considering the aforementioned coffee, but his mind had been on other things. Plus, since

Wes had called a meeting at the office, rather than the project site, that meant doughnuts would be available. Between Wes and the Montgomery Inc. administrative assistant, Tabby, there would be warm, delicious sugary goodness waiting for him. Those two knew how to throw a meeting.

He licked his lips as soon as he walked in, his nose twitching at the scent of fried dough and sugar. He lifted his chin at Storm, who stood by the box of glorious sugar-loaded pastries, then picked out a jelly-filled, anticipating that first bite. Sweetness with a slight hint of grease hit his tongue, and he held back a moan.

"That good, huh?" Decker asked as he made his way toward them.

Apparently, he hadn't held back that moan after all. Whatever, he was starving. He finished off his jelly-filled in one more bite then picked up a Boston cream as he made his way to his desk. He hadn't even set his shit down, and he'd already inhaled a donut. It was *that* good.

"These Hailey's?" Luc asked as he wiped his mouth off with a napkin.

He probably looked like a heathen—hence why he hadn't gone for a powdered-sugar-covered one. Storm, as it was, had a nice mustache and a chin full of powdered sugar—not that the man cared in the slightest.

Hailey owned a café called Taboo that sat next to the other Montgomery business, Montgomery Ink—a tattoo shop run by Austin and Maya. They even had a door that opened between the two, so Austin, Maya, and the others didn't have to go outside for the best sandwiches and coffee Luc had ever had.

"Yes," Tabby said as she shook her head, wiping up after them. She wore a nice dress that went to her knees and shoes so sky-high he wondered how she could walk in them. "And you are all pigs. Next time I'm bringing fruit instead of Hailey's doughnuts. She was nice enough to pack a fresh box for me when I stopped by this morning, but next time, hear me, *fruit*."

"I saw you chow down on *two* doughnuts before the others even arrived," Wes said, a smile on his face. "Don't lie."

Twin spots of pink danced on her cheeks, but she raised her chin and narrowed her eyes. "Yes, but I cleaned up after myself."

Luc had the grace to look ashamed but waved a napkin in the air. "I'm cleaning up. Plus, you didn't give us any time to do it ourselves. You wipe as we eat. We can't keep up with that."

"Try," she said sweetly, then picked up a folder and went back to her desk.

Decker grinned and bit into his second cruller. "Eat up, because we're going to work our asses off today. We need the extra carbs."

Luc nodded then went for a third. He'd been ordered to, after all. "I need to work on the specs for the entryway," he said as he sat down. "The last guy left a few kinks that I don't like."

Wes nodded, taking notes like he always did. "Whoever did the original rehab was a fucking idiot. We're cleaning up their messes as well as the wear and tear of a sixty-year-old building that no one bothered to maintain."

"We'll get it done," Luc said. "But it'll be a bitch of a job for a while. I'm having to rewire the whole place *after* I fix the shoddy job the other guy tried to pass off as legal."

Decker cursed under his breath. "Whoever owned it before was lucky the place didn't go up in flames as soon as they stepped foot inside. Luc's job is just the tip of the iceberg on this place. I have to work on shit that should have been done in the last phase. Thank God the foundation is set, or we'd be fucked."

Storm raised a brow. "We're making it better than it was before, and yeah, we wouldn't have bought the place if everything *and* the foundation was a piece of shit. At that point, you raze the building."

"You wouldn't do that," Wes said after he took a bite of his cinnamon twist. "You like the curves of the building too much."

"True," Storm said with a shrug.

Luc sipped the bottle of water—he'd have cold caffeine a bit later—Tabby put in front of him and listened to the others give their updates for their projects. They usually had one large project going on simultaneously with three or four smaller ones to fill in the spaces. Luc wasn't needed at the same time as Decker every day and vice versa. Tabby and Wes kept them on schedule to make sure they didn't have much downtime and didn't run over one another when they needed the space.

Montgomery Inc. was a well-oiled machine, and Luc was damn proud to be part of it.

"Sorry I'm late. Had issues with the truck today."

His body tightened at the sound of Meghan's voice, and he forced himself not to stand when she walked in. Ages-old chivalry had no place there.

"Fuck it, Meghan. We're buying you a new truck. This can't go on." Wes stood up, pulling out his phone, but Meghan snatched it out of his hands.

"Stop it. I don't need a handout. You know that." She tossed the phone to Tabby, who raised a brow. Her ponytail swayed as she shook her head. "It's at the shop now and should be fixed this afternoon. I'm not taking a truck from you because you feel sorry for me."

"That's not it at all, Meghan," Storm said softly.

"I'm not yours to take care of."

Then whose are you?

Luc pushed that thought away. "What about the things you need for the job?"

She shot him a glare, but he didn't back down. She was too stubborn to ask for help, too set in her ways. With all the Montgomerys around, he would have thought she'd have gotten over that, but she hadn't. Instead, she'd become more stubborn. As long as her kids were taken care of, she didn't ask for help.

Ever.

"I'm fine."

"You and Luc are on the same site today," Wes said, his voice a whip. "He'll help you load your shit in the back of his truck. It's not like you can carry everything yourself."

Meghan's jaw tightened, but she gave Luc a small nod. "Fine. I was going to ask him for help anyway."

He saw the lie for what it was. She'd gnaw her arm off rather than reach out to him, but it wasn't as though she had a choice today. She had a job to do, and if she wasn't going to take the truck from Wes and Storm, she'd have to deal with his presence.

Let the fun begin.

They ended the meeting, and he led the way to his truck. They loaded the truck quickly and in silence. When he opened the passenger side door for her, she stared at him, her arms folded over her chest.

"What? I'm not allowed to open the door for you? Fuck it, Meghan. I'm just trying to be nice." He slammed the door in front of her and stomped his way to the driver's side.

He jumped in, and she did the same.

"You know what? I'm tired of this. I told you before, but I'm telling you again. I'm a Dodd, Meghan. You know my mother taught me to open doors for women. She also taught me to help those who were carrying too much. If Wes or Storm needed me, I'd jump right in. You know that. But as soon as you need help from me, you jump down my throat and look at me like I said you that you couldn't handle it on your own. Well, fuck that."

He gripped the steering wheel and cursed himself. He hadn't meant to blow up like that, and frankly, she hadn't done a thing to deserve it. But with Tessa nagging at him the night before and the fact that he couldn't help Meghan, even if he wanted to, he was frayed at the edges.

"You're right. I'm sorry. I was just pissed off since my truck needed to go in the shop, and once I got the kids off at school, I had to take the bus to work. I hate it when my brothers look at me like they do, and I took it out on you with just a look. I'm sorry."

Now he felt like even more of an ass. "Let's call it even because you didn't deserve my words." He started the truck and pulled out of the parking lot. "But you might have just pissed me off more by saying you took the bus. You have forty siblings, and yet you didn't call one of them."

You didn't call me.

"I can handle it, Luc."

He just sighed and made their way to the garden center to pick up the things she needed for her site. He'd be running late, but it didn't matter. They'd get what they needed to do done and call it a day when the time came. Meghan might be stubborn, but it hadn't come out of nowhere.

Once they reached the site, they went off in different directions, focusing on their own jobs, rather

41

than each other. That was fine with Luc because he couldn't figure out what the fuck he was doing with the woman in the first place. Blowing up like that had done nothing but prove to himself, and her, that there was a reason they weren't as friendly as they had been.

He buried himself in work, and before he knew it, he heard the sound of children laughing and Meghan's low voice. Curious, he put down his tools and headed outside. Meghan's parents or her babysitter usually took the kids home after school, not to the job site. In fact, he wasn't sure he'd ever seen Cliff and Sasha here. Not that he minded since he loved those kids, but he hoped everything was okay.

"Uncle Luc!" Sasha screamed before launching herself at him.

He grinned, holding out his arms and catching her with ease—not that he had a lot of practice with her, but he was learning.

"Hey, baby girl. What are you doing here? Come to help me with wires?"

"Luc," Meghan said under her breath without even looking at him.

Instead, her attention was focused on a younger woman who looked close to tears. This must be the babysitter, and he had a feeling something was wrong.

"I wanna play with wires too," Cliff said, pulling at Luc's pants.

He winced then put Sasha down. He crouched so he was at their eye level. "No wires today. Maybe you can help your uncles with something later. How was school? Did you learn everything there is to know?"

Sasha nodded, her smile bright. "Of course. I wanna be as smart as Mommy."

Luc smiled full-out. "Your mommy is one smart lady."

"The smartest," Sasha agreed.

Luc faced Cliff and held back a frown. The little boy didn't smile. Instead, he gave Luc a serious look. "What's wrong, Cliff?"

"Nothing."

Clearly a lie, but it wasn't like Luc could pry it out of him.

"Cliff got an A!" Sasha squealed and did a little dance.

Luc couldn't help but smile at the little girl's attitude. "An A? Good job, Cliff."

The little boy shrugged. "Whatever."

"Did I hear you got an A?" Meghan asked. "I'm so proud of you."

Luc looked up to see Meghan alone, the babysitter long gone. He gave Meghan a look, but she shook her head.

"We get to do dinner out, right?" Sasha asked. "He got an A, so we celebrate."

Meghan opened her mouth, a smile on her face, then stopped before she took a breath. "Um, not tonight, honey."

Fuck. That was right. She didn't have a car. No worries. "I'll take you," he blurted out before he could think better of it.

Meghan blinked at him and shook her head before he could explain. "It's okay, Luc. As soon as the truck is working, we can head to dinner as a group. It just can't be tonight."

"Of course it can't be tonight," Cliff muttered. He sighed, and turned away. "It's okay. It was just a stupid test anyway."

Meghan reached out to touch her son's hair, but he shrugged her off. The look on her face made Luc want to pull her close, but he held back once again.

"We can do dinner tonight, Meghan. I want to celebrate, too. I can drive."

"We need boosters," Sasha said solemnly.

"Amanda left them here," Meghan said, then turned her wide eyes to his, as if she hadn't meant to say that. "I was going to beg for a ride home, but..."

"Let me take you all out to dinner," Luc said, on board with this crazy idea. "We'll celebrate good grades and your momma's fantastic day at work."

"Luc..."

"I won't take no for an answer." He dug his keys out of his pocket. "Go set up the boosters, and I'll go tell Decker what's going on."

"We both can't take the rest of the day off," Meghan put in.

"Yeah, we can. We'd only be missing an hour anyway. I'll make it up later, and God knows you will, too. Go on, Meghan. I've got this."

She gave him a look he couldn't decipher, but pulled the kids with her to his truck anyway. He had no idea what the fuck he was doing going along with this or, fuck, coming up with the idea in the first place, but he wasn't going to back out now.

Cliff and Sasha deserved something to celebrate, and Meghan deserved so much more.

If Luc could give her that much...well... then he'd do his damnedest to make it happen.

He just prayed he wasn't making another mistake when it came to Meghan Montgomery. He was already a master at that.

CHAPTER FOUR

Once again, Meghan ran her hands over her jeans and wondered how the hell she'd put herself in this situation. One minute she was working on planters, and the next, she was standing in front of a restaurant with Luc and her kids.

Seriously, she had no idea how it had happened.

He hadn't even let her go home and change, so she was still in her work clothes—as he was for that matter. It was as if he knew she'd find a way out of going if he dropped her off at the house even for a moment.

The damn man knew her too well.

No, scratch that, the man had *known* her too well.

He didn't know this Meghan.

And if she was honest with herself, she didn't know this Meghan either.

She shook her head, trying to clear her mind of philosophical issues that came from a lack of sleep. No good came from overthinking, as her father had always told her. Too bad she was the queen of overthinking these days. Jumping headfirst into situations was how she'd ended up married to

Richard, and she'd be damned if she'd do something like that again. So she lived her life according to lists and did her best to keep her children happy.

Going out to dinner with Luc to celebrate her son's good grade was not in that plan. It wasn't even a side note on a list where she could mark it off. This was out of the blue and so freaking confusing.

"If you don't stop clenching your jaw, you're going to break a tooth."

She froze at the feeling of Luc's warm breath on her ear and neck as he leaned closer to whisper in her ear. Damn man. What the heck did he think he was doing? They usually kept space between them.

Boundaries made for happy people.

"I'm not clenching my jaw," she retorted through clenched teeth.

She forced herself to relax, refusing to turn toward him. While he might have been the gentleman and her kids *might* have been acting reasonably calm, she was a freaking mess. She didn't like the fact that she'd been maneuvered into this, didn't like that her choices had been taken from her. It was stupid to even think that, since he was only doing a nice thing, one she would have done without him anyway, but still, it grated.

And the fact that it did made her feel like a first-class bitch.

Hence the clenching.

Luc snorted but pulled away and held up four fingers for the hostess. The younger woman gave Luc a speculative look then checked out Meghan and her kids. Once again, Meghan's jaw clenched, but this time it wasn't for Luc somehow convincing her to come out with him tonight. Whether the girl was judging that they were wearing older jeans and tops, that her kids looked nothing like Luc, or that she and

Luc were standing so close together in the first place, Meghan didn't know. In any case, it pissed her off.

"Ignore her," he whispered then kissed her temple. They both froze.

He used to kiss her temples all the time when they were younger. It had been a normal thing between friends where he'd calm her down. It had been *years* since she'd felt his lips against her skin, however, and now she didn't know what to do.

Luc seemed to be at a loss for words himself and moved awkwardly back to where he'd been standing. She didn't know what words might have followed after telling her to ignore the hostess, and frankly, she was glad he'd stopped talking. She needed a moment to compose herself.

For freak's sake, this was *Luc*. What the hell was wrong with her?

Cliff stood stiffly by her side; her baby boy was still not speaking to her. She had no idea what she'd done this time, but she wished she could figure it out. This was a celebration for him, yet he looked as solemn as usual. He used to laugh and smile so often before that she never imagined he'd go from a happy baby to this. He wasn't even a tween or a teenager yet, and his mood had changed dramatically. If there was something she could do to fix it, she would, but right then, she could only wrap her arm around his stiff shoulders and lead him to the table as they followed the hostess. At least he didn't pull away from her.

Sasha, on the other hand, had no problem blending right in. She chattered a mile a minute about her day, her tiny hand tucked safely in Luc's much larger one. She practically skipped her way toward the table, and Luc, being the good sport he was, kept her from knocking into other tables. He had his head bent, his attention on her words as well as the direction they moved.

The four of them looked as if they were a...family.

She swallowed hard, pushing that thought firmly out of her mind.

She had her family. Her, Sasha, and Cliff.

Luc was an old friend. Nothing more. She wasn't sure she could deal with more than what they had now. She'd messed up with Richard; she couldn't do it again.

Just because Luc was spending time with her babies didn't mean anything in the grand scheme of things. It would do well for her to remember that.

They sat down, Sasha pulling Luc in on her side of the booth, forcing Cliff to sit with Meghan. The fact that she'd even thought of it as force just then made a small part of her heart ache. However, she would push through the dinner just like she'd pushed through so much more.

"Can I have grilled cheese, Mommy?" Sasha asked, bouncing in her seat. Where her baby girl got her energy, Meghan would never know. "With the bacon?" She turned her bright smile at Luc. "I *love* bacon. Mommy won't let me eat it every day though. She makes me eat *oatmeal*." She scrunched up her nose, and Luc snorted, his eyes twinkling when he looked at Meghan.

Meghan closed her eyes for a brief moment. "You like oatmeal, honey. We put fruit in it."

Sasha nodded, her face serious. "But it's not bacon. Bacon is the masterpiece of breakfast."

Meghan couldn't help it. She threw her head back and laughed, the sound of Luc's deep-timbre laugh joining hers, making her warm from the inside out.

"Where did you learn that, Sasha?"

Sasha grinned, sticking her tongue against her loose tooth to wiggle it around. "Uncle Griffin. He says he's writing his masterpiece. That means the best ever."

Meghan laughed again. Her mystery and thriller writer brother did say that often, though most of her family knew he was joking. Or at least she hoped he was.

"You can get grilled cheese," Meghan said finally. "With bacon," she added with a wink. "Cliff, honey, do you want the beef sliders? I know you love those."

"Okay," he said softly.

She met Luc's curious eyes across the table and slightly shook her head at the questions she saw. It wasn't as though she had the answers.

The waitress came and took their drink orders as well as an order from Luc for nachos. Her stomach grumbled at the thought of melted cheese, and he grinned at her.

"Hungry?"

She felt her cheeks heat, but she shrugged. "Apparently," she said dryly. "Nachos are a weakness of mine."

"I know," he said simply, and Meghan had to pull her gaze from his.

After the waitress came back and took their dinner orders, Sasha began her point-by-point discussion of her school day. Her daughter did this nightly, but Meghan wasn't too sure Luc would want to hear it.

"Sasha, baby, why don't you wait to tell me about your day until we get home? Let's talk about something else with Luc."

Sasha lowered her brows, looking so much like her that it forced her to hold back a laugh. "But why? He's *Luc*. I want him to know about my day."

"I don't mind, Meghan," Luc said, his voice low, a little dangerous.

Dangerous? What the hell was going on with her brain tonight?

"See, Mommy?" Sasha said then began her story from the start.

Poor Luc.

She leaned closer to her son and lowered her voice. "Enjoying your coloring, Cliff?"

"I guess."

"Did you have a good day today?"

"Sure."

She took a deep breath and pulled away. Digging information out of her son in the middle of the restaurant was not going to happen today. Maybe when they got home, he'd be more open.

And maybe she'd find the cure for not enough hours in a day.

The waitress set down their nachos and Cliff finally sat straighter. He had her love of melted cheese as well.

"This looks great, Luc," she said.

He met her gaze and smiled. Damn, he had a nice smile. She missed it. "It does. Now should I have ordered extra sour cream, or will you be sharing this time?"

She snorted, her face heating once more. "You might need to order more," she mumbled, and Luc threw his head back and laughed.

"Good to know some things never change."

She met his gaze, an odd feeling going down her spine. "Some things do," she whispered then shook her head.

Her children were sitting right next to them, and here she was, her mind in the past and her body doing odd things in reaction to Luc's presence. She must just be overtired or something.

"Where did you live before?" Sasha asked, her gaze on Luc's.

From the way her eyes fluttered and her cheeks pinked, Meghan had a feeling her baby girl was falling in love.

Not good.

Luc was one damn nice-looking man, but it was the warmth in his smile, his easygoing nature she held dear that she figured Sasha loved. Meghan would have to do her best to ensure her daughter's heart didn't break once again if another man in their lives let them down. The scars that burned across her own soul had made her callous, but she refused to allow her daughter to go through anything like that again.

Resolute, she lifted her chin, her mind on her daughter and not the man who sat in front of her.

"I've lived all over," Luc said then took a bite of his nachos.

Meghan watched the way his tongue flipped over his lower lip as he caught a bit of salsa, and she blinked. She had no right to watch him that way. She must be hungrier than she thought.

Hungry for a man.

Not food.

Nope. Not going there.

"Where?" Sasha asked, munching on a chip.

Luc grinned then leaned back into the booth, putting one arm behind Sasha's head. "Well, I lived in Oregon for a bit, then Chicago, then I moved out East to outside New York City." He met Meghan's eyes for a second then turned back to Sasha. "I've lived everywhere, it seems."

"Why did you keep moving?" Sasha asked. "Why didn't you stay home?"

Meghan frowned. She would've loved to know the answer to that as well, but from the way Luc's face shut down ever so slightly, she had a feeling she wouldn't be finding out the true reason tonight.

"I'm home now," he said simply then bit into another chip.

Sasha, as young as she was, seemed to take that answer as truth because she proceeded to ask about puppies and if he had any.

"I don't," Luc said. "Not yet, anyway."

"We have Boomer," Sasha said with a smile. "You met him when you came over before."

Meghan deliberately refused to think of *why* he had come over that first time, even if it had been to a different house and her children weren't there. He'd picked her up from the floor of desperation, and she'd leaned on him.

She shouldn't have leaned on him.

She'd broken down at the sight of him and fell into his arms as if they hadn't been apart for years. He'd held her as she wept and wiped away her tears before he walked out of her home once more.

"I know Boomer," Luc said quietly.

"Boomer's at home now, but when we get home, I get to feed him." She paused. "Or Cliff. We take turns. When you get puppies, they can be best friends with Boomer. He will protect you. He's a good dog."

Protect you? Where had Sasha gotten that idea? Just one more thing to add to her Mommy Worry list. The damn thing got bigger and bigger every time she looked, but she couldn't help it.

She was a mom.

"Boomer sounds like a good dog," Luc said, his voice low, patient. "You're lucky to have him."

"I know." Sasha smiled sweetly up at him. "You can share him with us until you get a puppy of your own. That way you're not alone."

Meghan winced. "Honey, Luc isn't alone." For all she knew, he had a girlfriend, or something even more serious, with a dog of her own. Plus, he had his whole family, and everyone had to be glad he was back in town for good.

Luc gave her a sharp look but didn't say anything. Had she made a mistake? Hell, she used to be better at this whole thing...whatever this *thing* was. She was just too uncomfortable with the situation. She hadn't spent a lot of time with Luc since he'd been back, and now she had her two kids with her. From the outside looking in, they looked like a family.

And that scared the hell out of her.

"Thank you for offering to share Boomer with me, Sasha. That's a nice thing to say."

"Anything for you, Uncle Luc."

Meghan held back a groan when Sasha fluttered her eyelashes up at the man. Her little girl was going to be a handful when she got older. Heck, she was a handful now.

Luc's eyes danced with laughter, and he turned the conversation to movies just as their dinner showed up. The four of them ate with easier conversation, Luc actually pulling Cliff into the fray every now and then. Cliff didn't seem to have the same stiffness in his shoulders when he spoke to Luc like he did when he spoke to her. It hurt, like a sharp blow to the chest, but she ignored it. As long as Cliff spoke just a little, he wasn't hidden. She'd take anything she could get at this point.

If only she knew *why* he was acting that way.

Luc picked up the check, and she narrowed her eyes at him, promising later discussion. She wasn't about to get into an argument in front of her children, but the man needed to know she could care for her babies herself. She didn't need a man—even a man that had once been her best friend—taking care of her.

As if sensing her mood, he shook his head. "I wanted to celebrate Cliff's good grade. It's my treat." He grinned, a flash of teeth. "You can take care of it next time."

If she had her way, there wouldn't be a next time. He confused her, and she didn't have the luxury of being confused. She couldn't raise her babies, take care of her home, and run her side of the business if she was confused.

They piled into his truck, and he drove them home, Sasha keeping up the conversation for the four of them. If Meghan could harness Sasha's energy and sell it, she'd be rich.

Or at least not as tired.

When they pulled up to her small house, she quickly jumped out. "Thank you, Luc, for dinner and the ride. I can take it from here."

He raised a brow then got out of the truck. "I'll help you take them in. They have all their bags, and I could use a cup of coffee."

She raised a brow of her own at that. "Do you really need the caffeine this late at night?"

"You know me and my love of coffee."

"No, no I don't. You didn't drink it all that much when we were younger. It must have been something you picked up on the road." She wanted to kick herself when he raised his chin. She didn't miss the look of hurt that had passed over his face. Who was this shrew of a woman? Richard leaving her didn't mean she needed to act like a bitch to a man who was kind to her. If she'd been thinking clearly, she'd have invited him in for coffee anyway. It was a small thank-you for all he'd done for her that day.

Instead, she lashed out because she couldn't handle the direction of her innermost thoughts.

Those thoughts she refused to look at too closely.

"Come in for coffee, Luc. I'm sorry." She whispered the last part and met his eyes. He nodded then picked up Sasha's bag and helped her with the booster seats.

"Thank you."

"Don't mention it."

Please. Don't mention it.

He gave her a small smile then followed her into the house. It wasn't the largest place, and smaller by far than the one she'd shared with Richard, but it was all she could afford. Richard had taken most of the money in her accounts—including the children's college funds—when he packed his bags and left them. A technicality had allowed him to keep most of the money. Before he left, she'd spent her time raising her children and making their home warm and comforting, though the man who'd lived with them had been anything but.

There had always been something missing in the large home, however.

It seemed the smaller, slightly run-down place she'd been forced to find had that missing piece. Though not as grand, it *felt* homier. At least to her. It was *hers*. Hers and her babies'. Yes, she rented it, but it was still hers.

The children shared a room for now, but one day, when she had the money, they'd have their own rooms. They were getting too old to be sharing a room.

"Mommy!" Sasha screamed, and Meghan turned on her heel, dropping her bag next to the coffee table.

"What is it, baby?" she asked, going to her knees, clutching her child close. Luc was by her side in an instant, his body as stiff as hers.

"My tooth. I lost my tooth!"

Sasha pulled back and held up her hand, where a little baby tooth sat in her palm. It still had part of the bloody part attached, and Meghan did her best not to empty her stomach right there. Teeth freaked her out. She couldn't help it.

Luc reached over her and closed Sasha's hand over her tooth. "You're a big girl now, aren't you? Your first lost tooth?"

Sasha nodded, her smile wide.

Meghan stared at the gummy gap in the front of her daughter's mouth. Deep breath. She could do this. It was just a tooth.

From the corner of her eye, she saw Cliff smile. Yes, her son knew of her aversion to teeth, so at least he had something to laugh at. She'd take that any day. Bloody parts and all. Her stomach turned.

"It didn't hurt," Sasha said, and Meghan brushed her daughter's hair behind her ear.

"That's good, baby. Now let's go wash your mouth out and get you ready for bed. We'll need to put your tooth under your pillow to make sure the tooth fairy can come and get it."

Meghan internally winced. Sasha didn't sleep deeply until two or three in the morning usually. Meaning Mom would be up until at least then so she could tiptoe her way into the bedroom and play tooth fairy.

Sleep? Who needed that?

"Will Luc help?" Sasha asked, her eyes wide.

"Honey, Luc needs to go to sleep soon, too. In his own bed."

Now why the hell did she have to think about Luc and beds? He was just her old friend. That was it.

"I can stay a little while," Luc said softly. "I'll make sure your tooth is all ready for the tooth fairy. What do you say to that?"

Sasha jumped up and down, her tooth secure in her fist. "Yay! And will you read to me? I like your voice."

So did Meghan. But that didn't mean Luc needed to be there.

"Sasha, honey."

"I've got this," Luc said and stood up, picking up Sasha with him. "So I just throw her in bed right? Call it a night?"

Sasha giggled, and Meghan couldn't help but smile. She wasn't sure Sasha had ever had anyone but her or someone from her family tuck her in. She'd never even had a sitter do so for anything other than a nap. Richard had never done it. The idea that Luc would so readily help warmed her...and scared her to death.

She swallowed her hurt and went through the motions of getting the kids ready for bed. Luc listened to Sasha chatter through it all and even tried to pull Cliff out of his shell. It didn't work, but at least he tried. By the time the children were in bed, and Luc had read not one but two stories to her babies, Meghan knew she needed to put distance between her family and Luc. She didn't want them to get hurt again, and that was the only result of whatever was happening. That was a given.

"Thank you for taking time out of your day for them," she said primly as she stood with him by her front door.

"I'll pick you up tomorrow for work. What time is good for you?" His voice was low, dangerous yet again.

She shook her head. "No need. I can call Storm. Thank you again. Have a good night."

He leaned forward, his eyes on hers. She sucked in a breath but didn't back away. Why didn't she back away? Tingles shot down her spine; goose bumps ran up her arm.

"Afraid, Meghan?" he asked, his voice breathy.

"Always," she said honestly then shut her mouth. Why had she said that?"

She pulled away then, aware of what they'd almost done—what must never happen again.

"Thank you, Luc. I will see you at work." Her tone was cool, icy.

He searched her face then gave her a slow nod. "See you soon, Meghan."

She didn't say anything and forced herself not to watch him walk away.

She closed the door behind him and leaned her head against it, trying to catch her breath.

She'd almost kissed Luc or, rather, almost let him kiss her.

They hadn't done that as teenagers or young adults.

It couldn't happen now.

She'd had her happy ending and lost it.

She didn't have another in her.

CHAPTER FIVE

L uc wasn't an idiot, but hell, he'd sure been
acting like one. Almost kissing Meghan in her
house with her kids only a few yards away had
to be one of the stupider things he'd done. And he'd
grown up with the Montgomery boys, jumping off shit
and building forts too high off the ground only
because they could.

He knew he'd maneuvered his way into dinner
with her and the kids, then into her home to help her
say goodnight, but he hadn't really thought twice
about it. When he came back to Denver, it wasn't for
her; it was for himself.

Yeah, he'd left because of her—or, rather, his
reaction to her.

But he'd come back because, of all the places he'd
lived, Denver was home.

He'd come back and realized that what he left had
changed into something he couldn't quite quantify,
and he'd spent the past year trying to figure out what
he wanted.

He kept telling himself that he didn't want Meghan. Didn't want her like he had before, didn't want her like he could in the future.

Yet the more he was with her—surly attitude and all—he couldn't help but want to be by her side and get to know the woman she'd become. Maybe one day she'd let him show her the man he'd become.

So he might have lied to himself and his family that he didn't have feelings for Meghan, but he wasn't sure he could do it any longer.

He didn't love her like he once had. What he felt now...well, it was a new layer. A feeling he couldn't quite name that didn't have the same taste as before. Maybe he still loved her, but he wasn't sure. He needed to know her more. They'd both changed so much that telling himself he still loved her with every ounce of his being, as he once had, would be a lie to them both. Not just a lie, but it would be an assault on their hearts to even do so. Or at least that's what he told himself.

But he *liked* her.

Cared for her.

Wanted her.

Last night had proved to him that he wanted her more than he thought he could after all these years. He didn't want her for just one night, but he wasn't sure he could look too far down the road and see what else he could have.

It would hurt too much for all parties involved to do so.

Instead, he would need to do something that he hadn't done all those years ago.

Actually make a move.

Easier said than done, considering he had no idea how to go about that. He hadn't been a monk for the past decade, but none of those women had been Meghan Montgomery.

No, that wasn't her name anymore.

She'd been married, was now divorced and scarred.

And he wanted to know the woman Richard had thrown away because the man was such a fucking idiot.

There were many obstacles in his path, but the main one was the woman herself.

He'd seen in her eyes the desire that warred with confusion. He'd sensed the need in her and was aware she'd caught her breath when he leaned forward. She wanted him and didn't know what to do with the feeling.

He'd just have to lay all his cards on the table.

Because if he didn't, he'd be lying to himself once again.

He'd done that before, and he wouldn't hold back for another decade because he was afraid.

He cleared his throat and finally got out of his truck. Today, however, would not be the day he professed his feelings. Considering he'd been invited to the Montgomery family barbecue, pulling Meghan off to the side in front of all her brothers and sisters wouldn't be the best plan.

But maybe seeing him there would show her he wasn't going away any time soon.

Hell, he used to be better at this whole dating thing.

Apparently, he'd forgotten it all as soon as he'd seen her big blue eyes staring up at him.

"Are you just going to stand out here brooding all day? Or are you going to come in and say hi?" Austin Montgomery, the eldest Montgomery offspring, asked, his big arms crossed over his large chest.

Luc raised a brow at the bearded man. "You're talking to me about brooding? Doesn't Sierra call you her brooding, bearded husband?"

Austin grinned then, looking nothing like a brooding man. "True, but she calls me something else in bed."

Luc rolled his eyes and walked up and reached out for a tight hug. "Good to see you. I didn't know if you and Sierra would be here today since I'd heard Colin wasn't feeling too well."

Colin was their four-month-old son. They also had another son named Leif, who was around eleven or so from a previous relationship of Austin's.

"He's doing better today, and Sierra wanted to see the family. We were more worried about whether he was contagious since Dad's immune system is shot right now, but the doc said we were good to go."

The elder Montgomery's cancer treatments had been going well, but in the past couple months, things had started a downslide. The man was fucking strong, but sometimes pure strength wasn't enough.

Not that they wanted to think that way.

The Montgomerys were a force to be reckoned with.

"I'm glad he's feeling better," Luc said as he followed Austin into the house.

"Want a beer? I know you're driving, but it's early yet."

"Thanks, I'll stick to Coke for now. I don't know how long I'm staying."

Austin gave him a look, but Luc didn't elaborate. He needed to figure out his plan when it came to Meghan, and being able to think quickly on his feet would only help.

Sierra, holding Colin, came up to him and smiled. "You made it."

He'd known Sierra only since he'd moved back, but he liked her well enough to call her a close friend. Her honey-brown hair hung in waves down her back, and her bright eyes held a hint of pain every so often. But as soon as she saw Austin, that pain seemed to go away. Luc wondered what it would feel like to have that kind of connection to someone.

Colin held out his hands to Luc and he plucked the baby, who looked so much like Austin with blue eyes and dark hair, out of his mother's arms.

"Look at you, big guy," he said, snuggling the kid close. "You've grown like a foot since I was last here."

"Not quite that much," Sierra said with a smile. "You're so good with kids, Luc. I'm surprised you don't have any of your own."

He just gave her a small smile then blew raspberries on Colin's tummy. The kid laughed like crazy, the sound settling down into Luc's bones. He'd never been able to find someone to fit him like the dream girl he'd made up in his mind. If he hadn't been so hung up on Meghan, he might have been able to move forward and have a family by now, but that hadn't happened. Damn it, maybe he did love her still. Fuck, his brain hurt. Things were different than they were before. So different that he might even get to have Meghan for himself if things worked out. God, please let things work out.

Wait. He wanted Meghan for his in truth?

Hell. He needed to breathe, to think about what he wanted. On one hand, he was afraid of hurting what he had now with the woman he'd once loved with all his heart, on the other...well. He still cared for her. Was that love? He didn't know. It might be. He might be too chickenshit to figure it out. Shit. If he didn't breathe and take a step, he'd regret it. But he'd regret hurting Meghan more in the process.

He passed Colin back to his parents then headed out to the backyard to see the rest of the family. The Montgomerys were a large family, and they were tight-knit. Most times they had something like this barbecue, all eight kids and some of their friends would come, except for those who were away at school, but even then, they still visited on every holiday. At least that's what Decker had told him. Luc had missed all of that. He'd also apparently missed Meghan's ex being a right bastard at these things.

He wasn't sure what he would have done if he'd witnessed that.

"It's about time you showed up," Decker said as he gave Luc a one-armed hug.

Luc didn't remember Decker being so touchy-feely when they were younger, but he had a feeling it had to do with the pretty brunette next to him.

"I had things to do." Luc opened his arms as Miranda wrapped her own around his waist. "Good to see you, darling."

She kissed his cheek then looked up at him with a sparkle in her eyes. "It's good to see you too. I'm glad you're here. Mom and Dad were sad you weren't here last time."

He winced, knowing he had no true excuse for missing the last one. In fact, his only excuse was the fact that Meghan had been so cold to him. He hadn't wanted to deal with that. Only now he saw beneath the surface—or at least he thought he did.

Damn, he hoped he wasn't making a mistake.

"I'm here now," he said simply. "Now, when is the wedding so I can save the date? I feel like you two have been engaged forever."

Miranda and Decker shared a look, and Luc felt as if he'd stepped in it. Well, shit. "What did I say?" he asked, looking between the two of them.

Miranda sighed, but Decker just shrugged. "You're not the only person who has been asking when we're setting a date. I feel like we're letting everyone down by taking our time getting married."

"You need to get them out of your head, Mir," Decker said then kissed her temple. "We're enjoying life as it is. We'll get married when we're ready."

"It's not about getting married," Luc said. "Right? It's about the wedding and the fact that you have to plan everything for everyone else?"

Miranda winced. "I sometimes wish we could just elope. You know?"

"Then do it," Luc said simply.

She snorted, and Decker shook his head. "We can't elope," she said softly. "It would disappoint everyone."

"The only way you'd disappoint everyone is if you put their needs above your own about this. There are how many siblings and cousins in your family? There will be plenty of weddings. If you want to do something small, or something just with yourselves, then do it. I know I'm not family, so you can just ignore me, but do what you want to do to make your marriage work. Because, in the end, it's just the two of you in this, not the whole family."

Miranda's eyes filled with tears, and he opened his mouth to tell her to not listen to him, but then she flew into his arms, kissing his cheeks.

"What did I say?" Luc asked, doing his best not to hold Miranda too tightly since Decker was *right* there.

"Let him breathe, Mir," Decker said with a laugh.

"Thank you," Miranda said then kissed his cheek one more time before letting go. "Even with how often people are asking about it, no one is pressuring us. I need to remember that."

"We're the ones doing the pressuring, I think," Decker added. "The Montgomerys have done so much for me—for us—I just don't want to disappoint them."

Luc shook his head. "I don't think you could do that." He frowned. "Maybe you could just do something small with just the siblings and close friends in the backyard or something? You can even have one of your parents officiate. You know? Make it about you *and* them without dealing with all the things that make weddings hard as hell."

Miranda met Decker's gaze and smiled brightly. "That's a *fantastic* idea, Luc. Why didn't we think of that?"

"Because you were so worried about others and the grand scheme of things that you couldn't stand back and see a way to make it all work out for yourselves *and* them. You don't have to listen to me, honest. Just do what feels right. And remember to breathe."

Breathing. He could do that. If only he could take his own advice when it came to Meghan. Only he didn't think standing back and waiting for her to see him would work. It had taken a year after coming back for him to realize that this was the time—this was what he wanted. In fact, the realization had happened only in the past week. Although, come to think of it, he'd dropped everything the moment he realized Meghan needed him after he first returned to Denver.

Maybe he'd always be the one to drop things for her and try to help, but he'd take that. He wouldn't always beg, wouldn't always wait, but he'd show her what they could have. Or at least what he hoped they could have. Damn it. Now he was sounding like some whiney kid who wanted something he couldn't have.

He was a damn man over thirty. He should just buck up and deal with what came.

He talked to Miranda and Decker for a few more minutes then headed over to talk with Griffin, Storm, and Wes for a bit. He worked with Storm and Wes daily, so he was closest to them in most respects. Griffin was also close to him in age, but because the man shut himself off in his house to work on his stories, they didn't see much of each other. Luc had read every book Griffin released—not that he told him that. Griffin didn't like knowing if his friends and family were reading him, so Luc let it stay that way. He was damned proud of the man, though.

"Where have you been hiding?"

Luc turned to see Maya Montgomery making her way toward him, her blunt bangs setting off her blue eyes in the pinup star fashion she loved. Luc always thought she, of all the Montgomerys, was the one who stood out the most. Yes, Meghan was the one who called to him, but Maya had set herself apart. Why, he didn't know, and he didn't think it was his place to ask.

He held out his arm, and she folded into his side and gave him a tight hug. It didn't escape his notice that, of all the Montgomerys, there was only one who didn't hold on to him like this. And she was the only one he wanted to do so.

No, that wasn't right. There was one more Montgomery who kept his distance, but Luc didn't see Alex anywhere at the moment. He hoped the man wasn't off drinking in a corner, sulking over his divorce or whatever other demons haunted him. He knew the Montgomerys, and he felt helpless for Alex, but until the man wanted to help himself there was nothing they could do.

Luc shook those thoughts away and kissed the top of Maya's head. "I've been here for a bit now, Maya. I haven't been hiding."

She narrowed her eyes at him. "I'm not talking about *now*, dork." She poked him in the abs and shook her head. "You were gone too long, Luc. I know you wanted to see the world or whatever, but I'm glad you're home." She looked over his shoulder and smiled like a cat in the cream. "I know of another person who's happy you're back as well."

Luc refused to look behind him. The hairs on the back of his neck rose, and he knew who was back there. She must have just shown up because he hadn't seen her when he came in. Damn it, he was like a teenage boy, all limbs and sweat and no real words.

"Stay out of it, Maya," he growled. As much as he loved Maya, she had the habit of trying to help others in relationships. The woman refused to admit she had a thing with her own best friend, Jake, but she *loved* making sure others were happy with the ones they wanted. "I don't need your help."

"What is she talking about?" Griffin asked, and Luc suppressed a wince. He was so lost in his own thoughts that he'd forgotten he had an audience.

He turned to Wes, Storm, and Griffin. He wouldn't lie, but he could hold some of himself back. "Meghan and I are just starting to be friends again, and I don't want Maya to meddle."

Wes snorted. "Maya meddle? Say it isn't so!"

"Fuck off," Maya snarled, though she smiled as she did it. "I don't meddle. I...aid."

Storm studied Luc but didn't add to the conversation. Luc had a feeling he hadn't been able to hide everything as well as he'd hoped when they were younger. The Montgomerys saw too much, knew too much.

"Well, you can stop aiding," Luc said softly. "I've got this."

"Do you?" she asked, her gaze on his.

"I will." With that, he walked away, knowing he'd probably said too much. He was just coming around to knowing what he wanted, and he didn't need the others bearing down on him. In fact, if he thought too hard about it, he wasn't sure *what* he wanted, not in every detail. But he wasn't going to let his fears from when they were younger override what he could have now.

Even if Meghan wanted to be only his friend, he'd take that. He'd seen the look in her eyes the night before. Something had changed. He prayed he wasn't wrong, and she wanted more than being his friend.

And now it was time for both of them to deal with it.

"Uncle Luc!"

Luc bent down as Sasha ran into his arms. He picked her up and twirled her around, her laughter brushing away any uncertainties or doubts he had before. He wouldn't hurt these kids, and he damned sure wouldn't hurt Meghan. One day at a time. That's all he needed—to take one day at a time.

"I *knew* you'd be here." She grinned, showing off the gap in her teeth.

He set her on his hip and winked. "Oh, really? How did you know that?"

"Because Grandma *said* you'd be here. Duh."

At her expression, he threw his head back and laughed.

"Don't say 'duh', Sasha," Meghan said as she walked toward them. "You don't need to be rude."

Sasha just wrapped her arms around Luc's neck and snuggled close. "I didn't mean to be rude. Right, Uncle Luc?"

"I'm so not going there," he said smartly, knowing he was already wrapped around this little girl's finger. "Good to see you, Meghan."

She met his gaze then blinked before taking a deep breath. "Good to see you, too. Mom said you might drop by, but I didn't think you would."

"Of course I would. I love your parents. It's been a while since I've hung out with all of you. Have you eaten? I haven't had a chance yet."

She shook her head. "Not yet. I was just trying to wrangle the kids over there." She looked over her shoulder and frowned. "Cliff ran off with Leif as soon as we walked in."

He turned and followed her gaze. "He's with Austin and Sierra. They'll make sure he eats." He reached out and took her hand, surprising them both. "Come on. I'll eat with you."

She looked down at their joined hands then pulled hers away. He didn't let it hurt since they hadn't talked yet, but the fact that she hadn't done it quickly meant he might be on the right track. Plus, being in the middle of her parents' backyard wasn't the best place to start anything.

"I don't want to put you out. You looked like you were having a conversation with Wes and Storm."

"They'll be fine. Let's go feed this munchkin."

He tickled Sasha's belly, and she giggled much like her cousin Colin had. The sound made him realize that he didn't feel as awkward as before. Still, though, after all these years, he would have thought his time with Meghan wouldn't feel so tense. It was going to take time to figure it all out; he knew that. At some point, however, he'd have to find out exactly what Meghan wanted. That near-kiss and the attraction he felt from her had to mean something.

He hoped.

He led Meghan and Sasha over to the piles of food and helped the little girl in his arms make up her plate. He ignored the pointed looks from some of her family members. It had been a long time since he and Meghan had spent any time together, and it had never been with a child on his hip. Instead of dwelling on it, he sat Sasha down and made a plate of his own. The three of them ate their grilled chicken and potato salad while watching Leif and Cliff roll around on the grass. When Austin joined them, the rest of the Montgomery boys followed suit, and soon there was a game of touch football going down. Of course, Sasha wanted to play, and Luc made sure he was on her team. Under Meghan's watchful eye, as well as the rest of those who had decided to sit out the game, he led Sasha and their team to a victory, showing off their new end zone dance, which included spinning the little girl around until she squealed.

"Again! Again!"

He laughed and carried her over his shoulder to Meghan. "Not today. I'm exhausted." He met Meghan's eyes. "I'm not twenty anymore, it seems."

She smiled at him, a knowing gleam in her eyes. "None of us are. Okay, honey, we need to go ask Uncle Griffin if he's ready to take us home. You and Cliff have a few things to finish up for school."

"Your truck still not working?"

Meghan thinned her lips and shook her head. "It's going to take longer than they thought to fix it."

Luc put his hands on his hips and sighed. "You might need a new one altogether, Meghan, if that's the case."

She looked down at Sasha and gave a small shake of her head. "I can't talk about it right now. In any case, Griffin brought us here, so at least I asked for help. Right?" The tension in her voice told him this was something more. He knew he shouldn't have blown up at her in the truck that day, but he hadn't been able to help it. He hated the fact that she wouldn't normally ask for help. Hated that she tried to do everything on her own, even if she didn't need to.

She had a support system, but for some reason, it was as if she was blind to it. As if something had shielded it from her for so long she didn't realize it was there anymore.

He'd have to find a way to fix that and let her know he was part of it as well.

She did so much on her own, more than any one person should have to do. He didn't care that there were thousands of single mothers and fathers who did this every day. Meghan shouldn't have to. He didn't want her to wear herself out because she thought she had to do it all.

"I'll take you home, Meghan."

She shook her head. "I don't need to take you away from the party. Griffin will take us home."

"Let me help. Griffin is talking with your dad now. Do you really want to take him away this early?"

She narrowed her eyes. "I don't want to rely on anyone and force them to put things down for me. Don't you get that?" She took a deep breath. "Sorry. I'm a little touchy."

"I get it." And he did. Richard had been a fucking asshole to her, forcing her to rely only on herself and making her think she was failing even at that. "But I'm still taking you home."

"Luc."

"Don't worry about it. I wasn't going to stay long anyway. And I want to talk to you about something."

She licked her lips, and he held back a groan, aware Sasha stood between them, a curious look on her face. "We don't need to talk about that."

Good. She was thinking about that near-kiss, too. "Yes. Yes, we do. Go get Cliff and say your goodbyes.

I'll get Sasha cleaned up and get the boosters for my truck."

She opened her mouth to say something then shook her head. "Thank you. I hate that I'm sounding so ungrateful. But thank you."

He reached up to cup her face then thought better of it. "Anything, Meghan. You should know that."

With that, he did as he'd said, once again ignoring the glances from others. He'd deal with them later. First, he had to figure out what was going on between him and Meghan. Then they could deal with the outside world.

The drive to Meghan's was quiet, Sasha having fallen asleep as soon as he buckled her in. Cliff hadn't said a word to him, which worried him more and more. There had to be something going on with the kid, but from the look on Meghan's face whenever she stole a glance at her son, neither of them knew what it was.

He carried Sasha into the house, following Meghan and Cliff inside.

"I'll put her down if you want to get something to drink," Meghan said once they were inside.

"I've got it," he said. "I know where it is."

"Okay, let me get Cliff set up in their room with the last of his homework. Sasha already finished hers for preschool."

She gave him a small smile, and he met her gaze. What they were doing was so freaking domestic it made his heart hurt, but he wanted more of this. He hadn't known how much he wanted it until he'd gotten a glimpse. Now he knew he'd fight for it. Fight for more than he knew.

By the time Meghan came into the kids' room and settled Sasha fully, Luc had backed out to let her do what she needed to do.

"I know she needs to brush her teeth and everything, but we might just skip tonight. She's out for the count, which means she needed her sleep. She usually takes forever to fall asleep fully like this. Hence, why the tooth fairy had a *fun* time before."

Luc shook his head, smiling as he followed Meghan back to her living room.

"Thank you for bringing us home. I talked to Mom and Dad before I headed out, and I'm going to take Dad's truck." She took a deep breath. "I should have done it before because he's not using it with his treatments, but I was too stubborn." She shook her head. "So stubborn that I was making it hard to pick up my children from school. I can't keep doing that."

He let out a sigh then moved closer to her. Knowing he was about to do something very important or incredibly stupid, he cupped her face. She let out a small gasp, but didn't pull away. Progress.

"You're stubborn, true, but you know how to take care of your kids. Don't think the opposite."

"Luc, what are you doing? What are we doing?" Her voice was low, breathy.

He backed her up one step, two, so her back pressed against the door. He didn't want to cage her in fully, but he needed to know she was there, needed to feel her against him.

"I'm going to kiss you, Meghan. I'm going to taste your lips, your tongue. Then I'm going to do it again. Once I can't breathe anymore, once I can't do anything but crave you, I'm going to walk away and let you think about what this means. I'm here, Meghan. I'm not going away. I want you. I want us."

"You can't mean that. We're friends, Luc. We're not anything more. We never were."

His fault, he knew, but that was the past. *This* was the present.

"We could be. This is just a possibility. A possibility of something greater than us standing alone in a room with a crowd of people surrounding us. Let me show you what you could have, what *we* could have. Let me show you."

With that, he lowered his mouth, gently brushing his lips across hers, once, twice.

She froze then tentatively put her shaking hands on his chest, not pushing but touching. He licked the seam of her lips, and she opened for him.

They both groaned as he let his hands follow her neck and tangle in her hair at the back of her head, cushioning her as he pressed her harder against the door. Their bodies aligned, hot, hard melding to soft, want transforming to need. She tasted sweet and tangy, tasted of Meghan, the Meghan he'd never had but always wanted, always craved.

He pulled back and watched her eyes flutter open then kissed her again. Her tongue worked with his, a smooth seduction that held the hint of promise. Before he could go further, before he pushed them both to the brink, he pulled away, breathless.

"We'll do that again, Meghan."

"I...I don't know what happened."

He tucked a lock of hair behind her ear. "Yes. Yes, you do. And soon we'll find out more. Find out exactly what it means." He leaned down and brushed his lips against hers before taking a step back. "I'll see you tomorrow."

"Luc—"

"Tomorrow."

He said it knowing if he didn't leave then, he'd push himself and her for more than either could give.

He shifted his erection in his jeans, loving the way her eyes followed the movement, then he left her home.

He'd taken the first step. Probably taken the second and third, too. Now it was up to her. He prayed he hadn't made a mistake because, if he had, then he'd lost it all.

But that kiss? That kiss had been worth it.

Worth everything and more.

CHAPTER SIX

Maybe the world had tilted on its axis and Meghan now lived in a new dimension. It was the only possible excuse for what had happened the night before.

She swore her lips were still swollen from Luc's kiss. Kisses. Plural. He'd kissed her softly, taken a breath, then kissed her hard, pressed her against the door. Her body shivered once again at the memory of his hands on the back of her neck then tangled in her hair as he deepened the kiss.

Swallowing hard, she crossed her legs, praying her pussy would stop pulsating at just the memory of Luc's delicious lips. Of course, thinking of his lips kissing anywhere else on her body just made it worse.

Damn it. He was her *friend*.

He'd been her *best* friend.

That's all they were.

Right?

"Meghan? Are you okay? You're all flushed." Miranda frowned down at her, reaching out as if to feel Meghan's forehead.

Meghan instinctively moved back, pressing her back into the couch. "I'm fine." She cleared her throat. "I just need a drink."

Maya came up behind Miranda and cocked her brow, the piercing gleaming in the light. "You do look flushed, but I don't think it's from being sick." She grinned, a knowing look in her eyes. "I think it has to do with a certain someone who took you and the kids home last night."

Meghan raised her chin, refusing to kowtow to Maya. The three of them had always been decently close since they were the three girls of the Montgomery clan. Their parents had thought it was cute to name them all with M's, and their father even called them his M&Ms. It didn't matter that Meghan had nine years on Miranda and two on Maya. They were sisters and knew most of their ins and outs.

Each of them had their own secrets though—some darker than others.

This secret, however, wasn't so dark. That didn't mean she wanted to share it with her sisters though.

"Excuse me?" she said finally, putting as much ice into her tone as she could muster.

Maya rolled her eyes and tapped her foot. "Don't try that ice bitch tone on me, Meghan. I know you. You're all flushed and crossing your legs. You're thinking about *something* that makes you hot. Right? And considering you haven't looked like that in the years you were married to that right bastard, I'm thinking it's a certain electrician who came back to town. Am I right?"

Meghan narrowed her eyes but couldn't help the laughter that bubbled out of her. "Dear lord, Maya. Seriously? Did you just ask me if I was hot? How close are we sisters supposed to be?"

Miranda flopped next to her on the couch and grinned. "I don't really want to know the answer to that question, if that's all right with you. Now come on, talk to us."

"There's nothing to talk about," Meghan hedged.

Maya let out a dramatic sigh but smiled. "Well, it's a good thing the two of you came over to my house for margaritas. I'll ply you with booze, and we'll see what you say when your tongue is loosened with tequila."

Meghan folded her arms over her chest. "I think I'll opt out of tequila, thank you very much. I came over for a girls' night. I don't need to get drunk."

"Uh, Meghan? I think that's the point of a girls' night," Miranda put in. "A girls' day is where we go shopping, do lunch, and get a spa day or something. A girls' night is where we drink, do each other's hair, only to annoy Maya, and dish on men."

"We're not doing each other's hair," Maya said as she walked into the kitchen that sat behind the living room. "Last time we did that, Meghan got all pissy when I wanted to add food coloring to her hair. It would have washed right out."

Meghan fisted her hands and took a deep breath. "You know why I did that, Maya. It was when..." She took a deep breath. "Richard would have gotten upset if I'd come home that night with colored hair. He wouldn't even let me stay the night like I will tonight. He wanted me home with the children."

"Like that bastard couldn't have tucked Cliff and Sasha in himself." Miranda huffed. "Maya's right. He's a right bastard."

"Well, he's out of our lives," Maya declared, then turned on the blender.

"He's not out of our lives." Meghan spoke up once Maya turned off the blender. "He's my children's father. He'll never be fully out of my life." Tears pricked the back of her eyelids, and she sucked in a breath. "Damn it. I'm not even drinking yet, and I'm already spilling my guts."

"You needed this," Miranda said softly. "That's why Austin and Sierra took the kids tonight. We wanted Sierra here, but she said she needed to be home with Colin and crew." Miranda gave her an evil grin. "I don't think Austin could handle four kids."

Maya strode in, three large margaritas in hand. "Well, if they continue on with their plans of adoption, they might just get four kids eventually."

Meghan took the glass and sipped. The sharp and deadly taste zipped through her system at once, and she relaxed marginally. "They're going through getting into the system then? I know Sierra's pregnancy took a lot out of her."

"That's an understatement," Miranda added in.

"True. It almost killed her," Maya said bluntly.

"I know," Meghan whispered. "I might have been buried in my own pain, but I was there, remember? We were all there when she almost bled out on our parents' lawn." She shuddered, remembering the agony on her brother's face when he realized he was helpless in saving his wife. "They were so lucky that things worked out and she and Colin are healthy."

Maya tipped her glass forward. "Cheers to that. I know they want more than two because they have such freaking big hearts. I'm sure they can find and love a little boy or girl who needs a home." She gulped some of her drink then made a face. "Oh, boy, these are strong. Just how I like them. Anyway, enough with the depressing talk. Sierra is fine. They will have more children just in a different way. I mean come on. Leif entered their lives in the most fantastical way possible. Why not another?"

Meghan smiled, despite the fear that had slowly leached into her system at the memory of Sierra's pale form on the grass. "True. And tonight they are practicing with my crew. The two of them promised me they'd be on their best behavior, but you know them. They'll probably tackle Austin or Leif since they have so much pent-up energy."

Miranda laughed beside her. "Well, they can't help it. They're Montgomerys."

Truth. Despite her babies' last name, they *were* Montgomerys through and through.

If only Meghan felt as though she could still be one. She gulped more of her drink, draining it before she knew it.

"Let me get you another one," Maya said, snatching her glass away.

Meghan licked the salt from her lips and shook her head. "One is enough."

"You're staying the night tonight, Meghan. You can have more than one. Let yourself go for once and enjoy yourself. I'll get you water and aspirin before bed so you don't have a hangover in the morning when you pick up the kids."

"I thought I was the older sister," Meghan said, her tongue a little heavy. How much tequila had Maya put in her drink? "Why are you taking care of me? Shouldn't it be the other way around?"

Miranda laid her head on Meghan's shoulder. "Maya is getting you drunk. I think that's her job. My job is to cuddle and try to get you to tell me what's going on with you and Luc."

Meghan snorted. "Honey, if you're trying to be sly about it, telling me your plan isn't the way to go about it."

"I'm not sly," she countered. "I tried to be with Decker, and well...that turned out well. After, you know, he told me that I sucked at being sly."

Meghan wrapped her arm around her baby sister's shoulder. "I'm not talking about me and Luc."

"So there *is* a you and Luc not to talk about. We need to talk about that."

Meghan closed her eyes, the tequila working its sweet way through her system.

Must. Be. Stronger. Than. Tequila.

Oh, honey, how many times have those *words been said?*

"You don't make any sense," Meghan said softly, closing her eyes.

"Hey! No sleeping. Drink. Then spill." Maya thrust another drink in Meghan's direction and grinned. "Well, don't spill your drink. Spill the dirty details."

Meghan gulped another mouthful but didn't speak. She didn't know what was going on between her and Luc, and she didn't think she could talk about it.

She hadn't talked about her relationship with Richard either, and look how well that turned out.

Her fault.

Once again.

"Hey, you're having a party and didn't invite me?"

Meghan opened her eyes to see Maya's best friend—and possible hook-up—Jake, saunter into the room. He grinned at the three of them, that dark, bad-boy look of his too much to take on this much tequila.

"What the fuck are you doing here?" Maya snipped. "I told you this was a girls' night. You can't be here."

Jake just rolled his eyes at Maya's temper then wrapped his arms around her waist before bringing her in for a kiss on the temple.

Seriously, how could *anyone* not think the two of them were getting it on?

Jake threw his head back and laughed before pulling away from Maya. "Meghan, darling, Maya is my best friend. Not my fuck buddy. You know that."

Oh, dear God. Had she said that out loud?

Maya narrowed her eyes. "Yes. Yes, you did say that out loud. Jesus, Meghan. You're not usually this much of a lightweight."

Meghan set her drink down and closed her eyes. "Don't ask me any more questions until I eat something. For the love of God, have mercy on my soul."

Miranda gave out a loud snort next to her, and Meghan met Maya's eyes before breaking out into laughter. Jake joined in, and soon all three had tears running down their cheeks.

Miranda snorted herself away then looked around. "What? What happened?"

That only caused them to laugh harder. Soon her side ached, and she had to pee.

"Stop. Please stop it. I'm going to pee my pants."

"Go take care of yourself," Jake said, his eyes dancing. "I'll get you guys something to eat to soak up the booze. Seriously, Maya. You know not to liquor everyone up this early without having food out."

Maya just grinned, the alcohol not seeming to affect her like the rest of them. "I needed information from Meghan, and feeding her wasn't going to get it out."

Jake shook his head. "I swear, Maya. One day your curiosity for every ounce of information about your family is going to lead you into trouble." He met her gaze and frowned.

For a moment, Meghan thought she saw something pass between them—some long-ago hurt or perhaps something quite new and fresh. Either way, it wasn't her business, and she felt like an intruder. On shaky legs, she made her way to the bathroom, leaving the other three in the living room.

When she came out after taking care of her business and splashing cold water on her face, Jake had set out chips and dip, veggies, and cold pizza. He bent down and slid a batch of pizza rolls into the oven.

She shook her head then went over to him, wrapping her arms around his waist. She didn't know him as well as she should have. He'd become closer to Maya when Meghan was married and locked away, but she knew he was a good man.

"Thank you for taking care of us," she whispered.

Jake hugged her back before kissing the top of her head. "Anything you need, sweetness. I know it's girls' night, so I'll be out of here shortly."

"No, you can't leave," Miranda said from the counter as she munched on veggies. "We need you to help us deal with Luc and Meghan."

Meghan pulled away from Jake and folded her arms over her chest. "There *is* no Luc and Meghan."

"But, Meghan—" Miranda began.

"No. Stop it. He's my friend. He helped me out when I needed him." *He kissed me until I almost came.* "We're not in a relationship. We're not going to be. I don't want you putting those thoughts into anyone's head. Got it? I'm not going to fuck things up by thinking I can be with him."

She took a deep breath.

"You could, you know, be with him," Maya said.

84

"No. No, I can't. I'll fuck it up, and we all know that." Tears threatened again, and she cursed. "I'm done talking about this. We can talk about Decker or movies or whatever the fuck you want, but I'm not talking about Luc anymore. He's not anyone more than a man I work with and a man I used to be best friends with."

"He's more than that, Meghan, and you lying to yourself is only going to hurt those that matter." Maya frowned, but Meghan didn't want to hear it.

She'd made up her mind. She couldn't risk what she had with Luc—or at least the friendship she could have with him—by fancying delusions of something more.

"Shut up. I'm done talking about this."

Jake sighed. "When you're ready, I'm here if you need me."

"Me too," Miranda and Maya said at the same time.

She might not ever *be* ready to talk to them about anything. In fact, there wouldn't be anything to talk about. If she pursued a relationship with Luc, if she allowed him to pursue her, he'd see her for what she was.

Nothing.

She'd been lacking with Richard, and Luc was so much more of a man than her ex could ever be.

There couldn't be a way she'd be enough for Luc. She couldn't allow him to get closer. She wasn't strong enough to watch him walk away this time because he saw the truth for what it really was.

She couldn't have Luc.

Wouldn't feel his lips against hers again.

And one day, she'd be okay with that.

Today, though, was not that day.

****

Luc ran his hand over Griffin's shelves and let out a low whistle. "Decker do these?" he asked, recognizing the craftsmanship. In fact, something Decker made with his own hands stood in each of the Montgomery homes. Or at least would be soon.

"Yep. He made those last year when he and Miranda were dating." Griffin frowned. "Though I didn't know it at the time."

"And you handled it so well at the time."

Luc rolled his eyes when Griffin flipped him off, then sat down on the couch in the office. He'd come by his friend's house to talk about a few things Griffin needed if he was ever going to renovate. He put it that way since Griffin lived on a perpetual deadline. The writer tended to push things that didn't have to do with work to the side. In reality, Luc had just come by to talk with his friend.

Though now that he thought about it, guilt crept in.

He hadn't mentioned Meghan and wasn't planning on it. He needed to solidify his relationship with her—make sure they even *had* a relationship to begin with—before he talked to any of her family members.

Now he had a feeling he knew what Decker went through mentally whenever the big man had been around any of the Montgomerys.

"I apologized for hitting Decker," Griffin said calmly, though Luc saw the red flush on the man's neck.

"You fought it out. You drank a few beers. Saw a sports game. It's even in the ways of men."

Griffin laughed, just as Luc wanted him to. Griffin had overreacted for sure when he found out Decker and Miranda were dating, but they were all past that.

Luc rolled his shoulders, trying to keep his mind off Meghan and what they'd left unsaid. He could still remember the taste of her on his tongue, the feel of her in his arms.

Fuck, he'd been dreaming of that since he was fifteen, it seemed. And yet the reality was so much better, so much more exquisite than anything he could have ever imagined.

This wasn't the girl he'd fallen in love with when he was too young to do anything about it. And when he was old enough, she'd found Richard. This was the woman he wanted to know better. He'd give her a little more time to come to terms with it, and then he'd be back, showing her that he could be perfect for her, be part of her life.

Now, however, he needed to push those thoughts from his head. Getting a hard-on in front of the woman's brother probably wasn't the best way to go about things.

Griffin gave him a strange look then ran his hands through his too-long hair. The man needed a damn haircut, but it wasn't like he'd ever take time off to do it. Luc knew Maya sometimes showed up with scissors in hand when he refused to take care of himself. In fact, all three girls, and now Sierra, made it their goal to ensure Griffin ate right and slept. Marie Montgomery used to do it, but now she had a sick husband who needed her full attention.

That reminded him. "How's your dad doing?"

Griffin sighed. "He just finished up another round of radiation. He went through chemo before, so after this last round, we're off those treatments for a while, I hope. He got to keep his prostate since the tumor

87

wasn't as big as they thought, so he'll still have function and all of that hopefully, but damn, I hate seeing him like this."

Luc let out a breath. "I know. I came back to Denver expecting the same big man I grew up with and saw a shadow. If this is his last radiation though, that means he can hopefully start to gain some weight back."

Griffin nodded. "Yeah, that's the goal. We're taking turns making sure Mom and Dad are eating right and not wearing themselves down." He frowned. "Well, everyone but Alex, but getting him to do anything these days is like pulling teeth."

"What the fuck is up with your brother, Griff?" Luc knew Alex drank too much and had shut himself off after the divorce, though, really, he'd started doing so before the divorce.

"Hell if I know. He's not listening to us. Not letting us help. Fuck." He stood up and started to pace. "Just when one thing starts to go right in this family, two more things go to shit."

He knew Griff thought of Meghan and Richard in addition to everything else, but Luc wasn't going to bring her up. Not yet.

"You'll all figure it out. The Montgomerys are fucking strong. Just remember that."

Griffin gave him a sad smile. "I don't know if we're strong enough for everything, Luc."

He shook his head. "Don't think like that. If you set yourself up for failure, that's all you'll get." He checked his watch and cursed. "And I took up over an hour of your deadline time. Sorry about that. I need to get back to the house anyway and work up some plans for the project house."

Griffin and Luc said their goodbyes, and Luc headed back to his house, his mind going in a thousand different directions, but all of them led back to one person.

Meghan.

He wanted her. Needed her. Craved her.

He hadn't made a mistake the night before by kissing her and confessing his feelings. He hadn't. Like he'd told Griffin, if he thought about it negatively, then that's how it would come out. He just needed to think positive.

When he pulled up into his driveway, he had a feeling he would need all the positivity he could get.

"Meghan," he said softly when he got out of his truck. "What are you doing sitting on my porch? It's getting colder out here. Don't want you to freeze."

She stared up at him, blinking slowly. He forced himself not to reach out and pull her close. It wasn't time, not yet.

"Meghan?"

"I...I wasn't waiting here all that long. The kids are at Austin and Sierra's for a couple more hours. I'd been working at home but knew I needed to get this off my chest before I could do anything else."

Fuck, that didn't sound good.

"Let's go inside," he said gruffly. "Standing out here and letting the fall chill hit us isn't the best idea."

"Luc...I can't go inside."

He shook his head, one hand on the doorknob. "Meghan, standing out here isn't going to accomplish anything. You know that."

She narrowed her eyes. "You can't bully me into coming inside, Luc."

He closed his eyes and took a deep breath. "Don't compare me to him. Don't start doing that. Just come inside."

"I...I should go."

"No, you're going to come inside and tell me why you were sitting on my porch. I kissed you last night, Meghan. Kissed you more than once and told you I wanted you. You don't get to run away because you're afraid of how I'll react to what you say."

She shook her head but followed him inside anyway.

"I'm more afraid of how I'll react."

He faced her, still not touching her. He knew his limits. "What do you mean?"

"We can't be together, Luc. We're just now becoming friends again, and I don't want to lose that."

He knew she'd say something like this, but it still hurt like a hit to the solar plexus. "Why do you think being with me will make you lose anything? Won't it be gaining something? Something more?"

She shook her head, her hands firmly clasped in front of her. "It won't work out, Luc. You know that."

"What the hell, Meghan? You're giving up on us before we have a chance?" He didn't yell, knew better than to, but she still paled.

Damn it, that bastard had sure done a number on her. Knowing if he didn't make a move he'd lose her forever, he stepped forward and cupped her face.

"Meghan, sugar, you're everything. Don't you get that? Being with me, taking a chance, that's worth something. Letting me be with you is worth so much more."

She looked up at him, her face cradled in his hands, and his heart beat hard against his chest. "You just came back," she whispered. "When you go again, when you leave because you truly see what I am, I don't know if I could take it."

He shook his head then lowered his lips. He brushed his against hers softly before pulling away. "Darling, stop thinking like that. You won't ruin this.

90

You won't push me away. I won't let you. I'll let you be
Meghan. You'll let me be Luc. Together, we can find
out who we are when we travel that path."

"This is a huge step, Luc. We can't just jump in
headfirst."

"Can't we?" he whispered. At her look, he sighed.
"We won't jump. We won't even run. We'll walk
steadily. But, Meghan, I want you. Don't you want me,
too?"

She licked her lips, and his gaze followed the
movement. "I can't."

"That's not what I asked."

"I want you," she said, so softly he could barely
hear her.

His body relaxed, even as his cock hardened at the
words. "Then want me. Have me. We won't rush. We
can still be with one another."

She shook her head. "I already hurt my kids by
having Richard leave. I can't hurt them again, Luc. It's
not just me anymore."

He knew it would take a lot of work to make her
think of herself as not a failure when it came to
Richard. He wanted to kick the bastard's ass, but this
was not the time.

"Stop it, sugar. Just breathe and be you. That's all
you need to do. You didn't push him away, Meghan."

She opened her mouth, but he shook his head
once again.

"I'm sorry. We'll talk about that later. I'm not
going to push you, but I don't want you to give up on
us before we've even had a chance because you're
afraid. What happened in the past is a completely
different situation."

"If we do this, then we're risking everything, Luc.
Are you sure I'm worth that?"

She was worth more than that, but he didn't want to scare her away.

"Of course," he said simply, then kissed her. Her mouth parted under his, and he brushed his tongue along hers. When he pulled away, his body craved more, but he knew he could only have a sample.

"What are we doing?" she asked. "I came over here to push you away, and suddenly I'm kissing you. How strong does that make me, huh?"

He brushed a strand of hair behind her ear. "You were pushing me away because you were afraid. Now you're working through that fear. That seems pretty damn strong to me."

She snorted then rested her hands on his waist. "What are we doing?" she repeated, this time softly.

He hugged her close, letting her floral scent wrap around him. "Anything we want, sugar. Anything we want."

He held her and let this memory sink in, knowing it had to be the start of something. She'd come to him to leave him, but he'd convinced her to stay. He knew she would only relax for a moment before trying to push again. That was his Meghan—stubborn to the end. She'd run and protect herself as soon as things got to be too much. It would be his job to make sure she knew he was there.

Hopefully, for a long damn time.

CHAPTER SEVEN

There had to be a way out of this. Maybe she'd lost her damned mind. Yes. That had to be it. Meghan ran a hand over her face and tried to ignore her shaking limbs. She knew she was thinking overdramatically, but she couldn't help it. For some reason, she'd let herself be taken in, seduced, and needed.

Needed.

Odd word choice. She'd never felt truly needed except when it concerned the children, and that encompassed a completely different kind of need altogether. Richard never needed her—that much was true now that she looked at their relationship. He'd only needed her for his arm when he felt something required him to show her off. That, of course, had only been before the children. After that, her hips had gotten just a tad too wide and her breasts just a tad too low for him to want to take her out to functions. After that, he only *needed* her to care for the house and do her best to promote a healthy, happy family.

How much of a lie that had been.

Cursing, she pressed her forehead against the wall and tried to take a deep breath. Luc was not Richard. Richard was sure as hell not Luc. She needed to stop comparing the two. Only she didn't know how. Richard had been her first love, her first of so many things. She'd been too young to know any better and had fallen into his hands.

It hadn't mattered that her family didn't approve of him. At the time, she'd thought they would feel that way about anyone who tried to enter the family fold. She had no basis for comparison back then. She'd been the first to get married, with Alex finding his wife soon after. She held back a snort. Oh, yes, the two of them had done *such* a great job on that front.

Now, as a divorced mother of two trying to make it on her own, she had a date with the man who had once been her best friend.

It didn't make any sense. What was so special about her now? If she was what he'd wanted, then why hadn't he asked when they were younger? What had changed in all that time?

"Jesus, Meghan," she whispered to herself. Why did she keep doing this? Berating herself did nothing but strip her of the strength and independence she'd worked so hard for over the past year. She saw herself doing it over and over again, yet she couldn't seem to stop it. When she noticed it, she hated herself for it, and the cycle started all over again.

She rolled her shoulders and stared into her closet. Luc said he'd pick her up in an hour. She still hadn't chosen what to wear, but at least she'd showered.

The sound of a tail thumping behind her made her smile, and she turned to see Boomer staring up at her with adoration in his eyes.

"Sorry, buddy, you just ate and took a w-a-l-k. I'm not giving you a t-r-e-a-t." She grinned when he cocked his head. Boomer had long ago learned the words that were his happy spot. She had a feeling she'd need to rename them since he could probably spell at this point.

He got up and sniffed around her legs before collapsing on top of her feet, that put-upon sigh too much for her. She laughed as she bent down and rubbed his belly.

"I won't be out too late, darling," she said softly. He sniffed at her, his tail wagging like crazy when she continued her petting. Well, at least she hadn't changed yet, since dog hair covered her from hip to ankle. She'd just spritz some perfume on since eau de canine wasn't the most pleasant thing she could smell like for Luc.

She held back a shiver at the same time her stomach did a tumble at the thought of this...date with Luc. Seriously, what the hell was she thinking?

"Mom! Cliff won't play with me!" Sasha came running in and threw her arms around Meghan's neck.

Thankfully for Meghan, the force of the impact wasn't anything new, and the fact that Boomer still held her feet down kept her from falling on her butt like she had before.

She ran her hand down Sasha's back, even as she kept the other on Boomer. "Did he say he would play with you and back out? Or do you just want him to play?"

Sasha sniffed, and her eyes filled with tears. "He said if I played forts with him, he'd play the princess and knight with me."

Meghan sighed. She knew the fact that the kids had played so well together earlier would mean hell to pay for the babysitter tonight, but she'd held out hope. "Let me talk with him, honey."

"Thank you, Mommy." Sasha grinned and held out the tiara she had behind her back. "This is for Cliff."

Meghan looked down at the pink and gemstone tiara and burst out laughing. "So you're the knight and he's the princess?"

Sasha rolled her eyes. Seriously, this kid felt so much older than her years sometimes. "Of course. I want a sword. And I'll save Cliff from the dragon."

Meghan patted Boomer one last time and stood up, taking Sasha with her. Her back ached at the movement. She knew that one day soon her baby girl would be too big for this, but not tonight.

"Why can't you let him be a prince?"

"Because I don't have a crown. Only the pink tiara."

"Makes sense. Well, let's go see what we can do about that. Maybe you two can take turns being the princess and the knight."

Sasha sighed and rested her head on Meghan's shoulder. "Okay."

By the time she got Cliff to agree to the switch, let the babysitter in, and handled a Boomer bathroom break, Meghan had only fifteen minutes to pick out something to wear, put on makeup and do her hair.

Doable.

In a different reality maybe.

Cursing once again, she pulled out a black top long enough to go over her ass, a lacy tank, and sparkly leggings. Maya picked them all out for her during a shopping trip. Meghan hadn't wanted to buy any of it, but sometimes she didn't have the energy to say no to Maya. Luc had texted before, saying they weren't going somewhere fancy so she didn't need to stress.

On one hand, she warmed at the thought that he still knew her well enough to tell her it wasn't fancy. On the other, the man didn't know her at all if he thought she wouldn't stress.

She pulled on the leggings, wincing at the sight of her calves. Had they always been that big, or were the stretchy pants just accentuating them? Hell, she didn't have time to pick out another outfit, and the sparkles and studs on the black actually looked really cute. She pulled on the lacy tank that would show beneath the V-neck of the asymmetric top she picked out and hurried to her bathroom. The kids laughed downstairs, and Boomer barked, but she tried to tune most of it out so she could put on her face. At one point in her life, she'd been good at this. Now she was only good at making sure she didn't have mascara running down her face because she'd left it on the night before, too tired to wipe it off.

Just as she ran a brush through her hair, the doorbell rang, and she cursed again. Dear God. She'd forgotten to tell the children about the plan for tonight.

Fuck. Fuckity fuck fuck.

She'd been so worried about *how* to go about it that she'd just not done it at all. This was her first date—such a scary situation to begin with—since the divorce. What were her babies going to say?

She picked up her strappy sandals, buckling them on while trying not to fall flat on her face. She heard the deep vibrations of Luc's voice, and her body quivered.

No. No time for that. She needed to tell her babies that she had a date with a man who was not their father. Or maybe just tell them she had plans with a friend. They knew Luc. It was too early in their relationship to worry the children.

Relationship.

Oh, dear God. She could be in a relationship.

She took a deep breath, spritzed on that perfume she'd almost forgotten, and grabbed her smaller purse. She could do this. Weakness would *not* claim her as its own.

And maybe if she kept telling herself that, she'd be okay.

Why did she let Luc pick her up? She should have said she'd meet him at the restaurant. Wasn't that what smart, responsible single mothers did while dating?

Hell. One date in and she was already screwing up her children's lives.

She flew down the stairs, careful not to break her neck in her sandals and stopped short at the sight before her. Luc sat on the floor, dressed in dark jeans and a sweater over a button-down shirt. He looked damn good, but that wasn't what made her jaw go slack.

No, her surprise come from the fact that he sat cross-legged with that sparkly tiara on his head as Sasha danced around him, giggling like a loon. Cliff, despite the fact that he'd been so angry earlier in the day, chased Sasha but laughed as he sang a song that probably made sense in the past.

Their babysitter, a younger woman who lived in the neighborhood, stared at Luc with dreams in her eyes as she kept Boomer from the fun.

"Well, what do we have here?" Meghan walked into the living room. "Did the knights save the princess?"

Sasha stopped and rolled her eyes. Meghan added teaching her daughter not to do that to her internal mommy list. "No, Mommy. Not yet. I'm trying, but Cliff is the dragon now, so I have to run away from him."

"I almost had her too, Mom, but then you came downstairs." He didn't frown, nor did he smile, but Meghan saw a light in his eyes that had been lacking for so long. She swallowed the lump in her throat. She'd take that little bit of light and cherish it for as long as she could.

Instead of holding her precious baby close, she grinned at Luc, who still had the tiara on his head. "Great look for you."

He smiled at her, that flash of teeth so disarming that her heart practically skipped a beat.

"I'm thinking of adding it to my collection," he said simply. "I have a few hats, but I think this is what I've been missing."

Sasha wrapped her arms around Luc's neck and kissed his cheek. Meghan's eyes burned at the sight of Luc hugging her back and kissing her on the temple. Richard had never done that. Not once.

Dear God. Why did that run through her mind? One date. Only *one* date. Luc was *not* her babies' father. He hadn't signed up for the job, and she'd have to work harder at creating those boundaries. Without clear lines, people would get hurt.

"You can have the tiara if you want," Sasha said solemnly. "It's my favorite, but if you like it, it's yours. But when you come to visit, you have to bring it with you."

Luc smiled and shook his head before taking off the glittering toy and placing it on Sasha's head. "This is for you, baby girl. But when I come over, if you want to share, I'll take you up on it."

Sasha nodded then kissed Luc's cheek again. "Thank you, Uncle Luc."

Meghan refused to think about what had just happened. If she did, she'd break. Instead, she held out her arms and put on a bright smile. "Give me hugs and kisses, kiddos. Mommy and Luc are going out to dinner to hang out, but I'll be back before you know it." The kids came closer, hugging her tightly before pulling back.

Sasha pouted, sticking her lower lip out. "But why can't Luc play here?"

"Because your mom and I are going to play a bit, but I'll be back to play with you. Promise." He hugged her daughter before holding out his hand for Cliff. "I'll be back for you, too. Every princess needs a dragon."

Cliff studied Luc's hand, and Meghan opened her mouth to tell her son not to be rude, but she needn't have bothered. Cliff shook Luc's hand then let out a breath. Her kids weren't old enough to truly understand the events of tonight, but Cliff stood on the edge. She would need to sit down and have a discussion with them soon. Only she wasn't sure if tonight would be a one-night thing or not. Either way, she'd talk to them, but first, she needed to get through this date.

Luc smiled at her, and she had to remind herself to breathe. Dear Lord, had he always been so sexy? When they were younger, he had been attractive, though he'd grown into his wide shoulders over time, she supposed. His jaw had always been a bit square, but with age, it looked strong...fierce. She'd always loved his eyes, long, thick lashes over a honeyed brown. She remembered telling him that much back in the day, and he'd blushed under coffee-colored skin before he shrugged and said he liked her eyes, too.

That was so long ago, and once again, she reminded herself that they weren't those people anymore. This was the new Meghan and Luc—the old ones long since gone and covered in scars.

She said her goodbyes to her children and gave instructions to the babysitter once again before following Luc outside. Was it too late to cancel?

That would be weak, Meghan.

Weak.

Luc put his hand at the small of her back and frowned. "What's going on in that head of yours?"

She swallowed hard then shook her head. "Nothing important." Just doubts that had nothing to do with him and everything to do with her. "Where are we going tonight?"

He studied her face for a moment before leading her to his truck. He'd washed it apparently, and it gleamed. "We're going to Luciano's."

She relaxed. "I love that place," she said as she got into the truck.

"I remember." He closed her door then went around to his side.

The problem stared her in the face. They'd gone to Luciano's before. Shouldn't they be starting over?

"Stop thinking so hard. We're going to Luciano's because it's casual and a place we both like. I figured we'd go there instead of somewhere new so we'd be relaxed. We're not going down the same path we did when we were kids, Meghan. We're finding a new one. Just breathe. Okay?"

She breathed.

"Good." He gripped her hand, and she tensed before forcing herself to relax. He pulled out of the driveway and started driving. "That's better. Now, since we're not in front of the kids, I wanted to say you look great. I like the little gold doodads on your legs."

She grinned. "Doodads?"

"Sparkles? I don't know what they're called, but they make me want to rub up on them."

She swallowed hard. "Oh, really?"

"Really," he said with a grin. "I want to rub up on other places too, but I figured I'd refrain from doing that on the first date."

She'd be okay with the rubbing.

Not that she said that out loud.

They spoke of work and her kids, making things easier than she'd expected. They didn't discuss anything serious, just normal things that some people might talk about on a first date. Only they knew most of the things one would ask about when they first met, meaning she felt out of her depth more often than not.

When they pulled up to the restaurant, she didn't open the door but, instead, held on to his wrist.

"What is it?" he asked.

"What are we doing?"

He let out a sigh then turned so they were facing each other. The center console sat between them, but she could still feel his heat.

"This again?"

She snarled. "Yes. *This* again. I haven't been on a first date in over a decade, Luc. I've never been on a first date with *you*."

Luc reached out and cupped her face. "This is my first date with you, too, sugar."

"You know, when you call me sugar, it doesn't sound like you're patronizing me. That's the only reason I let you do it."

He grinned then, his eyes sparkling. "I know. And as for what we're doing? I'm about to get out of the truck and lead you into the restaurant. Then we're going to eat dinner, enjoy each other's company, and see if we work as a couple."

She licked her lips. "A couple?"

He nodded. "A couple. I'm not going to lose you as my friend, Meghan. I lost you before, and I won't do that again. But I want to see what happens if we try for something more."

"You're the one who left before, Luc," she said, that pain of his disappearance hitting home once again.

He clenched his jaw and gave a tight nod. "Yes, I left, but you left me before that, and we both knew it."

"Luc," she whispered. She didn't want to look at the past but knew they both had to do it.

"You were so in love with him, Meghan, and he hated me. He hated what he had together, and I get it. I was a man who knew his wife better than he did, and he wanted me out. You didn't fight for what we were, but I get that, too. You didn't know there needed to be a fight at all. You only saw the man you loved and the future you had. I don't blame you for that."

She shook her head. "It sure sounds like you do. I would have made a space for you in my life, Luc. I wouldn't have shut you out." Even as she said it, she wasn't sure that was true. Richard had cut her off from so much, and she was only just now seeing that.

"I couldn't stay, Meghan," he whispered. "I couldn't stay and watch you love another man."

Something clicked, and she pulled back, her eyes wide. "Even then?" she asked. What did it all mean? He liked her then? Could it have been more?

"Always," he whispered. "Always then and always now, but now is different." He cleared his throat. "Now we're both here, and this is *our* time. Come with me, Meghan. Take a chance."

Her mind reeled. All those years. *Why* hadn't she seen that? "Why didn't you say anything?"

"Because I was a coward," he said simply, only it wasn't simple at all. "I'm sorry for not saying anything. I'm sorry for missing out."

"But...but if you had, I don't know what I would have done, Luc."

"I know that. And I know if you hadn't married Richard you wouldn't have Cliff and Sasha."

Her eyes widened, and he brushed his thumb along her jaw. "So many choices, so many paths, and yet I had to go through them, Luc. I wouldn't change anything if it meant I had to lose my babies."

"I know that, sugar. That's why we're moving forward now."

"We can't forget the past, Luc. There's too much of it to ignore." She might want to forget Richard, forget that Luc had wanted her then, but she couldn't.

"I know that, but we can look forward while acknowledging the past exists. There's a difference."

If only she could see it. If only she could take the risk.

"Okay," she said softly.

"And try to have fun. I promise I don't bite." He met her gaze and smiled. "Unless you ask me to. Then I'll take a nibble."

She laughed even as her insides warmed. "I think I like this side of you. All rubbing and biting. Who knew?"

He licked his lips. "There's more. You just have to ask for it."

She sucked in a breath. They were parked on the backside of the restaurant near the streetlight but not in the light. Instead, it felt, for the moment, as if they were all alone.

Thank God the console was between them, or she might just fall into his arms right there—doubts or no.

Luc pulled on the center console, and it lifted up to form a bench seat.

Well, fuck.

"If you keep looking at me like that, I'm going to press you up against that door and kiss you until neither of us can breathe."

She swallowed hard, her nipples pressing against her bra. "You like pressing me up against doors."

He grinned, sexy and slow. "Hell, yeah. I can't help it. I kind of like you at my mercy." He frowned suddenly, and she tilted her head. "Am I scaring you? Going too fast? Too hard?"

Those words brought up images she couldn't quite push out of her mind. Luc thrusting, backs arching, fingernails digging...

She cleared her throat. "I'm not scared." *Much.* "I...uh...no one's really spoken to me like that before. I didn't know you spoke like that at all."

He tucked a strand of hair behind her ear. "I'm just getting to know who I am around you. If I go too fast, you tell me. I'll back off." He met her gaze, and she knew he was serious. "If I do *anything* that takes you to a place you don't want to be, you tell me. I won't hurt you, Meghan, but you need to know you can speak up."

Just hearing those words, having his voice wrap around her, let her relax. She hadn't even realized she'd tensed up. She knew he spoke of Richard. He didn't know what her ex had done to her, and she would have to explain soon, but the fact that he worried told her he knew more than she liked.

The fact that he cared...the fact that he'd made it a conscious decision...she knew she could do this. If only for a night.

"Kiss me," she said softly. "Kiss me."

He smiled. "Necking with you in a car? I can get down with that."

She snorted. "No one says necking anymore, Luc."

"We're older, sugar. We don't have to be hip with the slang."

Meghan's eyes crossed, and she laughed. Yes, they were older, and he was far sexier than he had been when they used to speak the lingo. She liked this Luc and how he blended with the Luc she'd had in her head.

She laughed again but ended it on a moan as he held her head, crushing his mouth to hers. His tongue tangled with hers, and she arched her back, wanting more. Somehow he'd ended up on her side of the truck, and her back was pressed against the door like he'd wanted. Her breasts rubbed along his chest, and they both moaned. He licked at her lips, nibbling here and there, sending shockwaves down her body.

He pulled away, leaving them both breathless. "Damn, you kiss good."

"You're not too bad yourself." She straightened as he moved away then blinked. "We steamed up the windows. In a parking lot. At a restaurant."

Luc raised a brow then wiped her lip gloss off his mouth. Oops. "Apparently we're still young."

She met his gaze, knowing he meant more than just steaming up a few windows. "I like the sound of that." Most days she felt old as hell, working until her back ached, then working a bit more. But right then, in his arms, she felt the years melt away.

"You ready to go inside and get food, and try to act responsible? If not, I'll gladly take you to a lookout and make out with you some more."

She shook her head, even as she grinned. "I'm hungry, and I think making out with you in your truck is only a one-time thing."

"Is it?" he asked, his voice low.

She raised a brow of her own then opened the truck door. "We'll have to see. Won't we?" She had no idea who this teasing Meghan was—the one who made out in a truck where anyone could see her—but she liked her.

It reminded her of the laughing girl she used to be, the one with no troubles and only a bright future ahead. Was Luc giving it to her? Or was she merely living in the past?

It didn't matter. Not this night. The world would return tomorrow, and she'd take the next step. But for tonight, she'd do what Luc said and live in the moment.

She liked the Meghan in this moment.

If only she was real.

CHAPTER EIGHT

"Knock, knock! We come bearing goods!" Luc cursed and set down his book. He'd been planning on doing nothing that Sunday afternoon to prepare for a hard week. Now it seemed he wouldn't be getting much of what he wanted.

"Mom, you know I gave you that key for emergencies. You could have just knocked for real." He stood up and took the bags from his mother but didn't move. Instead, he watched his mother move to the kitchen island and smile at him.

"Why? You have that woman hiding here?"

He met his mother's eyes at Tessa's outburst and bit his tongue. He didn't want to make a scene in front of his mother. Wait. Why was he bothering to be nice to Tessa when she acted this way?

"What did I say about calling Meghan 'that woman', Tessa?"

Tessa sniffed and set her bags on the counter. "God. You're harping on me after I spent the morning getting your groceries? Some nice baby brother you are."

Luc crossed his eyes, his hands fisting at his sides, and his mother sighed.

"Tessa, shut up," Maggie said then put her hand on her hip. "We're not having this conversation again."

"Mom—"

"I said, no more!"

Luc raised his brow at his sister, who stuck her tongue out at him. And *she* was the older sibling. He walked into the kitchen and leaned down to give his mom a kiss on the cheek.

"You know I love you, Mom, but why did you buy me groceries? I went two days ago."

She shrugged, but he didn't miss the gleam in her eyes. She wanted dirt, and taking care of him was just a ploy. Damn, she hadn't changed in all the years he'd been gone. It warmed him inside, even though it annoyed him at the same time.

"I just want to make sure you're taking care of yourself, baby. You're a growing boy."

Tessa snorted again, and he smacked her on the back of the head. "Mom! Luc's hitting me."

"I swear to God, you two. You're grown adults. Act like it."

"You just said I was a growing boy and called me a baby," Luc said with a smile. "Am I grown or not?"

Maggie waved her finger at him, her eyes sparkling. "Don't use your fancy logic on me, boy. Now put away the milk before it goes bad."

"I have milk, Mom." But he put the milk away anyway.

"No, you have white water, not milk. You need fat on your bones."

"Maybe if you had a better woman, she'd take care of you," Tessa mumbled, and Luc growled.

That was it. Fuck this shit.

"Okay. Get the fuck out, Tessa. If you're going to be a bitch, just leave."

"What? I don't know what you see in her, Luc. She's not good enough for you."

"Because she married someone else? Because she had a life before me?" His voice rose, and he shook his mother's hand off his arm. "Because, if that's the case, you can get the fuck out of my house and never come back. I thought better of you."

Tessa's eyes filled, and she shook her head. His sister had her own issues, but he'd *never* heard her say something like that before. "Fuck. I'm sorry. I don't mean that. God, you know I don't. I just don't like that she hurt you. Damn it. I didn't mean to say what I did. I don't even think that. She left you high and dry before, and now you're following her around like a lapdog. I don't want you to break when she leaves you or when she can't handle a relationship with you."

Luc closed his eyes and counted to ten. His mother whispered to Tessa beside him, but he tuned her out.

"If you think Meghan's going to leave me because she didn't love me before, then you don't know her. If you think she's going to leave me because she left me before, then you're thinking wrong. She didn't leave me. She didn't *have* me. We've had this conversation before, Tessa, and I am not having it again. I loved her when I was a kid. I won't deny that, but as an adult, I have strong feelings for her. I might love her. I don't know. That's something that takes time. But I'm going to fucking take that time with my eyes wide open. If you can't handle that, then it's your problem. Not mine."

"Luc, language." His mother didn't sound sincere, and he heard the anger under her words. Some reprimands were just instinct.

"It's Sunday, folks. I wanted to take the day off, read a book, and veg. Tomorrow, I'm up to my ass in work shit, and I get to see Meghan and try to figure out how we're going to work and be together. Plus, I need to deal with all the Montgomerys I work with. I would love to be able to say everything is going to work out, but we don't know anything. Nothing is set in stone, and you guys know that. I love you guys, but I'm not going to sit here and defend my relationship to you. I'm fucking pissed that I have to do that at all."

"Luc Dodd, you do not need to *defend* Meghan to me. You know I loved that girl like my own. I want to know her now, and that means you *will* bring her by for a meal once you're ready." She winked, and he relaxed marginally. "Or when I think you're ready and I invite her myself."

"Mom."

"Shut it. You're allowed your privacy, but I want to know about this girl and you. I want to see you happy—and she used to make you so happy even if she put sadness in your eyes at the same time. I pray that sadness came from the lack of momentum in your relationship and when she married that poor excuse for a man. Now, I'm taking Tessa away, and you can have the rest of your Sunday." She kissed his cheek when he leaned down for her. "Baby, if you talk like that to me again, I'll spank your ass. Okay?"

He smiled despite himself. "I'm sorry, Mom. I was angry with Tessa. Not you."

"I'm right here, you know. And I didn't appreciate your tone either."

He flipped his sister off, and his mom slapped his arm. "My house. My rules." He grinned as he said it, not wanting to piss his mom off, considering she really *would* spank his ass at his age. "And watch your mouth about Meghan. Got me, Tess? I love you like a sister, but I don't like the person you become when you hate on Meghan."

"I *am* your sister, asshole," she muttered, but kissed his cheek anyway.

By the time he got them out of the house and the groceries he didn't need in the first place put away, his head ached like a bitch. He sank into the couch and closed his eyes, trying to push Tessa's words out of his head. It would hurt like hell if Meghan left him; he knew that, but she'd taken a chance and things had gone well the night before. He could still taste her on his lips if he kept his eyes closed. They'd had only one date. He needed to stop thinking the worst and let things happen.

Of course, he could do his best to make sure she kept thinking of him.

He pulled out his phone and sent a text to the woman on his mind.

Enjoying your Sunday? Hope you're taking care of yourself.

It pinged right away, and he grinned. At least she wasn't avoiding him after their first date. That was progress. He hated the fact that she constantly had doubts, but he couldn't blame her. She had her kids to think about and an ex-husband who'd fucked things up long before Luc came back to Denver.

The kids wanted to build a fort, so I'm buried under blankets with the dog and ignoring bills. So yes, I'm enjoying my Sunday. You?

He smiled, thinking of her under blankets and pillows with her kids. He couldn't believe he'd put on that damn tiara for Sasha the night before, but the kid had him wrapped around her finger, and she knew it.

Guard my dragon and knight. See you Monday, sugar.

As soon as he hit Send, he cursed. He'd downright claimed her kids in a text. Well, that was stupid. He knew she'd put up that barrier—or at least tried to—as soon as she walked into the living room and saw them together. Calling them his, even in a silly text message, was idiotic and moving way too fast.

Will do. See you Monday.

He let out a breath. Well, she didn't sound angry. That was something. Maybe he was thinking too hard. Or maybe he wasn't thinking at all. Meghan sure as hell kept him on his toes.

The next day, he strode into Montgomery Inc. and froze at the looks on the brothers' faces.

Well shit.

They knew.

How they knew, he didn't know, but the Montgomery grapevine was one of legend.

He let his gaze leave theirs for a moment to search the room, but he didn't see Meghan. He hadn't seen her truck in the parking lot, but that meant nothing since she was either getting it fixed or using her Dad's at the moment. Still, he needed to keep his attention on the two men in front of him who looked as though they wanted to wring his neck.

This could either end fucked up or only a little shitty.

Mixing business with pleasure was never the best thing. Adding in family? Well, that was just a recipe for disaster.

"We need to talk," Wes said, frowning.

Storm tilted his head. "Take a seat."

Luc didn't want to take a seat. These two were the ones who pulled Griffin off Decker when their brother went after their best friend for a very similar thing, but that meant nothing now. Different sister. Different set of circumstances.

"I take it you heard."

"Heard what?" Wes asked. "That you and Meghan went out on a date? Her first date since that dickwad? Yeah. We heard. Sasha told Leif. Leif told Austin. News travels."

"She's an adult," Luc said. "She's making her own choices. You know I would never hurt her."

Storm nodded. "We know that. That's why we're not acting like Griffin and kicking your ass. You're a good man, Luc, and I know you loved her when you were younger."

Luc blinked at that revelation then froze when someone sucked in a breath behind him.

Fuck.

He turned on his heel and spotted Meghan at the door, her eyes wide, her cheeks flushed with color.

"What?" she gasped then held up her hand. "No, that is not something I need to find out from my brothers." She met Luc's gaze then came to his side. She didn't take his hand. This was their place of work, and it made sense, but the feel of her body next to his let him relax a bit.

"You two...I can't believe you two."

Her brothers held up their hands at the same instant, looking so much like the twins they were that Luc almost laughed.

"We didn't hit him," Wes said quickly. "Honest. We just needed to do the brother thing. You're ours."

"We were worried," Storm said softly. "We shouldn't be. It's Luc. But we love you."

Meghan sighed, and Luc looked down to see her wiping a tear. He wanted to help and wipe away her sadness, but doing that in front of her brothers, at their place of business, wouldn't be smart right then. Instead, he fisted his hands by his sides and did his best to keep in control.

"I love you two idiots. And really, you shouldn't be worried. I'm the one who's supposed to be worried."

Luc turned then. "You're worried?" he blurted out. He knew she had doubts, but the way she said it right then didn't sit well.

Meghan threw her arms up in the air. "See? This is why I didn't want to talk about this at work...no. Well, crap. I need to go to the job site, and all of you need to do the same. Wes and Storm, I love you both, but this is my life. Not yours. You're welcome to keep your opinions to yourselves. Luc? We can talk about everything later. Promise."

With that, she stormed off, leaving the three men staring in her wake.

"We weren't going to hit you," Wes rasped out. "We just wanted to know your intentions."

Luc snorted. "I'd tell Harry my intentions first, dude. You know that."

Storm shook his head. "She's yours. She's always been yours. I get that. We'll leave you be. But, Luc, you hurt her, we hurt you."

"I hurt her, I'll *let* you hurt me."

His mind heavy, he picked up his papers from his desk then headed back out to his truck. So far, not the best way to start the day but clearly not the worst. They'd figure it out together—he just hoped there'd be a together to figure out.

He pulled up to the job site to see Meghan frowning over her plans. He knew he should give her some space, but he didn't like how they'd left things.

"Meghan."

She looked up and gave him a small smile. Progress. "Sorry for storming out. I was just so embarrassed."

He stopped moving and blinked. "You're apologizing? I was the one who should have done that."

"No, it was me. We needed to talk about how work was going to go, and if my brothers hadn't come at you, I think we could have left it professional."

He looked at the foot of space between them then up to her eyes. "We're pretty professional right now. Want to get a little unprofessional later?"

She snorted. "That has to be one of the worst lines ever."

He wiggled his brows, relieved to see her smiling at him. "I try. What do you say? I know it's a Monday, but I could come over and have dinner or something. Or if that's too soon with the kids, it's no big deal." He was acting like an awkward fool, but he'd find his footing once again.

"Actually today and tomorrow are teacher work days. The kids are with Maya overnight."

He coughed at that. "Really?"

She smiled brightly. "Really. They wanted a sleepover with Aunt Maya, and Maya had the time off so I have the house free." She froze, her cheeks going pink. "Uh..."

"How about I come over for dinner?" he said softly. He didn't touch her, didn't come closer. They were at work after all. Grinding her against the truck probably wasn't the best way to show they could be professional and together at the same time.

"Dinner."

"Just dinner, Meghan."

"Dinner," she repeated. "I can do that."

He smiled. "Good." Before he did something stupid like kiss her, he went back to his area of the project site, smiling like an idiot.

Dinner sounded pretty fan-fucking-tastic.

When he pulled his truck into her driveway, he took a deep breath before shutting off the engine and getting out. He didn't know what it was about this woman, but she set him on that sweet edge and made him overthink even the littlest things. He swore she brought him back to being that young kid without any experience, without the ability to speak to a woman without stumbling over his words.

He took another deep breath and rolled his shoulders.

Tonight he'd just be Luc.

She'd just be Meghan.

And together, well, together they might just be something more.

Meghan opened the door before he had a chance to knock, and he held back a smile. It seemed he wasn't the only one just a tad nervous since she'd apparently been watching for him. She wore a different set of leggings and a long flowy top that hugged her curves when she moved. He wanted to strip her out of it and lick every inch of her.

His damn cock perked up, and he tried not to think of Meghan naked. Starting the night off with a hard-on would hurt like a bitch if it lasted for too long.

"I heard your truck," she said before stepping back. Boomer came up to him, sniffed at him, and then headed back to his doggie bed. "You didn't say what you wanted for dinner so I made chicken and rice." She wrung her hands, and he frowned. "But if you don't want that, I can make something else. Or order in. Just let me know what you want."

Fuck. This wasn't his Meghan. It was going to take more than a few sweet words for her to know he wasn't Richard. He *knew* that, but the bastard sure had done a number on her.

If he ever saw Richard again, he'd probably kick his fucking ass.

He reached out and cupped Meghan's jaw. "Stop worrying, Meghan. Anything you make is nice." She didn't relax, and he had to hold back a curse. "I should have been clear about what *we* should do. Not just you. I invited myself over for dinner, but I should have brought something or made it myself, sugar. I really just wanted to be with you. I couldn't care less what you make because I'll like it because *you* were the one who made it. Get me, sugar?"

She let out a breath then pulled away. "Damn it. I don't know why I keep doing that. I swear I have a spine."

She started to pace, and he rooted himself to the spot. Crowding her wouldn't help. "I know that. I've seen your spine. You've stood up to me plenty of times."

"It's not enough."

He moved toward her then, running his hand down her arm to tangle his fingers with hers. "If it's not enough, then you'll change it. You're stronger than you know."

"You say that, but I don't feel it. And the fact that I'm complaining about it just annoys me."

He lowered his head and brushed his lips against hers. "You work your ass off and keep trying to prove you're worth something, Meghan. You're proving it each time I see those kids of yours smile. They are happy, healthy, and loved. You work yourself to the bone because you not only want to show your brothers that you're perfect for the job but because you actually *like* your job. I've seen it, hon. I've seen the way you work, the way you move. When you stop thinking about how you should act to make someone else happy, you're the Meghan you used to be, or at least the Meghan I think you want to be. So stop thinking so hard and just...*be*."

She tilted her head at him then ran her hand up his back, her fingers tentative over his Henley. "You've seen all that?"

He nodded. And more, but he didn't want to scare her away. He might have lied to himself for the past year that he was fine without her in his life, but he couldn't do that any longer.

"Luc...what are we doing? I'm not sure if I'm ready for something serious."

He shook his head. "Meghan, you're only meant for serious. If this was just a fling, a one-night thing where we'd walk away afterward, you wouldn't be so tense, so nervous. I won't disrespect you with anything less."

She licked her lips. "If we do this, if I take you to bed and have you in my life for longer than a night, then things change." She winced. "And that was beyond obvious. You know what I mean." She studied his face and frowned. "What did Storm mean earlier in the office when he said you've always had a thing for me? What exactly?"

He was the one to wince this time. He would be nothing less than honest with her. "I did. I liked you then, Meghan. You know that."

"I do," she said slowly, drawing out each word. "But the way he said it...it sounded like it was something more than that. Something more than what we'd talked about before."

It was all or nothing. "I loved you, Meghan. I never said anything because I was a coward. It was more than like. I wanted you for more than just my friend, more than what we had, but I never did anything about it. That's on me. And when you married Richard, I knew I had to leave. That was then, Meghan. I know we're different people." He cupped her face. "I'm falling for the Meghan in front of me. I know you're not the same Meghan as before, but I like this one, too. Is that okay? Too much?"

She swallowed hard. "It would have been if you hadn't added that last part. It scares me. I'm not going to lie about that. I'm not ready to...well, I'm just not ready to fall."

His heart ached, but he took it in stride. It wasn't a surprise after all. "Just because I'm somewhere doesn't mean you have to be too."

"But I didn't know before. I should have. Should have seen who you were before, but I didn't, and *that's* on me."

"It's not before. We're in the here and now. So let's push aside falling and think about the path we're on." He kissed her slowly, a tentative brush of lips, of tongue. "Are you ready for me, Meghan? If you want me, then say so. If not, if you need more time, then we'll eat your chicken and rice and just talk. I won't push you. But know this: As soon as I'm in your bed, as soon as you let me hold you, I'm not going to be easy. Not going to be sweet. I'm demanding. I'll want every inch of you. Want to taste you, feel you, fuck you, make love to you. I'll want it all. You ready for that? Because if you're not, then you're going to have to tell me now."

Her eyes darkened, and her lips parted. He put his hand on the back of her neck, his thumb brushing over her rapid pulse. He could tell she liked his words.

He saw heat in her gaze rather than fear. But he needed to hear her say it. He could *see* it, but it wasn't enough.

She smiled slowly. "I think I like this side of you."

He grinned, knowing his smile was a little feral. "Is that a yes?"

A heartbeat.

"Yes."

He crushed his mouth to hers, pulling her closer so their bodies were aligned. With one hand still on the back of her neck, he slid the other down her back, cupping her ass. She moaned into him, and he rocked.

His lips trailed up her jaw, and he bit her earlobe. The shocked gasp escaping from her mouth pushed him further.

"Is the oven off?" he asked, his voice a growl. "I want to eat up every inch of you, and I don't want the house burning down around us."

She nodded, though it was a jerky movement. "Everything's off." She shuddered a breath as he licked her pulse point. "I...I'm not good at this."

He froze then pulled away. "Excuse me?"

"I'm not good at...this."

"What's this, Meghan?" he asked, anger burning in his gut at the bastard who'd put that look in her eyes.

She raised her chin, reminding him of the Meghan she truly was. "I'm not good at sex."

He shook his head then pulled her hand so it rested on his denim-clad cock. He let out a groan when her pupils dilated. "You feel that? You make me hard by just standing here, Meghan. You arch into me when I kiss you. You moan when I touch you, and you don't hold back. So you're wrong. You're going to be fucking amazing at sex. And if we need to try over and over again for you to get that, then we'll keep at it."

She snorted, and he let out a relieved breath. "It's not that I don't get turned on, Luc." She licked his lips then squeezed his dick, shocking the hell out of them both. "I have a vibrator. Three actually. I know how to get myself off." She swallowed hard. "It's the only way I've been able to in a few years, actually."

His jaw tightened, but he pushed Richard out of his mind. "That man doesn't belong between us, Meghan. That man doesn't belong in our bed. Whatever that fucker told you, ignore it. You're better than that."

"I keep telling myself that I'm not what he made me, but no matter what I do, it comes back." She sounded as annoyed as he felt at the idea she'd been beaten down. "I don't like acting this way."

"The fact you recognize you're doing it means you're on the right track, sugar." He kissed her again. "Now show me your bedroom so I can get you out of these clothes. I want my face between your thighs so I can see if you're as sweet as I've imagined." He paused. "And Meghan? I've imagined plenty."

She blushed, even as she pulled him upstairs. His heart raced, his need building as he followed her. She was so goddamn sexy. He'd do all in his power for her to see what he saw.

A strong, capable, sexy-as-fuck woman.

As soon as they entered the bedroom, he pulled her close then caught her knees under his arm.

"Luc! Put me down."

He grinned and carried her to the bed before setting her down on her feet right at the edge. "I've always wanted to do that. Now shut up and let me love you."

Her eyes widened, and he kissed her again, this time framing her face in both hands. They rocked into each other, deepening the kiss with each passing moment. His hands roamed her body, and he cupped her breast, the heavy weight pushing him closer to the edge.

"More than a handful," he whispered against her mouth.

"They aren't as high as they used to be," she said softly.

He growled and pinched her nipple through her shirt and bra. "You think I care about that? You think I care that neither of us is twenty anymore? You're with me now, Meghan. The woman in front of me is the one I want. So don't tell me that you don't have the body you once had because, woman, you're fucking gorgeous. So let me love on it."

He kissed her again then lifted her shirt over her head. Her breasts were covered by pink lace and so fucking sexy. He lowered his head and licked her nipple through the lace, causing her to moan. He sucked the tight bud and fabric between his teeth before releasing her and paying the same care to her other breast. Her hands roamed over his face and shoulders, as if she couldn't help touching him.

Good.

He lowered the lace. Her dark nipples were hard peaks. "Fuck. I dreamed about the color of your nipples."

She let out a rough giggle. "Oh, really?"

"Hell, yeah. I wanted to know if they were pink or red or maybe a little dark. I wanted to know if they were large or small, if they were sensitive and could make you come." He met her eyes. "Can they make you come, Meg? If I lick and nibble, can I make your pussy clench without even touching your clit? Tell me."

She swallowed hard, the long line of her throat working. "I...I don't know. They're pretty sensitive."

"How do you know that, Meg?" he asked, his fingers tracing the tight buds. "Do you play with yourself? Tell me."

She licked her lips, and he imagined that pink tongue on his cock. Soon. "Yes. I pull and squeeze them when I'm fingering myself. Or when I have my vibrator inside me or buzzing on my clit."

"Holy fuck, Meg. I like it when you talk dirty to me. You keep doing that. You hear me?" When she did, she broke through the barrier that she'd put between them, the barrier that time had put between them.

"As long as you keep talking like that to me."

"Deal." He sucked on her nipples, taking turns on each until she moaned and rocked against him, her body squirming.

"Luc...Luc."

"That's it, say my name." He bit down, and she froze before her knees went out. He pulled back and caught her before she fell, her body limp and warm. "You okay, sugar?"

She blinked up at him, bright blue eyes framed in black lashes. "I...I came. And my pants are still on."

"Hell, yeah. Want to come again?"

"Only if you do."

He smiled and kissed her. "I think that can be arranged." He wanted her to come again, wanted her to squeeze his cock until they both passed out.

He had Meghan his arms, and he'd never let her out of them if he had a choice.

Bliss, he thought.

Fucking bliss.

CHAPTER NINE

"Let me touch you," Meghan moaned. "Please." Her mind whirled. She couldn't believe she'd come from his mouth and hands on her breasts alone. She'd never had that happen before. Sure, her nipples had become more sensitive when she hit thirty, but she didn't think they'd become *that* sensitive.

"I want inside you so fucking bad, Meghan. I should wait. Go slow. Taste you, but I need to be inside you." The low growl of his voice rolled over her body, and she sucked in a breath.

"Your clothes are still on," she said with a laugh. She looked between them, their bodies tangled but still standing. "Kind of hard to do that with my pants on, too." God, she loved what he did to her, what he let her become. If she let herself go, maybe she'd stay this way for longer than the moment.

Or maybe she'd break again.

No. Damn it. Luc was here. *She* was here. She'd be damned if she lost whatever it was that she held in front of her.

"Maybe I need to put my mouth between your thighs anyway," he said softly, his hand in her hair, the other cupping her ass.

"What are you talking about?" She blinked, the heat that had been rushing through her slowly cooling at her thought. His words, though, stalled the cooling for the moment.

"Sugar, your mind is so far from where we are right now. I can see it on your face." He tugged on her hair, forcing her gaze to his.

She let out a little gasp at the movement but didn't try to pull away. This was Luc. *Her* Luc. At least for the night. If, after this, he decided he didn't want her anymore, then she'd have the memories to get her through. He'd promised her that their friendship wouldn't end, but there could be no such promises as to what might happen.

He tugged on her hair again, and she forced those depressing thoughts out of her mind.

"Eyes on me, Meg. I want you here with me while I fuck you. I want your thoughts on my dick sliding out of that sweet pussy of yours. I want you to ride me and show me what you can give me. You think you can do that? You think you can be here with me instead of where you just were?"

She stood there topless in front of him, in his arms, and she'd never felt so vulnerable. He wasn't asking for merely her body. He was asking for...*her*...body and soul.

She could do that. Tonight, she could do that.

"Okay."

"Okay, *Master*."

She froze, her eyes going wide.

Luc grinned at her then leaned down and kissed her fully. "Kidding. I might want to tie you up at some point and have you at my mercy, but I'm not your

Master. I also might spank that pretty little bottom of yours"—he squeezed one cheek and she moaned—"but I'll only do it if you want it. Do you want it, Meghan?"

She swallowed hard. "I..." She moaned again when he rocked his denim-clad cock against her belly.

"I'm going to take that as a yes since you've lost the ability to speak." He pulled away, putting a foot of space between them. "Now let me strip off these pants of yours because I need to taste you."

He stripped her leggings down her legs, taking her panties down with them. She lifted one leg at a time to help him, her body shaking at the sight of him kneeling before her. She ran a hand over his head, the coarse hair tickling her palm.

Luc looked up and smiled. "I might have to shave it again if you're going to pet me like that."

"I like you either way," she said honestly. "Although I think I like you more with a bit of scruff on your face."

He leaned forward and kissed her thigh. Her body shook once more, wanting him, *craving* him. "You just want my beard scraping the inside of your thighs when I eat you up."

Her clit throbbed at his words. Luc sure knew how to dirty talk—something Richard never did. She froze once more at that errant thought. No. She would *not* think of that man right now.

"Looks like I'm not doing my job properly," Luc growled.

Before she could think, her ass was on the bed, her legs spread, and the man before her had his mouth firmly latched onto her clit.

Her back bowed off the bed, but he had one hand on her belly and the other on her hip, locking her into place. His tongue worked magic, flicking her tight nub even as he sucked. She forced her eyes open so she could watch him. The darkness of his skin was stark against the paleness of her own. She'd never seen anything so erotic...so *right*.

He licked her then, teasing her opening with the tip of his tongue. When his gaze met hers, her inner walls contracted at the heat in his gaze. He licked her once more, this time slowly, his eyes never leaving hers. When he circled her with his fingers before entering her with two fingers, she sucked in a breath, her eyes closing.

No. I want to see him taste me.

His fingers found that spot inside her that only she'd been able to find before, and he pressed down. Her mouth opened, her body shivering in heat and sparks. Her nipples contracted, her inner walls clamping down on his fingers.

And still, he licked, teased, and sucked.

With her legs wrapped around his head, she tried to push him away so she could get a break from her endless orgasm, but Luc was having none of that. Instead, he sucked harder, bringing her over the edge once more.

Impossible.

Yet not so much.

When she came down for the second time, her eyes finally closed, her body sated yet still at the edge of a precipice she never thought existed.

"Meghan, sugar, look at me. Look at *us*."

She opened her eyes to see a naked Luc hovering over her, his eyes dark with need, his muscles straining. "Luc..."

He smiled before kissing her. She could taste herself on his tongue. She'd never kissed a man after he'd gone down on her before. In fact, it had been *years* since anyone had gone down on her.

Luc pinched her nipple, and her mind came back to the present, her body raring to go again. This man was a machine, and she was greedy. For once, she'd let herself be that greedy.

"With me, Meg?"

"With you," she whispered, her voice hoarse. She vaguely remembered screaming his name when she came the second and third times—hence the strain on her voice. She looked down and sucked in a breath. With the way his body remained over hers, not touching, but oh-so-close, his condom-covered cock lay on top of her mound. The weight of it, the sheer thickness of it made her blink.

"Um...Luc?" How the hell was she going to fit all of him inside her?

He chuckled then, that manly chuckle that went straight to her insides. "You're all wet and ready for me. I'll fit."

She raised a brow. "Sure you will. And how did you know that's what I was thinking?"

"You said it out loud, sugar." He kissed her again when she would have cursed at her not-so-inner monologue. "Now look down at us as I fill you. I want you to watch my cock fill your sweet-as-fuck pussy. Once I'm balls-deep, then I want you to move your hips, move your body, just *move*. Be with me when I fuck you. Fuck me back. Make love. Have sex. Do it all. Okay, Meg?"

Tears filled her eyes, and she nodded, knowing this was *her* Luc. No matter what happened next, no matter if he found her lacking as Richard had, this was *her* Luc. She'd never forget this moment, never forget who was inside her.

He kissed her cheeks, licking up the tears she didn't know had fallen.

"You're mine, Meghan. Mine for now, mine for far longer." Then he pressed forward, stretching her with that exquisite burn.

She sucked in a breath, watching him thrust slowly in and out, working until he was fully inside her.

So. Full.

She'd never felt so full, never felt so much a part of something she couldn't understand, couldn't comprehend beyond who was with her now, who was with her.

"Mine, sugar. You're *mine.*"

Her gaze shot to his, and he kissed her then, pulling out, then slamming back home. Her body bowed, her hands going to his back. Her nails dug in, and she wrapped her legs around his waist, wanting *more.*

She did as he'd asked and moved her hips, meeting him thrust for thrust. His cock slid in and out, hitting home each time until she could barely keep up, barely keep her eyes open.

"Come for me, Meghan. One more time." He met her gaze, and she came, her body already on that crest when he'd spoken. He shouted her name then crushed his mouth to hers as his body jerked, his seed filling the condom within her.

When she would have lain limp, Luc rolled over so she was on top, his still-hard cock deep inside her.

"I can't do anymore," she rasped out, her body beyond spent.

He cupped her ass with one hand, the other casually running down her sweat-slick back. "It's okay, darling. I just wanted you on top of me. Didn't want to crush you."

"But you're still hard."

He let out a rough laugh. "Yeah, but I came fucking hard, Meg. Let me rest for a minute, and then I'll take care of the condom."

She lifted her head and swallowed hard. "Stay the night?" she asked, not knowing where that had come from. She should want to hide, to deal with the feelings she didn't understand. Instead, she wanted him with her. Her children weren't home, and Luc's car would stay in the driveway where her neighbors would see. But they wouldn't care too much, and Meghan couldn't find it in her to care at all. At least not right then.

"Of course," he said simply then kissed her again.

They cuddled until Luc took care of the condom and left her a limp pile of limbs in the bed. He came back and cleaned her up with a warm cloth before sliding back into the bed, pressing his front to her back. She fell asleep in the warmth of his arms, the comfort of his presence.

And she didn't think of Richard.

Only Luc.

"I knew you had ink. I've seen it before but never this close." Meghan lay on Luc's chest, her fingers tracing the lines on his pec that wrapped up his shoulder and down his arm. She knew part of the tribal went on his back, but she hadn't seen all of it yet. She'd grown up with ink surrounding her—even had two siblings who ran a tattoo shop. Yet, for some reason, she loved this ink more. She frowned. "Wait. I know this ink."

Luc shrugged then sat up so she could see his back too. "Austin did it."

"But...Austin?" She couldn't think of that though. Her gaze latched on the designs etched into his skin.

He had a full back piece of a tribal dragon and the head of the magnificent dragon rested below the tribal that flowed over his chest. The tail of the dragon wrapped around his right thigh and Meghan had to suck in a breath at the sight. Seriously…it was magnificent. "When did Austin do this?"

Luc turned and brought her close again so they were lying as they had been before. "He's been meeting me where I've been living since I moved away. I trust only him with my ink." He winced. "I trust Maya too, but I knew Austin would show up like he was on a vacation and see the world with me. Maya would have probably tried to force me back to town."

He was right about Maya, and once her sister heard about Austin's work on Luc's body, she'd be pissed. Maya and Austin had rules with family and close friends—they shared their human canvasses. Except for Sierra, Austin's wife, the two of them traded ink off and on. Luc had been close to all of the Montgomerys at one point, and this wasn't going to end well.

"She's going to kill you," she said softly. "Or Austin."

Luc let out a sigh. "I have more skin for her to ink. I didn't know if I was coming back, and at the time, Austin needed to leave town for his own reasons anyway."

Meghan nodded at that. Her eldest brother had his own demons that Sierra had soothed, but that was beside the point. "He knew where you were this whole time and never told me."

"You had your own life, Meghan. All of that is in the past. I'm here now." He pushed her so she was on her back and his hand went to her hip. "Now your ink, it's fucking sexy."

She blushed and looked down at the Montgomery Iris on her hip that usually rested under the seam of her panties. Neither she nor Luc had spent much time looking at the other's ink the night before. Each of her family members had the logo on their skin—even her parents. The MI with a circle and flowers surrounding it was the logo for each of their companies as well as their family. Sierra had gotten one of her own when she married Austin, and Decker had even had it done when he married Miranda. Richard had never even thought about doing it. In fact, he hated her ink. She was also pretty sure that Alex's ex-wife had never put ink on her skin. Other than Richard's contempt for it, she'd never judged either of them for not getting the tattoos. Ink was personal, even if sometimes the world could see it all. She'd never force anyone to get something etched on their skin forever. However, the fact that her ex had called it dirty and beneath him hadn't made things easy. Of course, the man had never made things easy.

Luc's fingers traced the tattoo at her hip. "Sexy as hell, sugar." He leaned down and kissed it, sending shockwaves through her system. "I have a few things to get done today, but can I see you?"

She pulled her thoughts from Luc's hands and frowned. "I'm picking up the kids and doing lunch with them before handing them over to Mom and Dad." She let out a sigh. "Mom and Dad really wanted them for an afternoon, even though Dad is so weak. I couldn't say no. Wes is there helping out with a few things in case they need someone else. I have errands to run, but then I said I'd meet some of the girls at Taboo for an afternoon coffee. Maybe meet me there after that?" It was weird, making plans with someone else, but she thought she could do this. It's what friends did. They were friends after all. Even if they got naked sometimes. Or naked just this once.

Live in the moment, Meghan.

Worry about your children.

Take one thing for yourself.

If she kept chanting that, maybe she'd believe it.

Luc traced her jaw with his finger, his head tilted. "I can do that." He lowered his lips, a soft caress. "I should go. I don't have a change of clothes."

She nodded, her tongue feeling heavy. "Luc...what are we going to say to others?"

He frowned as he sat up, the sheet barely covering him. "What do we need to say? We said plenty at work yesterday."

"People will talk," she said then cursed at the hurt in his eyes.

"I know they will. We all talk. Are you going to have a problem with that? It's not like we're keeping it secret. The horse has already left the barn on that one."

She smiled at the reference and let out a breath. "This is new to me."

He cupped her face and smiled back. "It's new to me as well. I never made love to my best friend before." When he kissed her that time, she parted her lips, eager for more, though she knew they both had to leave. "And now I really need to go, or I'll never leave." He lowered his forehead to hers. "Stop thinking so hard. Just be. I know that's almost impossible for you, but at least try. I'll text you when I'm done for the day and see if you're still at Taboo. Be safe."

With one last kiss, he left her lying in bed, her body sore and achy. Yet, despite the fact that they hadn't slept more than a few hours, she'd never felt so revved up. Luc had slid right back into her life, but this time in a completely new and unbelievable place. If she kept telling herself this was casual, then it wouldn't scare her so much. Only she had a feeling Luc was anything but casual.

"You got laid," Hailey, owner of Taboo and her friend, said as soon as Meghan walked into the café. The woman's blunt bangs had a stripe of hot pink today as well as another stripe on the other side that fit right into her iced blonde bob.

Meghan came up short at the counter and looked behind her. Thankfully, the place was almost empty, as the rush had ended earlier. Too bad the counter wasn't quite so empty.

Miranda clapped her hands and did a little chair dance. "It's about time!"

"Luc, right?" Maya said as she bit into a cookie. "You look all spent and glowy. He gives good glow."

Meghan was sure her cheeks were a bright red but forced herself to sit down on the other side of Miranda at the end of the bar.

Sierra, who sat near Maya, grinned. "Oh, I'm so happy for you. Luc's a great guy."

"I like him," Callie, one of Montgomery Ink's tattoo artists and another of Meghan's friends, added. "He's coming in for more ink, I think. Maya claimed him, and Austin gave up too easily. I think the bearded bastard is planning something."

"That's my husband you're calling a bearded bastard," Sierra said with a smile.

"Well, he's not really a bastard, but I liked the ring of it." Callie grinned and took a sip of her milkshake.

Sierra closed her eyes and rubbed her temples. "Why didn't I just stay home? I have bills, chores, laundry, and work to do. I don't have time to deal with this."

Miranda leaned into her side and wrapped her arm around Meghan's waist. "You love us. Come on. You never used to hang with us like this. Now we can talk about everything."

"And she does mean *everything*," Hailey said as she set a red velvet cupcake and coffee in front of Miranda. The woman always knew what Meghan wanted without her saying it. Made for good business, even if it startled her from time to time. "Last time I got to hear all about Decker's love for tabletops."

Meghan groaned. "That's my baby sister, folks. Can we not talk about sex?"

"But you got some," Maya said. "That's a good thing. It's about time you had your pipes cleaned."

Meghan choked on her cupcake, even as the other woman laughed and pushed at Maya. "Jesus Christ, Maya. I think you need to leave the shop more if that's what you call it."

Maya grinned then flicked her tongue ring against her lips. "I can't help it. I like watching you get all stern-mother when I do. Anyway, I'm glad you're finally hitting that. He's a good man. You two look good together."

Meghan didn't want to talk about this. She was still reeling over the fact that she'd had sex to begin with. Good sex. Fantastic sex. She'd come at least six times the night before, where she'd never come with Richard. Sure, she'd never had sex with Richard in that bed, but her ex had never made her come. He might have when they were first together, but now that she'd orgasmed so hard with Luc, she was pretty sure she'd been lying to herself for far too long.

Damn it. She had no idea what the next step was. What was she going to do? If things got too serious, she'd get hurt. She might get hurt anyway, but there was a type of hurt she'd never recover from. Plus, her children needed her more than she needed a man. If she let Luc into their lives more than he already was, what would happen when he thought better and left?

"Stop it."

Meghan blinked up at Maya, who had moved to stand beside her. "Stop what?"

"You're thinking about what could go wrong and blaming yourself. That fucking asshole is out of your life, and you need to remember that he left because he's a pencil-dick freak. He didn't leave because of you."

Meghan pressed her lips together, refusing to look at the other women, who gave her pitying glances. She didn't need their pity—she had enough pity to last a lifetime.

"Maya. We're not talking about this."

"Maybe we need to," her sister snapped. "Maybe not now, not here, but soon. As for Luc? If you push him away because you're scared of what happened before, then you're only hurting yourself—and Luc. Just breathe and let him in your life. Or keep him as he is. He's already burrowed his way into a layer of you that I think is good for the two of you."

"Maya..."

"What's going on?"

Meghan gave her sister a sharp look then looked over her shoulder at her brother, Griffin. He frowned at her and Maya, and the other ladies at the bar.

"I didn't know you were coming in today," Meghan said, keeping her voice light. She lifted her face, and he brushed a kiss on her cheek before moving down to do the same to all the women— including Hailey—at the counter.

"I needed caffeine, and I'm out of coffee in the house."

"The horror!" Miranda rolled her eyes and wrapped her arm around her brother's waist. "You know, there's this thing called a grocery store. You go out in public, much like you're doing now, and you pick up things you need to survive."

"It's ingenious really," Sierra said with a grin.

"I'm surrounded by comedians," Griffin replied dryly.

"Do you need me to pick you something up when I go tomorrow?" Meghan asked, worried about her younger brother.

Griffin waved her off. "I'm calling in a service to do it. I just have to set an alarm to remember to go online and buy it."

"Meaning you don't have to leave your man cave," Maya muttered. "I'm worried about you."

Meghan agreed. She'd never seen her brother look so...tired. Tired and a little lost if she had to put her finger on it. She wasn't sure what she could do, but she'd do her best to find a way to help. She had a lot on her plate, but family was everything.

"Looks like a full house," Luc said as he walked in.

Meghan's spine went ramrod straight. Crap. She didn't know how to react. Her cheeks heated, and her insides spiraled. She caught the teasing looks of the girls and the curious look on Griffin's face but didn't have time to think about any of it.

Instead, Luc took matters into his own hands and kissed her softly. It wasn't overtly sexual, and he kept his hands to her face, but she closed her eyes for that moment, reveling in it. Only this man, only Luc, could do that to her.

"Hi," she breathed.

"Hi," he said softly, laughter in his eyes.

138

Oh, the damn man knew what he'd done and wasn't ashamed of it. Hell. There was nothing to be ashamed of. She was a grown woman in a...in a relationship. She could do this.

Whatever...*this* was.

Griffin cleared his throat beside them, and Meghan braced for his reaction. He hadn't done so well when Miranda and Decker started dating, so who knew what would happen. However, instead of anger on his face, she saw...longing?

He blinked it away before she had a chance to think too hard, instead smiling. "Nice. Want some coffee, Luc? I need a caffeine fix."

Luc ran his hand down her back, and she relaxed. "That sounds perfect."

Instead of a fight, instead of questions and cautious glances, she sat at the counter with her girls, Griffin, and Luc, and drank coffee. The world hadn't ended with her and Luc being together in public.

One small step and all that.

Only she felt like she'd taken a much larger leap.

A leap to what, she didn't know, but she had a feeling she was about to find out.

GRIFFIN

L ife wasn't supposed to be this hard, this messy. Yet Griffin Montgomery had no idea what the fuck he was doing. He stood in his office, the piles of papers, folders, and books looking as though they had bred when he was at the café getting coffee.

When was the last time he'd had a cleaning lady in?

When was the last time he'd cleaned up his own shit?

He ran a hand over his face, knowing he had to do something about his life before he fucked it up for good. His family kept getting married, divorced, having kids, and moving on, yet he hadn't done anything for himself except fall deeper into his work.

Writing was all he had, but he couldn't do it.

Couldn't write down a fucking word.

He'd never been late on a deadline, yet his last one had passed in a blur of agony and self-doubt.

If he couldn't write, what else did he have?

Nothing.

That's right.

Nothing.

He didn't even have the energy to play big brother with Luc and Meghan. He'd fucked up with Decker and Miranda, reacting before he could think, and now he didn't know what to do with his sister getting serious with a man Griffin trusted.

Sure, he trusted Decker, but he'd had lashed out, screwed up royally and paid the price.

Now the words wouldn't come, and he couldn't figure out what to do next. Because without writing, without the characters that drove him to the next level, put food in his belly and a roof over his head, what did he have?

Nothing, he repeated once again.

And wasn't that a damn shame?

Something needed to change, that was for sure. Yet he had no idea what.

Griffin Montgomery was in a rut and had no idea what to do about it.

CHAPTER TEN

L uc cursed up a blue streak then forced himself to take a deep breath. He wasn't in the mood to deal with another supplier who had no idea what the fuck he was talking about. The man Montgomery Inc. had used for years had retired, closing down his business rather than selling it. When that happened, Luc and the others had been forced to look around for a new supplier. Of all the people who worked for the Montgomerys, Luc actually needed the least amount of materials most days. However, what he *did* need meant the difference between faulty wiring and a home someone could live in safely.

The current asshole who was supposed to deliver the new boxes and wiring hadn't shown up on time. Luc pinched the bridge of his nose, trying to keep his temper in check. He'd have to go to Wes and Tabby to see what he should do since he couldn't work on the old wiring in their project house without something to replace it. It might not be his fault he didn't have the things he needed, but it still felt like a kick to the nuts nonetheless.

"What's going on?"

Luc sighed as Wes walked into the project house, his ever-present tablet in hand. "Stan didn't show up with our supplies. He said he'd be here today because he didn't show yesterday. I'm shit out of luck on this next part since I don't have what I need." He put his hands on his hips and tried to tamp down the anger. Fucking something up because it was his fault was one thing—that was in his control. Fucking it up and disappointing Wes and the crew because of someone else? That he hated more than anything.

Wes frowned and touched a few buttons on his tablet screen. "Well, hell. This is the second time Stan has done this. We went with him because he had a decent reputation and pricing, but this is shitty."

Luc ran a hand over his head and mentally went through his list for the day. "I can work on a few things that don't require new parts, but most of this house, as you know, needed to be gutted. The wiring needed a complete overhaul to come up to code. Most of that shit was from the fifties, and the rest was short circuiting."

"I know," Wes said, still frowning as he worked. "I almost wanted to just tear down the whole place and start over, but Storm would have killed me."

Luc snorted then pulled out a couple sodas from his cooler and handed one to Wes. "The place has good bones. It's everything else that sucks ass."

Wes sighed and ran a hand through his hair. The man had worn jeans and a flannel shirt, rather than his normal slacks and button-down. Wes might like to dress nice, but when it came to worksites, he wasn't an idiot.

"I have another supplier we can use since we're not going to work with Stan anymore."

Luc raised a brow as he sipped his drink. "Dumping Stan then? Not that I'm complaining, but most places where I worked before would have blamed me or another person rather than finding a whole new supplier."

Wes flipped him off then took a sip of his own drink. "Thanks for thinking so little of us. Tabby and I have been watching Stan for the past couple of months since this is our first big project with him. He sucks ass. I don't work well with ass suckers."

Luc nodded, his mind going through what he could do without supplies for the time being. Not much, he concluded. "When you get a new supplier, I'll let you know what I need, but I'm going to be running behind on this site for a while as it is." That grated, but there was nothing he could do to make the house safe without new wiring.

"We're all going to be behind since Decker needs shit, too, today. Fuck. Okay, Tabby and I will get on this right now. Do what you can for now, and when you run out of work, go to another site or help Decker and Meghan. I'm sure they have shit for you to do if you're free."

With that, Wes pulled out his phone and started out of the building. He was always moving from one thing to the next, planning and organizing things so everyone else could breathe. The fact that Stan had fucked it up for all of them wouldn't sit well on his shoulders. Fuck, it didn't sit well on Luc's shoulders, either.

He drained the last of his drink, tossed the can in the pile he'd take to the recycling bin later, and made his way to where he'd left off the week before. He had a couple boxes to check before he completely ran out of shit to do in this room.

As soon as he walked in, he froze, then cursed. "What the fuck, guys?" he asked, stomping toward the newly finished drywall. "I wasn't done with this wall."

He pulled out his unit and looked at where he'd placed the box before. It was now three feet to the right. Luc knew his plans like the back of his hand, and someone had moved the fucking box. Who knew what else they had done?

Jason, one of the younger drywallers came to his side, his hands in his pockets. "Steve said to put up the sheetrock yesterday. Did we do it too early? 'Cuz that's not what he said."

Luc pinched the bridge of his nose yet again. Jason was a nice kid, but he only did what others told him to do and didn't have many opinions of his own. Or common sense really. "The box is moved, and the wall is up before I'm done. Now I have no idea what the fuck is going on behind the drywall. We're going to have to tear this up so I can get a good look. That's going to add more time that we don't have on a project that is already a pain in my ass." Luc's temper ramped up, but he pushed it down yet again. He might get angry, but he didn't act on it often. He'd explode if he did.

"What the fuck are you doing, Jason? Get your ass over here!" Steve yelled from the other room, and Luc balled his hands into fists. He didn't particularly like Steve. The bastard was older, set in his ways, and didn't like working for the younger Montgomerys. And, for some reason, Steve hated Luc. It usually didn't matter, but now Luc's job got only harder because people were acting like fucking assholes.

Luc stomped after Jason and folded his arms over his chest once he entered the kitchen. "Steve. Mind telling me why you had them wall over my workspace? We weren't done, nor was it on your schedule."

Steve raised a bushy brow. "Mind not telling me what to fucking do? You were done. Don't blame me if you fucked up. You're the asshole who only got the job because you're fucking the boss's sister."

Luc blinked, the burning rage that had cut through him turning to ice. "Excuse me?"

"You heard me. You were done. If the boxes are messed up, must have been you. Maybe you're not as perfect as you thought. You put them in the wrong place. Wes, Storm, and Decker will have to deal with your shit at that point."

Luc prowled toward Steve. He towered over the man but refused to break the dick's nose. "First. You ever, and I mean *ever*, talk about Meghan like that again, I'll end you. You get me?"

"You threatening me, boy?"

"No, I'm fucking promising you. Any problems you have with me outside of the job we do here can be dealt with after hours. Fucking with my work because you have some twisted-up version of whatever the fuck you're thinking isn't going to cut it. Now tear down that fucking wall and let me fix the problems you caused. If I find out you were the one to move my boxes, or do anything else to sabotage my work, then I'll make sure you're out. You hear me?"

Steve's face reddened, and he sputtered. "You think because you're fucking that little bitch you can talk to me that way?"

Luc moved, his fist connecting with the man's nose. The satisfying crunch was not good enough. He sucked in a breath, knowing he'd fucked up. He'd let his personal life get in the middle of work, and he'd hit a man. It didn't matter that Steve probably was the one messing up his work, he'd hit the fucker because of his words against Meghan. Shit.

"What the hell?" Wes yelled as he stormed in, Meghan on his tail.

Fuck.

Meghan's face had paled, her body shaking. When he reached out, she took a step back, and he froze. Holy hell, was that fear on her face? She was afraid of *him*?

Well, Jesus Christ.

"Steve, get the fuck off my project site. You're done," Wes snarled.

Luc gave Meghan one last look, the anger that had been building going full steam now. The fuckups of the day just kept piling up, and he had no idea what to do. He'd needed to let off the aggression, the rage, but in doing so, it looked as though he'd scared the one woman who mattered more than anything.

"I'm filing charges, you fucker," Steve wailed, clutching his nose. "He hit me, unprovoked."

Luc lifted a lip in a snarl, but Wes was the one to speak. "I heard what you said about Meghan, what you said about Luc. I also have a pretty good idea who fucked up Luc's station. I'd have grounds to fire you for that alone, but when you bring in family? Then you're out. We're not a big firm. We're the Montgomerys. You don't fuck with us."

"Fuck all of you, then. I don't need you." With that, Steve scrambled out of the room, leaving a blood trail in his wake.

Jason blinked rapidly between them, shuffling from foot to foot. "I...I'm sorry. I didn't know I messed up."

Luc couldn't speak. Anything he had to say would come out as a yell, and he'd scared Meghan—and Jason as well, it seemed—enough for the day.

"You didn't do anything wrong, Jason," Wes said, his barely restrained anger leashed just enough. "Why don't you and the rest of your crew work on that wall. I need to talk with Luc for a minute."

This was it. He'd lose his job because he'd lost his temper. He normally held it in so well that no one knew he could break at any moment. Only today he couldn't do it.

He still refused to look at Meghan. If he did, he'd see the pain on her face, the fear. Just the thought of it cut through him. Instead, he lifted his chin at Wes and strode out of the house, aware that every eye in the place was on him.

"Am I out?" he clipped.

Wes shook his head, his hands balled into fists at his sides. "Fuck, no. I heard what Steve said. I'm surprised you didn't do more than break his nose."

Surprised, Luc blinked. "I hit a man on the job, Wes."

"Yeah, and he deserved it." The other man winced. "Though he might file charges. We'll deal with them if we have to, but you're not losing your job. I saw the mess they made of your work, and I know that's not you. That's on them."

Relief should have spread through him, but instead, all he could think about was what would have happened if Wes hadn't been as smart as he was, and added on to the fact that Meghan hadn't spoken a word to him and had looked at him the way she did, he had nothing left to give.

"We don't have your supplies, and the tension is high enough as it is," Wes said softly. "Why not go home and work on estimates for the next job or go punch a bag or something. I might call it early for everyone today. I'm fucking pissed that the little fucker would say that about Meghan and that he messed up our timeline. With Stan being a douche as well, I just need to get drunk."

Luc nodded understanding. "I'm heading out then. I'll be back tomorrow." He gave one last look at the project house then turned away when he didn't see Meghan. He'd scared her. He'd yelled, hit a man, and waved his arms around. He didn't know about everything she'd been through with Richard, but he'd crossed a line. He wasn't sure the other man had ever laid a hand on her, but the fact that she'd looked scared told him enough.

He wasn't good enough for Meghan Montgomery. Hadn't been before and sure as hell wasn't good enough now.

When he pulled up to his house, he punched the steering wheel. Too much anger raged in his veins, and he needed a way to get it out. He got into his house, pulled off his clothes, and then put on an old pair of sweats that hung on his hips. If he'd been just a tad angrier, he'd have started on the bag in his garage without taping his hands first. However, he retained enough presence of mind to take care of his knuckles since he had a job to do. If he showed up unable to work because he'd been a fucking idiot, then he wouldn't blame Wes for firing him.

He let his mind focus on the bag in front of him, his form meticulous. He'd learned with Decker years ago, but while he was gone, he'd perfected his stance. With each hit, he tried to let out the anger.

The anger over supplies.

The anger over destruction.

The anger over Steve.

The anger over his sister's attitude.

The anger over Richard.

The anger over Meghan's fear.

The anger over his own actions.

Sweat poured over his brow, but he shook it away. He didn't relent, the bag beating back on his hands. His arms began to ache, his legs burning from his positions. Yet he didn't stop. He didn't know how much time had passed before he became aware of a harsh buzzing noise. He held on to the bag and cursed while he cleared his head.

Someone had to be lying on the doorbell for it to keep going like that. Not bothering to towel off, he stomped toward the front door. It seemed his anger hadn't cooled off. Instead, he'd only tired himself out some, but the tension radiated.

He let out a breath when he opened the door to see Meghan standing there, a frown on her face. Fuck. He wasn't ready for her to dump him. He probably deserved it with how he reacted. She also didn't need the looks and whispers that came with him and her being together at work. He'd done his best to keep the distance between them on the job, but people didn't care. They thought what they wanted, and Luc would have to deal with that. It didn't mean he wanted Meghan to have to do the same.

"You didn't even say a word."

He blinked but didn't move from the doorway.

"You're still not talking, Luc." Her gaze raked up his body, stopping on his bare chest, and he forced his dick not to react. Just because he saw the heat in her gaze didn't mean she wanted him. It was just a reaction. He'd scared her. She needed to dump him and leave.

"What is it you want me to say?" he ground out. His dick wasn't paying attention to his commands. Instead, the damn thing tented up his sweats, rock hard and eager to be inside Meghan's sweet heat.

Little fucker.

Megan narrowed her eyes. "Are you going to let me in?"

"Not if you're going to dump me. You can do that right on the porch step if that's okay with you." Fuck it. He knew he was acting like an ass, but he didn't

150

want to scare her more. If she left, then he wouldn't hurt her. He'd be the one left standing in pain, but it was better than her aching. He was too angry, too pent up, to deal with her then. If he reached out, if he gave in, he'd press her up against a wall and fuck her hard. She was too fragile, too precious for the kind of attention he could give at the moment.

Meghan rolled her eyes then pushed past him. He moved out of her way, confused as hell. "You're an idiot."

"Excuse me?" He closed the door behind him and followed her to the kitchen.

She pulled out a couple of water bottles and threw one at him. He caught it, still confused. "Drink something. You look like you sweated out every ounce of water in you. Not that you don't look damn sexy all sweaty and mostly naked, but you don't need to be dehydrated on top of everything else."

He twisted off the cap and drank the whole bottle down, his gaze never leaving Meghan. She licked her lips, and his dick, once again, pointed right at her.

Traitor.

"Why are you here?" he asked as soon as he set the bottle down.

"I'm here because you left without saying anything." She set her half-empty bottle near his and prowled closer. She set her hand on his chest over his heart, and he swallowed hard.

"What was there to say? I got pissed off and scared you."

"Yes, you got pissed off because that asshat hurt your business, hurt my family's business, and made lewd comments about me. That pissed me off, too. Did you scare me? No."

He shook his head. "I saw the look on your face."

"You saw me look startled for a moment. I walked in to hear that prick saying shitty things about us, and then you hit him. I'm surprised you didn't hit him harder." She narrowed her eyes. "I grew up with the Montgomery boys and Maya. I'm used to using fists when words would work. However, this time, I don't think words would have worked. I don't like the fact you might get in trouble because he's the type to make waves, but I'm not upset over that."

Finally, he let himself cup her face. She leaned into his hold and turned to kiss the center of his palm. He swallowed hard, his body on edge. He wanted her, but if he took her now, he'd be too rough.

"You flinched, Meghan."

"Yes, but it wasn't your fault." She met his gaze, even as she moved closer. Her hand went from his chest to the top of his sweats.

Jesus Christ, he wanted her touch.

"Richard never hit me. He only hurt me with his words, his actions. I'm not afraid of men. I am damn lucky that I'm not. I know I have issues, and we're both working on those. You're helping me so much with the whole thing, in fact, by you just being you. However, I don't have a problem with what you did today. Maybe another woman would, but not me."

"I...I don't know what to do with you."

"Just be you, and you're everything I need you to be." She tugged on his waistband, and he reached down, gripping her wrist.

"Meghan," he warned. "I won't be gentle. I'm not in a sweet kind of mood."

"I don't need you to be sweet. I need you to be you. I already told you that. The whole point of this...relationship is for us to be able to take care of each other. Isn't that what you told me? Well, you've spent most of it taking care of my problems. Let me take care of you."

He ran his thumb over her lower lip. When she bit down, he let out a little growl. "And touching me, letting me have you, will take care of me?"

"I think you need to let go, and I'm here to make that happen. If you want to talk more, I'm here. Don't think that because I feel weak you need to treat me as such."

He let out a breath, lowering his forehead to hers. "I've never once thought you were weak. You're the strongest woman I know, Meghan. I don't want you doing something you'll regret."

She pulled away, her gaze on his. "I want you to fuck me, Luc. Make love to me. Have sex. Do it all. I want you to do what you need to do because it's want I need, too. We have all the time in the world for words, and I know they'll be said. But right now? With you mostly naked and all sweaty in my arms? Now I need you to be *with* me."

Right then, he saw the light in her eyes that reminded him of the temptation known as Meghan he'd once loved. He thought it had all but burned out. If he could give her that fire, that fight, he'd do anything.

"Tell me what you want, sugar," he said, his voice a growl.

"I just did."

He wrapped his hand around the back of her neck and tipped her head up with his thumb on her chin. "In detail. Tell me what you want me to do to you. What you want to do to me. Tell me all of it."

"I thought you were the one who couldn't go slow."

He lowered his head and nipped at her lip. "Tell me what you want, and I'll give you what I think you need. It won't be slow. It'll be hard and fast. You okay with that, sugar?"

"God, yes."

He grinned. "Good. Now tell me."

"I want to suck your cock until you're shaking. Then I want you to fuck me hard on the kitchen counter. How does that sound?"

She gave him a siren's grin, and he reached down between them, squeezing the base of his dick through his sweats so he wouldn't come. Holy hell, he loved it when she talked dirty. There was a vixen hidden beneath the layers of protection she wore, and he wanted to strip her down until she was bare to him in every way possible.

Bare to only him.

He pulled back, his hand still on her neck. "Then get my dick out and suck it. I'm going to fuck your mouth, Meg. So you better keep it wide so you get all of it."

She went to her knees immediately and pulled down his sweats. He kept his hand tangled in her hair, wanting her to know he was there, in control. Though as soon as she sucked on the tip of his cock, he had a feeling he'd lost the upper hand.

"Holy shit."

She hummed against him then worked him, swallowing as much as she could while using her hands on what she couldn't take in. She pulled back, hollowed her cheeks, and then flicked her tongue along the slit. As her head bobbed, he sucked in his stomach, trying to keep from coming down her throat. As much as he wanted to, he needed to come inside her instead.

He pulled at her hair, and she looked up at him, his dick in her mouth; she looked so fucking hot he almost exploded. "I'm going to fuck your mouth. Keep your jaw wide."

She hummed again, and he thrust his hips, tiny little movements until he hit the back of her throat. When she didn't gag, he kept moving, taking care not to go too far. He didn't want to hurt her, but holy fuck, she felt so good around him. When his balls tightened, he pulled away then lifted her up into his arms. He crushed his mouth to hers, even as he moved so she sat on the counter. She wrapped her legs around his waist, his cock pressing against the seam of her jeans.

"I need a condom. Don't move," he said with a curse then pulled away, sliding out of his sweats fully before running to the bathroom. His dick slapped against his belly as he ran back into the kitchen, only to come up short at the sight before him.

She'd sure stripped naked quickly. Meghan pulled up her legs so she sat spread out, her hand between her thighs, her fingers working hard in and out of her.

"Couldn't wait," she panted.

"Holy fuck. I'm the luckiest guy in the world." He quickly tore off the package and slid the condom over his dick. "I'm going to need to keep condoms in all parts of the house from now on." Or maybe they'd go without one day. Not the time to talk about that though.

He kissed her, his tongue sliding in and out of her mouth. She moaned, her hand moving from between her legs to his cock.

"Get inside me. Please, for the love of God, fuck me." She squeezed the base of his cock, and his eyes crossed.

"Hands on the edge of the counter. I'm going to fuck you hard, Meg. Don't want you sliding off." With that, he gripped her hips then slid into her in one thrust. They both let out a groan, her pussy clenching around his cock. He hadn't prepared her, hadn't tasted her, yet she was ready, so fucking wet and waiting.

He kept his eyes on her as he fucked her, sliding in and out, hard and fast. Their breathing synced as they panted in shallow breaths when they both came hard. He pulled her close, keeping his cock inside her, even as he spilled inside the condom. Her cunt squeezed him like a vise, her body shaking as she came down from her high. He brushed her hair from her face, his own hands shaking.

"Too hard?" he asked.

"Never," she whispered, kissing his jaw. "Again?" she asked, her smile warming him from the inside out.

"I've created a monster. Give me a minute and we'll do it again. Maybe on the table this time."

She leaned into him, her legs still wrapped around his waist. "Anything you want. I like it. Though I don't know how I'll feel eating in your kitchen now."

"What? You don't think you'll be able to eat where we fucked? Because I plan on fucking you on every piece of furniture and counter I have, so you'll have to get over that."

She rolled her eyes, her hands running down his sweat-slicked back. "You doing better?"

"With you in my arms, sugar? Hell, yeah. Sorry I was an ass."

"I'm sorry you had to be an ass. But don't pull away, okay? I...I'm not good with that."

He cursed himself then kissed her temple. "I'm sorry, Meg. So fucking sorry."

"It's okay. I know you." She smiled up at him. "I really do, you know. I know *you*."

He nodded slightly then rested his head on hers. She knew him just as he knew her. Meaning they were both going to fuck up again. They couldn't help it.

They'd been friends for so long it was inevitable they'd make mistakes. But that didn't mean things had to end because of it. And, next time, he'd do his damned best to remember that. Because the woman in his arms was it for him. He didn't want to let her go.

CHAPTER ELEVEN

Sometimes, if she let herself go, she could imagine that her life held the perfection she needed. At other times, Meghan knew that wasn't the case. It didn't matter, however. Today, she felt like things were going her way, and she needed to embrace that for all it was worth. She wrapped her arms around her waist and took a deep breath that ended on a happy sigh.

Contentment, dare she say happiness, rolled through her, and she closed her eyes, letting the memories of Luc's embrace and touch settle her. Seriously, if she had a freaking notebook, she'd draw little hearts on it with their initials. That's how giddy she felt at the moment. There hadn't been talk of love, and she wasn't ready for that as it was, but sincere *like* was on the table.

Okay, so she might sound like a high schooler rather than a mother of two in her thirties, but right then, she didn't care. Luc made her smile, made her remember that she was a woman with needs, with feelings, and she could never repay him for that. What made it better? He said it was her, not him, who'd done that. As if she had that inside her all this time but had buried it.

That could be true, and if she really thought about it, she'd like to have that be the case. It didn't matter where it came from though. The smile on her face was well worth the worries as to whether she could keep it up. She was *happy*. She might not have all the answers—might not know where the future led—but she didn't feel as overwhelmed.

Boomer barked, and her kids screamed over something, and Meghan closed her eyes once again.

Okay, so she might be overwhelmed, but this time, it was something she could deal with. It wasn't that she'd needed a man to complete her, but the idea that someone wanted her for who she was, rather than what they wanted her to be, made all the difference.

"Is everything okay?" she yelled from her room. She needed to finish putting the laundry away then work on the countless other chores before they headed to see her parents. The kids had pent-up energy because of the rain and were not happy about it. They'd been doing okay together playing in the living room for a little while, but a whole day with just each other was a lot to take. Hell, it was a lot to take for her as well.

"Cliff won't play dress up!" Sasha yelled. She ran toward Meghan's bedroom, the sound of her little feet getting closer and closer. "Why won't he play, Mommy? What did I do?"

Meghan blinked at the words. What did Sasha do? Those words sounded so freaking familiar, except it was always, *What did Meghan do*? Had she'd shown her baby her own personal scars?

Damn it. Meghan set down the laundry basket and went to Sasha. She kneeled in front of her baby girl and cupped her face. "You didn't do anything wrong. Cliff simply doesn't want to play because sometimes he wants to play something else. Nothing you did caused that."

"But you always say it's your fault. So it's mine, too."

Pain. Sweet pain like a dagger slicing through her heart. What had she done? What had *Richard* done? She should have left the man long before she did. All his taunts and threats of keeping the children since he was the one with an income had been for naught. He hadn't fought for custody when he left and sure as hell hadn't done anything in their lives since.

Meghan took a deep breath, knowing if she didn't tread carefully this could blow up in her face. She might be just getting used to who she was now— thanks to herself *and* Luc—but she'd be damned if she'd let any of that mar her baby girl.

"It is *not* your fault," Meghan said firmly, her hands on Sasha's shoulders. Out of the corner of her eye, she saw Cliff and Boomer walk up behind Sasha, but she didn't move her focus from her daughter. "What I said before? About things being my fault? That wasn't always the case. If you do something that actually results in hurting someone, then yes, that is your fault. But if something doesn't happen in a way you want it to, or in a way that others want it to, it doesn't make it automatically your fault. Do you understand me?"

Sasha nodded, her eyes wide. Cliff reached forward and put his hand over Meghan's, and she sucked in a breath. She met her son's eyes, and he pulled away. That small touch though, that had to mean something. It *had* to.

"I'm going to do my best to not make everything my fault," Meghan promised. She tucked a strand of hair behind Sasha's ear. "We've all been through a lot, and I know it's been tough, but we're getting better, right? We're happy?"

"I'm happy," Sasha whispered.

"Cliff?" Meghan asked, afraid of his answer.

He gave a small nod but didn't say anything. She let out a relieved breath. It was progress.

Boomer's tail thumped loudly on the floor, and Meghan couldn't help the laugh that escaped her. "I guess Boomer is happy too."

She leaned forward and kissed Sasha's forehead before reaching out to Cliff. He hesitated a moment then wrapped his little arms around her shoulders. She sucked in a shaky breath and hugged him. Not too tightly, but just enough so she knew he was there. Sasha hugged her on the other side, and Boomer stuck his nose between them.

Family.

This was her family.

God, she loved them. Add in Luc and what he brought out in her, and the happiness slid right through her once again. Things were *good*. Finally.

Someone rang the doorbell, and she frowned. She'd planned on meeting her family at the main house in a couple hours. Since she had her dad's truck, she didn't need a ride. Maybe it was Luc stopping by instead of meeting them there. Although, now that she thought about it, he said he was having lunch with his family before coming to dinner with the Montgomerys.

She made her way to the door and opened it without looking through the peephole.

Stupid fucking mistake.

Her stomach tightened, whatever was left in her stomach threatening to come back up. Her palms went sweaty, her shoulders immediately hunching forward.

"Richard."

That wasn't her voice. Not the voice she'd heard in the past couple of months. No, that was the voice of the woman he'd made, the woman she'd let him make. Why was he here? Oh God, why?

He'd slicked back his hair, the sneer on his face more pronounced than before. He'd also lost some of the weight he'd put on. In fact, it looked as though he was taking better care of himself than he had before.

Or another woman was taking better care of him than she had.

No. Stop that, Meghan. You did nothing wrong. Richard is the fucking abusive prick. You are not a doormat.

His gaze traveled over her jeans, tank top, and shrug. She'd been cleaning and doing other chores that morning and afternoon. She was planning on changing later, but right then, she looked out of place compared to his suit and tie. No, fuck that, *he* was the one out of place. He was the one who had forced her to move to this not-so-great neighborhood.

It didn't matter what she wore because he had no right to an opinion. He'd been out of her life, out of her children's lives for a year.

Her children.

Shit. She moved so she stood between the crack of the door and the rest of the house. She would *not* let him hurt her children. Hers, not theirs anymore. He'd lost that right when he'd feigned interest and not bothered to try for custody during the divorce proceedings. Instead, he'd taken their money and moved on.

Yet he was here.

"What do you want?" she asked, praying the kids didn't come and see who was at the door.

"Mommy?" A tug on her shirt.

Shit.

Richard's expression didn't change. Instead, he kept his gaze on Meghan's rather than looking down at Sasha, who had inserted herself at Meghan's side.

"Go back to your room, Sasha," Meghan whispered.

"Daddy?" Sasha asked, her voice quiet as a mouse. Her daughter was never that quiet. Damn this man. "Daddy?"

"I need to speak with you, Meghan. Do take care of the children."

That tone. That fucking tone. She hated that tone. "No, you will not speak with me. This is my house. If you want to talk with me, you can talk to my lawyer." She went to close the door, but he put his hand on it, keeping it open. Her heart raced for just a moment, and she pulled Sasha behind her.

"Go to your room, Sasha."

"Mommy..."

"Now."

"Come on," Cliff whispered behind them, and she heard, rather than saw, the two of them head to the back of the house.

Boomer rested on her leg, and she calmed somewhat. Her dog wasn't an attack dog, but he was big enough to help her feel slightly better.

"Get your hand off my door, Richard. There is nothing I need to hear you say."

"I have visitation rights, Meghan. You know as well as I do that you can't keep them from me."

Meghan snarled. "You didn't even *fight* for them. Don't think for a minute I think you care."

Richard just smiled. "Actually, that's exactly why I'm here. My fiancée, Ambrosia, and I are talking about children."

Fiancée.

Ambrosia.

What. The. Ever. Loving. Fuck.

"Cliff and Sasha, to be exact," Richard continued. "Do I really need to discuss this on your porch like a common salesman?"

Meghan clenched her jaw. "You're not coming into my house. I don't care if you get married." Her babies would have a stepmother, but that was something she'd deal with later. She didn't care about Richard in any other respect. "Now get off my porch before I call the cops."

"My children are inside that house, Meghan. You can't stop me from seeing them."

Meghan raised her chin. "Go. Away."

Richard frowned, his gaze raking her body once more. She'd need a shower after this. "I don't know where you got this backbone, but I don't like it. I'm here to give you warning. Ambrosia and I want children, but she doesn't want to ruin her body like you did to have them. Children would be good for our image and since I have two to spare..."

The hollowness that had once taken over her body at Richard's presence filled with fury. "What? No. You *will not* have my children."

"Our children, Meghan Warren. Our children."

"I'm a Montgomery, you asshole. You aren't taking my babies. You didn't want them when we were married, and you didn't fight for them in the divorce."

"You mean when I left you because you weren't good enough? Is that when you're talking about?"

The barb stung, but she ignored it. Her children were more important than any hurts of her own. "You can't have them. Don't threaten me, Richard."

"Oh, but I can. I have more power than you could ever dream of. Ambrosia wants the children, and she will get them. You're just a dried-up housewife who had to go back to Mommy and Daddy for money. Your brothers took you in and gave you a job you don't deserve. You live in a rundown neighborhood. And now you're fucking the help in the same home where you raise our children. Compared to what I can give them, you have *nothing*."

She buried each word, each remark. She'd deal with them all later. What she felt, what she cried for, that was hers and hers alone. Not Richard's. How he had found out about Luc, she didn't know. The fact that he might be watching her or, knowing him, having her watched made her skin crawl, but once again, she ignored that.

"I give them love, attention, and my soul. You're the one who gives them nothing." She prayed her babies had locked themselves away in the bedroom. They did not need to hear Richard's painful words. She needed to close the door on him physically and metaphorically.

"You make them weak like you. Ambrosia will have the body she has now, and we will have the children for what we need. She's not a weakling. She comes from money. You come from tattooed trash. Blue collar garbage."

"You married into the family, Richard," she bit out.

"I married you thinking you were smart enough to leave the pathetic idiots you call family behind you, but no, we had to see them every fucking week. With Ambrosia, I don't need to do that. And with her, we hire the best people to take care of me, as I deserve. She doesn't fuck up my shirts like you used to. She doesn't lay cold in bed and act like a damn corpse when we're fucking. With Ambrosia, I am now with the people I deserve. I have an important job and know people who will help me get to better places.

With the children, we will have the perfect family, and I don't have to deal with fucking babies again."

Dear God, this man's emotional abuse knew no bounds. Everything he said about her he'd said before. She'd had eight years of him telling her she wasn't good enough, and yet she'd stayed with him for her kids. Because she was scared. Well, she wasn't scared anymore. No, that was a lie. She was fucking terrified, but her newfound strength would provide any motivation she needed. She *knew* the children would be shipped off to boarding school as soon as they weren't needed anymore. There would be no way in hell she'd let her babies get anywhere near him.

"You're not touching my children."

"I came here as a courtesy," Richard snapped. "My lawyer will be drawing the papers soon. It would save you time and money you clearly don't have to back off now and give them to me."

"They aren't something to be won, Richard. They are my *babies*."

"And you aren't good enough for them."

She balled her fists at her side. "No. *You* aren't."

She stepped back and slammed the door in his face, locking it with shaking fingers. Holy God. This couldn't be happening. She couldn't lose her babies. No judge would give them to Richard after her ex hadn't fought.

Except the bastard *did* have money, and as she'd learned, money talked. She put her hand over her heart, praying it would stop beating so hard she could barely think. She wouldn't put it past her ex to bring everything he had to court. If the woman who lavished him in money and self-importance wanted children, then he'd get them for her. It didn't matter that he'd be breaking up a family—the same family he'd broken so callously before. Everything was always an end game for him.

She couldn't lose her babies. She'd give her life for them. Her throat worked as she swallowed hard. What was she going to do? She didn't have the money for a lawyer or a long custody battle. She also didn't want to have to rely on her family for it. They each had their own problems—her father's medical bills alone were putting a strain on her parents. The family might own two businesses, but as Richard put it, they were still blue collar. She had never once thought ill of that fact—except now she wished she had the money to keep her babies safe.

"Mommy?"

Meghan quickly wiped the tears from her face, not even aware she'd let them fall in the first place.

"Yes, Sasha?"

"Is Daddy gone?" she asked, her little lip wobbly.

Meghan nodded. "Yes, baby."

"Good. I don't like him." With her arms spread, Sasha ran to her mother. Meghan fell to her knees, holding her daughter closer. Cliff moved forward but didn't touch them, putting his arms around Boomer instead.

Sasha's words broke her heart, but not as much as the tears that leaked onto her shirt. That bastard had made her babies cry. She held her daughter close for a moment, her eyes on her son who had pulled away when Richard had left. Her ex had done this. Had tried to break them.

She wouldn't allow that to happen again.

She didn't know if she could lean on her parents and family for this. It might be too much, and she'd spent enough time learning to stand on her own. However, *standing* on her own didn't mean *being* alone. There was only one person she wanted to call right then, if only to hear his voice.

The fact that she wanted to at all should have scared her, yet she couldn't find the fear…only a need to have someone next to her when she faced the greatest challenge of her life.

Luc would come if she called, would be there.

And finding the balance between giving in and leaning on would be something she'd fight for. It was the only thing she could do.

****

Luc wanted to leave. He loved his family, but weekly meals were grating on him. Tessa was still being a bitch, even if she might have toned it down some, and his mom kept badgering him to bring Meghan over. He knew Meghan wasn't ready for that so he hadn't pushed, but he had a feeling it wouldn't be long until his mom invited her over herself.

He didn't want to think about how that would end.

Luckily, he had only a few more minutes, thirty tops, until he could leave and go see Meghan. It wasn't that he didn't like or appreciate his family. It was more that they thought he needed to be there every hour of every day since he'd been gone so long. He didn't blame them. Hell, he loved being near them most days, but every weekend, when he didn't have a lot of time to begin with, was too much.

"Luc? Are you listening?" Tessa snapped.

He took a deep breath, determined not to get in a fight with his sister once again. She didn't understand that he didn't care about her opinion when it came to

Meghan. Tessa still thought he and Meghan were the same people they were years ago. Neither of them was, yet Tessa couldn't get that out of her head, although in reality, his sister hadn't much liked Meghan even before Luc left town. He couldn't change that, couldn't fix it, and he hoped one day Tessa would get over her misconstrued feelings.

"I wasn't," he said honestly.

"You're thinking about that woman again."

"Tessa," he warned.

"Tessa, I don't know when you became so bitter, but you need to stop badgering your brother about Meghan. What has she ever done to you?"

He could have kissed his mother. She really got it sometimes.

"She made Luc leave, Mom. Why are we forgetting that?"

"Meghan didn't make me leave. I left of my own accord. She didn't even know I was leaving town. Frankly, this is an old conversation, one we've had over and over. I'm done with it. I know you don't like it, but Meghan is in my life now. So if you can't figure out how to live with that, then I don't know what to do. Your anger is misplaced. If you had any other argument, then I'd try to help, but I just can't see it."

His phone buzzed, and he checked out the screen.

I know you're with your family, but can you come over soon? I need you. Richard came by.

Are you okay?

I'm fine. We're fine. I just...come here when you can?

He stood up before he even knew he was doing it. "I've got to go. Meghan needs me."

Tessa threw her napkin down on her plate. "Seriously. She says come, and you trot right to her?"

Luc pushed in his chair and picked up his plate. "Her ex stopped by the house. I don't know what's going on, but she's there with the kids. So, yeah, I'm going. If you got a problem with that, then fuck you, Tessa."

"Put your plate down, baby," his mom said, worry in her tone. "Go see what that dick did to your girl. Let us know if you need us. We're here for you." She narrowed her eyes at Tessa. "All of us."

He set his plate down and kissed his mother on the cheek. "I'll let you know. Thank you. I love you." He nodded at the rest of his family then made his way his truck. It was only a fifteen-minute drive to Meghan's, but it felt like the longest fifteen minutes of his life. He had no idea why Richard had shown up at her place after so long, but the fact that he'd been there at all pissed Luc off.

He pulled into the driveway and was out of the truck as soon as he turned off the ignition. Meghan stood in the doorway, her face pale, but she appeared unharmed. She held up a hand as soon as he got near her. He pressed his chest up against her palm, needing her touch but not wanting to crowd her.

"The kids are inside. So we're going to be calm. Okay?" Her voice shook, and he wanted to rip Richard's balls off.

"What happened?" His voice came out as a growl, so he took a deep breath. "What happened?" he repeated, this time calmer.

She closed the door behind her so they both stood on the porch. "Richard came by to tell me he was going to sue for custody." As she told him word for word what the fucking prick had said, his shoulders tensed, raw fury roaring through him.

"That's not going to happen," he said as softly as he could. He didn't want to rage, didn't want to scare her with the depth of his anger. "I'll fight with you. We'll do everything we can to keep him out of their lives. You tell me what you need, and I'm here. I'm not going to say I'll take care of it because I don't have the first clue, but you need me? I'm here. Hell, even if you don't think you need me, I'm here."

A single tear slid down her cheek, and she leaned forward, kissing his chest. "Thank you. I knew you'd come. I don't know how I knew, but I knew. What you just said? That was perfect. I don't know the exact game plan because my mind is still whirling, but thank you. Now, the kids are inside, and they know something is wrong, but I haven't told them everything yet. I need to formulate a plan of action."

He nodded, giving in and pulling her close. His hand rested on the small of her back, and he let out a breath. "You want me with you when you do that?"

She bit her lip then nodded. "Yes. I know we're not clear on the future between us, but no matter what, you've always been good for my kids. I'm selfish, too, because I need you."

"Never think you're selfish for that." He kissed the top of her head. "Are we still going to your parents' tonight?"

She nodded under his hold. "Yeah. I need to tell them, and since most everyone should be there tonight anyway, I can get it over with all at once."

"Are you going to let them help you?" he asked. She tried to do so much on her own when she didn't need to, so he honestly didn't know the answer.

"I...I don't know."

"Okay then. You ready to go inside?" He pulled away and lifted his chin toward the window. "I just saw Sasha look through the curtains, so she knows I'm here."

"I guess so." Meghan stood on her toes, and he leaned down, letting his lips brush along hers. "Thank you. Thank you for dropping everything."

"You're worth it, Meghan. That and more."

She gave him a wobbly smile, and he followed her into the house. There was no way in hell Richard would get his greedy hands on those kids. He'd find a way to help, find a way to keep that bastard out of their lives forever.

Even with all the tension in the air, the uncertainty, one fact remained.

Meghan had reached out to him when she needed help. And that was progress.

One step closer, he reminded himself. One step closer to everything.

CHAPTER TWELVE

"That's not happening."

Megan let out a breath at the heat behind her father's words. He might not have the body mass or strength he once had due to the cancer ravaging his body, but beneath it all, the Montgomery will burned deep.

Luc squeezed her hand, anchoring her in a way she'd never thought possible. He hadn't said a word since they walked in, but he was there, her rock, her sanctuary.

It scared her how much she wanted to rely on that. She pushed that thought away, knowing she'd have to deal with her fear and dependency sooner or later.

"I'm not going to let it happen," she said softly. She hadn't meant to speak softly. In fact, when she'd come over to her parents' house and had spoken with the entirety of her family and Luc, she wanted to yell and scream. Only her voice emerged soft, a calmness that veiled the sheer panic growing within her.

"We're getting you a lawyer," Wes said as he pulled out his phone, presumably to either call or look up someone.

Storm put his hand on his twin's, stopping him. "Doesn't Meghan already have a lawyer?" He raised a brow at her. She loved all her brothers, she really did, but sometimes Storm got her better than the others. He might look like the calm and collected one, even with the scruff on his face, but he'd blow up when he had to. His temperament matched her own, which, considering that her organization skills matched Wes's, just reminded her that the twins were close to her heart.

"I do, but he was what I could afford at the time." She winced as she said it, trying her best to ignore the accusing glares on the faces of most of her family.

"Well, you wouldn't let us help last time," Maya put in, her voice not as loud as Meghan would have expected. In fact, her sister hadn't blown up at all. That, in itself, told Meghan how worried Maya was for her. When her sister had shown up at the house with Jake, she'd taken one look at Meghan's face and told Jake to watch the kids. To his credit, he simply kissed both women's brows and did as he was told. He wasn't a submissive man by nature—even with the force of Maya's personality—so he must have sensed what the others clearly had.

"We're helping this time," Miranda said, her hand in Decker's. "Between all of us, we can get you a top-notch lawyer. That fucker isn't touching those babies."

Decker grinned slightly, mirroring Meghan's own quirk of the lips. The man loved it when his fiancée got all fiery. Meghan loved it as well since her sister had been through hell and back. It was good to see that none of that had tempered the woman within.

"I know a few people," Griffin said, the sadness she'd glimpsed in his eyes before becoming more apparent. She didn't know what was wrong with her brother, didn't have time to dwell on it right then, but she promised herself that she'd find out. "I've worked with them before for research in a couple of my books. If they can't take you, then they'll know someone who specializes in custody cases. They're damn good at what they do, too. So, no, you won't be using the same lawyer as last time."

She narrowed her eyes at his tone, but Luc squeezed her hand once again, pulling her back from anything she might have said.

"Your lawyer got your kids for you last time, but this is different," Austin put in. "This time Richard is actually saying something. I don't even think the guy we used when we were officially taking in Leif would help."

"He wouldn't," Sierra said. "Completely different situations in all cases. Even the lawyers I used in the past with my own legal battles won't work for you. But we'll find you someone that is perfect."

"Does it bother anyone that we all seem to have lawyers on speed dial?"

Meghan inhaled through her nose and looked at Alex. He didn't have a drink in his hand, but by the way he spoke—slowly as if he was trying to keep each word precise—told her he was either hung over or already drunk. Decker and Miranda had picked him up, thankfully, so he wouldn't be behind the wheel, but she didn't know this brother. The two of them had married Richard and Jessica within a few months of each other, and both unions had ended in divorce around the same time. She knew her own pain, knew the battles she'd fought, but she didn't know Alex's. Didn't know anything about them. She hated herself for not knowing, for not being able to help, but her kids had to come first.

Only she had a feeling her own worries had come at Alex's expense. Her brother was on a path to destruction, and no matter how many times her siblings tried to help, he wouldn't find his way until he wanted to.

She just prayed he didn't hurt himself or others in the meantime.

"We've overcome a lot, Alex, and we will overcome this as well," their mother said, her tone sharper than Meghan had heard it in a while. "Let me get some coffee for the room."

Alex snorted. "I don't need coffee. Scotch would be nice."

"Alex," Marie snapped.

"Never mind," he mumbled.

Meghan's heart broke for him, but she needed to focus on her babies. That killed her, but she didn't have a choice. There were other Montgomerys to take care of him, but first, he had to *want* to care for himself.

Luc moved his hand from hers and rubbed the small of her back. She took a deep breath and continued the conversation about lawyers and Richard's accusations. Yet, the entire time, a small part of her mind focused on that hand—on the person who owned that hand.

He'd been by her side since he pulled up, and she leaned on him. He hadn't thought twice about jumping into her messes, her problems. He'd held her hand, touched her back, kissed her temples...everything and so much more. Not only had he let her rely on him, but he'd always controlled that quiet anger she knew he hid from Sasha and Cliff. She could see the rage in his eyes now, and his need to fix it all.

Luc deserved more from her. He needed a woman in his life who could share and relish each moment. He needed someone who didn't have as much baggage as she did. God knew what would happen in the future with Richard and the proceedings that could come. Just because her ex hadn't fought before didn't mean the right people and the right amount of money couldn't change everything in just a mere whisper of time.

Luc didn't need to give up his time and future to fix her problems. He was already doing that. Between the rides home when her car wouldn't start, cutting dates short when her kids needed her, the strength it took to deal with her when she ignored him...it was too much. She'd already hurt him once before by not recognizing what stood in front of her, and she refused to do it again.

Something broke inside her, a sharp snap echoing in the hollowness of her heart. He couldn't sacrifice a bright future with a woman who could love with the depth and breadth of her soul without restrictions and ties to a past paved with pain and heartache. He'd told her himself that he loved her once yet only cared for her now that they were adults and starting over. If she pushed him away now, he wouldn't hurt so much.

It would break her, but it was nothing more than she deserved.

She needed to focus on her children—not on the man she knew if she looked inside the cavernous ache that had once been her heart. Luc deserved more than a fraction of a woman long since damaged.

She rolled her shoulders back, her body going numb. Tears threatened, but she pushed them back. There was no room for tears. This was needed for the good of a man who deserved a future filled to the brim with hope and promise.

Throughout all of her thoughts, she kept talking, planning with her family. Luc's hand froze on her back, and he looked down at her.

He couldn't know what she planned. Yet she wouldn't meet his gaze. That would be for private. For later. When she had the courage to do what must be done.

He'd be hurt, but not as much as he would be if she let him love her.

Her babies would cry and want Luc back in their lives, but she couldn't hurt Luc more than she already had. Because if she let him in, she'd rely on him too much and break them all.

This was for the best.

And maybe one day, she'd heal from the sacrifice.

****

Luc knew something was wrong. There was no way to miss the look of defeat in Meghan's eyes. Oh, she might have found a plan of action with her family when it came to her children, but something else had broken within her.

From the way she ever so slightly pulled away from his touch and refused to look in his eyes, he had a feeling he knew what she'd given up.

Him.

Well, fuck that. She was scared. Damn if she didn't have a right to be, but he wouldn't let her take the easy way out, and letting her walk away without a second thought would be the easy way out. The woman always had to do things on her own. That she'd let her family help her now spoke of her determination to protect her children.

But she refused to protect her heart.

Or, rather, she'd encased the damn thing in such a shield that she refused to let him in. He wouldn't break her, damn it, and once the kids were put to bed, he'd show her running was not an option.

He fucking loved Meghan Montgomery-Warren, and he'd be damned if he would let her go because of the fear of what could happen when she fully relied on another. He could already hear the so-called reasonable excuses for why she'd leave him, but he didn't care about any of those. Meghan was his, and he refused to allow her to risk a chance at something more because she was scared or, for fuck's sake, worried about him.

He loved her.

Damn it.

He knew it of course. It wasn't as though it was a surprise, but tonight wasn't the time to tell her. Not when the woman he loved had it in her to push him away to protect him or, rather, protect herself. The true reason lay somewhere between the two, but either way, he wouldn't let her throw away everything they had because of it.

Instead, he said his goodbyes to the Montgomerys, seeing the looks on their faces at his hold on her and the kids. It wasn't curious or even wary. No, they approved of him, and that made him feel that much more sure he wasn't making a mistake by not allowing Meghan to push him away.

A tug on his hand and he looked down into Sasha's wide eyes. They'd been back at Meghan's for about thirty minutes. Enough time for Meghan to avoid talking to him, other than letting him inside.

The kids would be going to bed soon, and then they'd discuss matters.

First, though, he had to make sure this little girl knew he would *always* be there. He knelt down and smiled. "Yes, Sasha?"

"Will you read to us?" she asked, her voice oddly soft.

"Of course. You know what book you want?"

She nodded. "Uh-huh." She paused, biting her lip. "Uncle Luc?"

"Yeah, princess?"

"Is Daddy really going to take us away from Mommy? Because I don't want to go. He never smiled at me, and his eyes were mean. I know he's supposed to be my daddy, but I want you instead. Or just Mommy. Don't make me go to Daddy. Okay?"

His heart broke into a million pieces for this little girl. He couldn't make her promises he wasn't sure he could keep. Money spoke, and sometimes the courts didn't work for those who were honest and hardworking. But he'd be damned if he'd scare her right then. Instead, he told her the only truth he knew.

"Your Mommy loves you." He took a deep breath. "I love you too, princess. No matter what, neither of us is leaving you."

"I love you too, Uncle Luc." She wrapped her arms around his neck, and he held on as tight as he could without squeezing too hard. "Book now?"

He took a deep breath then stood up, taking her with him. She kissed his cheek then babbled on about what she wanted to do at school the next day as they made their way to her bedroom.

Seriously. Adorable kid.

And he'd protect them as fiercely as Meghan would. The woman he loved would just have to get that through her head. Meghan stood in the doorway, her arms wrapped around her middle. He nodded at her then tucked Sasha in. By the time he read two stories, both Cliff and Sasha were out. Cliff hadn't said much other than goodnight to him, but he could see the toll of the day on the little boy's face.

He had a feeling he knew what was wrong with Cliff, but he needed to feel the kid out more before he confronted him. Some things were too fragile to handle without grace.

He touched Meghan's elbow and met her gaze finally. The stark fear and loss knocked him back, but he swallowed hard, letting the determination in his face show in his eyes.

"Let's go to the bedroom and talk," he said softly.

She looked around him at the kids.

He pulled her gently to the hallway, shutting the door behind him. "They're sleeping, and they know we're together, Meghan. I don't have to stay the night, but we need to talk."

She licked her lips then turned toward the bedroom. He didn't let go of her, knowing that once he did she'd find a way to try to keep him from touching her again. Instead, he followed her to the bedroom and, once again, shut the door behind him. This time he locked it, aware there were children in the house who didn't know to knock.

"Luc."

"Meg." He pulled her close and cupped her face with one hand while keeping the other on her wrist. "You can't push me away to protect me."

"I have to," she whispered. "You deserve so much better than me."

"Bullshit."

Her eyes widened. "What?"

"You don't get to tell me what I deserve."

"And you don't get to tell me what I feel."

"Right back at you," he clipped. "Damn it, Meg. I know you're scared. You have every damn right to be, but that doesn't mean you get to push me away because of it. I'm here *for* you, just as I'm here for me. I want you, Meghan. All of you, every part of you that you keep trying to hide. But you don't get to leave me because you're scared of what's to come. I'm sorry, but fuck that."

Anger sparked in her eyes, and he let relief spread through him. Anger he could work with. Fear at the tone of his words, he couldn't. But his Meghan was stronger than she gave herself credit for.

"Fuck that? I'm making sure you have options. It's for your own good."

"I'm not your child, Meghan. I'm your lover, your friend, your boyfriend. You can't tell me it's for my own good when I clearly think the opposite. So don't push me away telling me it's all about me when it's not."

"If you stay, I'll take too much from you."

"If I stay, I'll give all I have to give."

Her eyes filled with tears, and she shook her head. "I don't cry. Yet all I seem to do lately is cry."

Luc leaned forward and brushed his lips along hers, a soft caress filled with so much more. "Don't cry, my Meghan."

"You have to go, Luc. I'll only end up hurting you."

"Why do you say that? You can't hurt me more than I let you, Meghan. But pushing me away right now? *That* will hurt me. So don't push me away. Let me fight with you, rather than fight for what we have. I'll do the latter if I need to, but I'd rather not be forced to. I don't want you to push me away. Let me be here. Let me be yours."

"It's all too much, Luc," she whispered, her eyes closed.

"Then let me help. That's what I'm here for. If it's all too much, then let me carry the burden."

"I can't do that to you."

"You're not doing anything to me if I'm freely offering myself. Open your eyes, sugar."

She did, the sadness inside reaching out to him. "I don't want to lose you, Luc."

"Then don't let go."

He lowered his head then, taking her mouth with his. She leaned into him, her body pressed tightly against his. When he pulled back, breathless, he met her gaze.

"Don't do it, Meghan. Don't push me away because you're scared. If you want me to leave, make it be for something I've done or something you need, not for something that might never be."

"I promise," she whispered. "I was just so scared of losing you because I need you."

That agonizing confession broke him once again, but instead of dwelling on it, he kissed her again, this time walking her backward to her bed. He kissed her, his tongue tangling with hers.

She arched into him and moaned. He slid his hands down her back and cupped her ass, pressing his cock against her belly.

"You feel that, Meg? You feel my cock hard as a rock? That's for you. I'm going to slide in and out of you, stretch you until your tissues cling to me and you come. How does that sound?"

She wiggled against him, and he smiled.

"Strip. Do it slowly."

He stood back and folded his arms over his chest. She blinked up at him then did as he told. She ever so slowly stripped off her clothes, being so fucking seductive and sexy without even trying.

"Touch your breasts. Show me what you like."

"Seriously?"

He smiled then. "Yeah, cup them and play with your nipples."

"Only if you touch yourself, too."

He licked his lips. "That I can do, sugar. Sit on the edge of the bed and spread your legs as well. That way I can see that pretty cunt of yours get wet."

"Get wet? What if I'm already wet?"

"Fucking minx," he growled out as he stripped off his clothes. He fisted his cock and gave himself two strokes. "Now play with your nipples then slowly slide your hand down your body until you touch your clit."

"I want you to touch me, Luc," she panted as she swirled her finger around her clit.

"And I will." He squeezed the base of his cock so he wouldn't blow right then. "But first, I want you to make yourself come before I fuck you. Can you do that for me, sugar? Can you make yourself come so you're all swollen and silky when I slide my dick into your cunt?"

He watched her fuck herself with her fingers, her hips moving up and down as she moved faster.

"Luc, I'm almost there."

"Come for me, Meghan. Come for me."

She met his gaze, her mouth partly open, her eyes dark, and she came, her body shaking. He quickly tore open the condom he'd placed by his clothes and slid it on. He cupped the back of her neck and forced her eyes on his.

"Mine," he growled then thrust into her. Hard.

Her pussy clenched around him, and they both groaned. He moved his hips, sliding in and out of her, but his hand never left her neck.

"You're not leaving me, Meghan. You don't get to leave because you're scared you'll take too much. You're mine." Her fingers dug into his back, and he let the pain ramp up his intensity. "Say it, Meghan."

"I'm yours," she panted. "I'm yours."

"Good." He crushed his mouth to hers and fucked her hard. She wrapped her legs around his waist, moving her hips with his.

Just as he felt his orgasm coming, he pulled out, ignoring her whimper. He flipped her over on her stomach and slammed back into her.

"Grip the sheets, sugar. Press back on my cock and fuck me as I'm fucking you."

Her toes barely touched the floor so she had to use her hips to fuck him back, but she did it. Every thrust, she moved on his cock, making it harder and harder to hold back and not come right then.

He slapped her ass and grinned when she looked over his shoulder.

"Did you just spank me?"

"I'll do it again if I have to. Your pussy just clenched around my cock, baby. You liked it."

She narrowed her eyes, so he slapped her again. This time her eyes rolled, and he kept moving his hips.

"It's my choice to be with you, my choice to stay. You don't get to say I've had enough. Okay, sugar?"

"Anything, Luc. I promise. Just let me come."

He slid his hand around her and flicked her clit. She came again, but he still didn't let go. Instead, he gathered her juices and slid his finger between her ass cheeks.

"Luc?" she moaned.

"Feel this, Meghan. Feel *me*."

He slowly prodded her ass with his finger before gently breaching her. She let out a groan, and so did he. He used only one finger, gently thrusting as he fucked her pussy with his cock.

"Can you come one more time, Meghan? Can you come for me?"

"I don't know if I can," she moaned, her words slurred.

"Just try, baby. One more time."

He twisted his finger, and she came again, clamping onto his cock. This time he couldn't hold back and came with her, her cunt milking him for all he was worth.

This woman was his, his alone to cherish, his alone to fall in love with. Fear threatened to take them both, threatened to break them, but he wouldn't allow that. She was stronger than she'd ever been before, and he'd be damned if he let that fear take what they had.

He'd fight for her, fight for himself, fight for them.

CHAPTER THIRTEEN

The buzz of the needle on her skin didn't hurt. Instead, Meghan smiled down at her brother Austin's work. Each of her tattoos meant something to her—as they should, considering they were permanent. Richard had hated the first one she had, and she forced herself not to get any more, despite the fact that her family lived in the ink business. With all that had been happening with her lawyers and Richard though, she knew she needed to get something that was all about her and her family. Luc wanted to be there with her, but he had an emergency at the job site—cleaning up the mess Steve the asshat had left for him. She'd told him she could wait, but Luc said he'd see the finished product later. He'd kissed her and gone on his way.

She still couldn't believe she'd almost lost him because she'd been an idiot. Running away from her problems had never been her way, yet that's what she tried to do. Luc had loved her up and made her feel like a queen—a queen who could rely on him in every way possible. She needed to get it through her head that was okay.

The tattoo on her hip had hurt like the dickens, even with Maya being as careful as possible. The tiny flower surrounded by her children's initials on her wrist didn't hurt at all.

"Seriously, I don't get it," she said, her eyes on the lines of ink and blood.

Austin wiped away the leftover ink and plasma, his focus on his work and not on her. "Different spots hurt on different people. I know one guy who had a huge back piece done and the left side hurt way fucking more than the right."

Meghan smiled and looked over Austin's shoulder at his co-worker, Callie, and winked. "Are you talking about Morgan?"

Callie grinned at them, a sketchpad in her hands. If the woman wasn't working with a client, she was always drawing. "Actually, yes, though we do tons of back pieces so it could have been anyone. Some people have odd reactions to tattoos and ink. If you add in the different sensitivity of nerves, muscle memory, and layers of fat or bone placement, it's a toss-up for what will hurt more. It's not like what some random website says about pain levels on different parts of the body. It might seem that way if you average people out, but not in each individual case. I will say that I didn't press harder on his left than I did his right, but he felt the pain just the same."

Meghan winced as Austin went over a vein. "I spoke too soon. Ouch, bro."

He grinned at her, his big beard hiding most of his mouth, but she didn't care. She loved her big broody, bearded, inked brother. Even if he currently had a needle on her wrist.

"Wuss."

"Prick."

"Love you, too," he said then changed out the needles. "I need to do some shading. I left some space around the sides for more initials by the way."

Meghan froze then raised a brow at her brother. Her ever-meddling brother. "Excuse me? What do you mean more initials?"

He raised his own brow at her but didn't say anything.

"What our idiot brother is saying is that he doesn't want to have to change up the design and try to do a cover-up or some shit if and when you and Luc have more kids," Maya said from her station. Her sister stood slightly bent over a very large biker who gave Meghan the chills for some reason, but she didn't really care about that right now.

"More kids?" she asked, her throat suddenly dry. "Luc?" She coughed.

Sloane, another artist and friend, handed her a cup of water. "Drink up, buttercup."

The word buttercup coming from the bald man, who had to be over six-two and was two hundred and twenty pounds of pure muscle, had her laughing up her water. Austin waited patiently, holding his tattoo gun while she caught her breath and cleaned up the mess she made.

"Buttercup?"

Sloane winked at her before heading through the door that connected to Taboo. Hopefully, he was off to visit Hailey. While she would love to think more about whether those two would ever just get it on, Austin's words still rang in her mind.

"Kids," Austin said softly once she looked at him again. "You're still young. You can have more. Or adopt like Sierra and I might. You never know. Don't close off your future because you're still scared about the past."

"It's a tattoo, Austin," she whispered, knowing the ramifications were much, much more than that.

"It's your life. And I'm not telling you how to live it."

"That would be a first," Maya mumbled, and Meghan smiled despite herself.

It was true that Austin tended to try to micromanage his siblings' lives, but since he'd married Sierra, he'd toned it down. Somewhat. Now he had two children and a wife to try and manage. Or at least keep happy.

"Luc and I aren't serious," she lied. She *knew* it was a lie. Austin knew it was a lie. Callie knew it. Maya knew it. They all did.

"Meghan." Austin's deep voice rolled over her like it always had when they were younger. He really was her big brother in every sense of the word. "Don't be an idiot."

How could she not be? She and Luc had made love and passed through boundaries she never knew existed, but she still held that innate fear that she'd never be enough. Stupid didn't even begin to cover that particular feeling, but she couldn't help it. There was a little part of her that kept telling her she'd never be enough, never be able to hold on to him and he'd leave town. Again.

She needed to kick that little part's ass.

This whole flip-flop emotional mess was too much. Fuck her doubts.

If only that kind of attitude would stay around longer.

Between her doubts, Richard, her kids, her job, and Luc working overtime on the house because of issues with work, she figured her brain was having its own pity party of doom.

It needed to stop. Now.

"You done overthinking?" Austin asked, his hand still holding her wrist.

She swallowed hard and nodded. "Yeah, but I need a minute before we finish."

He tilted his head. "We have like ten minutes left on this one, Meghan. It'll take longer to wrap you up than to finish the shading."

"I need a minute to breathe. Plus, I have to pee." She smiled softly when he rolled his eyes at that last part.

"Fine then. Pee but don't fuck up your wrist. Use your other hand to wipe." He lathered goo on her wrist so it wouldn't dry out in the minute she was gone and stood up from his stool. "I could use a break to stretch my back anyway. Got a new client coming in right after you."

"You're busy these days," Meghan said as she stood on her toes. Her big brother leaned down so she could place a kiss on his bearded cheek.

"I'm always busy, but I like it. Now go pee so I can finish up your ink."

She took her phone with her to the bathroom and locked the door behind her. She'd missed a call when she was in the chair so she might as well listen to the message while she went about her business.

As soon as she heard the snide tone on the other line, she knew she'd made a mistake in not checking who'd called.

"I'll be seeing the kids this weekend. I have visitation rights, and you can't keep them from me. Ambrosia wants to meet them so she is prepared for when they eventually move in with us. Because, Meghan, they *will* move in with Ambrosia and me. It doesn't matter what little lawyer you bring in. I will always win. You are nothing, and you need to remember that. That spine you found from fucking that blue-collar pissant won't last long once I'm through with you. It never did."

He hung up, and the message ended, leaving her shaking. She put her phone away then washed her hands, splashing water on her face. A single tear hadn't fallen, and for that, she was grateful. However, just the man's voice made her want to curl in on herself—new spine be damned.

God, that fucking bastard. He thought he could just come in and take whatever he wanted. There was no way he'd take her babies that weekend. Their agreement stated he needed to ask through his lawyer and get approval ahead of time. He couldn't just show up when he wanted and take them. He'd never gone through the process before—never bothered to see his children in the past year, so he didn't understand that.

Richard didn't understand a lot of things. Well, she was about to make sure he understood *everything*.

She looked down at her phone, ready to call Luc and tell him what had happened. Before she could dial though, she stopped herself. He was at work dealing with other people's errors. She couldn't bother him every time something happened. However, she *would* tell him that night. There was no way she could hide that from him, and she'd promised them both she'd learn to rely on him, even if it was only for a shoulder to cry on.

Besides, she had her family outside the door waiting for her. She could talk to them. Meghan looked at herself in the mirror, surprised at the woman she saw. Yes, her face had paled since the phone call, but that darkness in her eyes she'd long since taken as her new look was absent. Instead, the fire inside shone through. She'd fight for her children, and Richard couldn't take that away from her.

After taking a deep breath, she opened the door and slammed into a redheaded woman. Meghan took a step back, teeth rattling.

"Shit," the other woman muttered. "I'm sorry, I didn't know anyone was in here. I shouldn't have been so close to the door." She had an accent Meghan couldn't place. It was more of a mix of accents rather than one particular one. Just a slight lilt that told Meghan that she wasn't a Denver native, where the lack of accent was their claim.

The woman's long auburn hair lay in soft curls around her head, and her bright brown eyes looked truly apologetic. Meghan probably had an inch on her height-wise, but the other woman had curves to kill for.

"No, I'm sorry," Meghan said. "I shouldn't have stormed out of the bathroom like that."

The other woman smiled, and Meghan did the same. "Well, anyway, are you done? Because I had a really long drive and I kind of have to go."

Meghan laughed and stood out of the way. "Sorry about that. All yours." She made her way back to Austin's station and sat down on the chair.

"Looks like you met my new client," Austin said, his attention on his wrist.

"I did. She's gorgeous."

Austin looked up at her, a smile on his face. "I thought you were taken. And, you know, straight."

"She can look and not touch," Maya put in. The biker in the chair laughed deeply.

"Thank you both for that," Meghan said dryly. "And it was just an observation."

Austin snorted. "Which Montgomery do you want to set her up with? I thought that was Maya's job."

"Matchmaking isn't a job I take lightly, thank you very much."

Meghan just shook her head and let the buzz of the needle wash over her as her siblings bickered. They settled her in ways she couldn't understand, and she loved them so damn much. Once Austin had the needle out of her skin, she'd tell them what Richard said on the phone then deal with it. She'd deal with it all, but maybe this time she'd learn to lean on someone. Luc was teaching her that.

Another part of her heart ached, and she took a deep breath. The man had taught her so much, and if he ever opened his eyes and left her...

Well, she didn't know what she'd do then. She didn't want to learn that lesson.

Ever.

AUTUMN

Autumn Minor walked out from the shop bathroom, drying her hands on her pants as she did so. She hoped the woman she'd bumped into was okay. It looked as if she'd needed a hug or someone to talk to, but Autumn didn't have the time to see if she could help. She saw the other woman getting her ink done by Austin, the man who would work with her soon, so she held back, waiting in the wings while the other woman composed herself. It took only twenty minutes, and it didn't matter too much to her. She didn't want to intrude, and she'd heard the woman mention she was related to the artists so she gave them space.

Maybe she'd see her again one day and be able to do something about it.

That was Autumn. Full of the need to help and "one days".

"You ready to go?" the big, bearded tattoo artist asked. "Thanks for waiting."

Autumn nodded. "No problem. I was early."

"I know we talked about your ink, but let's talk more." He patted the seat in front of him, and she noticed the big band on his finger. He was hot, but married. Too bad.

Oh, well, it wasn't as though she was looking for someone. She'd just moved to town and didn't need to put down roots. She held back a shudder. Hell no, she didn't need roots. Or connections.

"I just need a touch-up today, but if things go well, I'd like to get something fresh."

Austin nodded. "Where did you get your other work done?"

She shrugged. "Everywhere. I'm a nomad."

"Well, you have nice work from what I can see," he said with the tone of man appreciating art, not picking up a woman. Good for him. She hated cheaters.

"I don't like shit ink."

"Good, because I don't give shit ink." He sat back in his chair, studying her tats. "So, you're new to the metro area then?"

She didn't like questions, but being cagey would just raise flags. "Yeah. Pretty new."

He raised a brow at her tone. Apparently, she hadn't hidden her worries enough. "Okay then. No more questions. Tell me about your ink."

She let out a breath and talked about the things she could without having a panic attack.

She didn't know these people and didn't want to. Because once she did, they'd be in the line of fire.

Others always were.

CHAPTER FOURTEEN

"**I** now pronounce you, husband and wife. You may kiss the bride."

Luc threw his head back and laughed as Decker dipped Miranda practically to the floor, devouring his new bride with his mouth. He wasn't the only one laughing amongst the catcalls and hollers inside the Montgomery house.

Of course, not everyone laughed. Each of the Montgomery brothers who stood by Decker's side up front looked as though they were ready to pound their new brother-in-law into the ground. The ladies on Miranda's side just smiled and wiped their eyes.

He met Meghan's gaze and smiled full-out. She stood next to Maya in a light blue dress that fit her curves perfectly. She did a little finger wave, and he tipped his chin at her. He couldn't wait to have her in his arms, and he swept her across the dance floor the Montgomerys had made of the dining room.

Decker and Miranda had done as Luc had suggested and planned a very small wedding with just family and the closest of friends in the parents' backyard. Of course since Colorado winter had set in, they'd opted for inside the large home that had raised the family. Since they were Montgomerys and pros at having parties at the house, they'd gone all-out to ensure it was a day they'd never forget—even if it was small and intimate.

Each of the siblings was there, standing up for their family. Decker had chosen Griffin to be his best man while the others stood in order of age. Alex wavered on the end. The man looked worse for wear. However, Luc couldn't quite keep his eyes of Meghan. The sisters were by Miranda's side, of course, and Miranda had added Sierra, Callie, and Hailey to even out the numbers. There were a few too many Montgomery men out there to make things perfectly even without help.

That was one reason Luc hadn't felt slighted at not being asked to stand for Decker. He might be as close to the man as some of the Montgomerys—more so in some cases—but the Montgomerys were Decker's family—blood or not. Luc would go home with his own Montgomery tonight, so that was all that mattered.

Cliff, Leif, and Sasha had acted as ring bearers and the flower girl before sitting down next to their grandparents in the front. Baby Colin slept peacefully in Marie Montgomery's arms as she leaned into her husband, the same husband who had surprised the hell out of all of them when he'd walked his baby girl down the aisle. He'd told the hushed crowd that he'd be damned if he'd let his baby walk alone—cancer or no cancer.

Of course, the crowd wasn't all that big. Since the wedding party was filled with Montgomerys, there was only one row of seats for the rest of the crew. Marie and Harry took up Miranda's side with the children while Decker, Sloane, and Jake took up Decker's side.

Small, but perfect for Decker and Miranda.

After all, Decker once said he'd lost everything before he found Miranda and the Montgomerys. What else could he need?

"If I ever get married, I'd want something like this," Jake said from Luc's side.

Luc turned to Maya's best friend and nodded. "I get that, though I don't think my parents would let that happen. My mom would want all her friends to be there, and it'd turn into a big thing."

Jake looked toward Maya and Meghan, who stood laughing as Decker continued to kiss Miranda. Seriously, the two of them were animals.

"Well, as long as Meghan is happy, I guess your wedding will be whatever it needs to be," Jake said then stood up and whistled. "Get a room!"

"Or not," Harry called out. "Get your hands off my daughter, son. Time to party. Then you can take your new wife away, and I don't want to hear about any of it."

Luc laughed again and shook his head as Decker carried his bride down the aisle. Instead of waiting for the wedding party to follow, Luc stood and took Meghan by the arm. "I'm walking you back, sorry to Austin."

She rolled her eyes. "He can take Callie," she quipped then kissed him softly. That she'd kiss him in front of her family spoke of how far they'd come in the past couple of months.

"Kiss me, too!" Sasha bounced up and down, and he picked her up, settling her on his hip. He placed a small kiss on her cheek, and she sighed, resting her head on his shoulder. "Thank you."

He chuckled and wrapped one arm around Meghan's waist. Cliff stood on the other side of Meghan and gave him a shy smile. Progress.

Again, he didn't miss the knowing smiles of the Montgomerys and crew at the picture he and Meghan presented. Like a family.

God, how he wanted this. He'd never realized he wanted more than just the open road and a roof over his head when needed. But, damn, he couldn't help but picture Cliff and Sasha growing older with him by Meghan's side through it all. Yeah, Richard might be huffing and puffing, and doing his best to fuck up everything, but they'd prevail. There wasn't another option when it came to Meghan and her kids.

He still hadn't said he'd loved her yet. That would come. The shell she'd encased herself in for so long was just beginning to crack, and he knew the words were ready. She wouldn't run away from them. That didn't mean she'd say them back. One thing at a time, he reminded himself. One thing at time.

"So now that the vows are said, and it's just us, we can eat and dance," Meghan put in as she played with Cliff's hair. The kid rolled his eyes but didn't move away. Again, progress.

"Save me a dance?" Luc asked. "Or all of them."

Meghan smiled and leaned forward. "You can have as many as you want."

"Kiss! Kiss!" Sasha squealed from his arms.

Well, he couldn't disappoint her. He lowered his head and brushed his lips softly across Meghan's and sighed. Damn, this was perfect. So fucking perfect he was afraid for it all to come crumbling down. He pushed that thought from his mind knowing it was best to worry about things he could fix, rather than what he couldn't prevent.

"I need to fix the kids' plates," Meghan said, breaking into his thoughts. "Do you want me to get you something?"

He shook his head. "No, I'm good. You need help?"

"I've got it. Go talk with my brothers and make sure they're okay. I know they're happy for Decker and Miranda, but they're still freaked that their baby sister is married."

He grinned despite himself and kissed her temple. "I can do that. Don't want them beating the poor guy for groping his wife."

"Little ears," she said with a smile, and he rolled his eyes.

"Gotcha." He set Sasha down on her feet, nodded at Cliff, and headed back to where Griffin stood in the corner, nursing a beer.

"Hey, Griff. You thinking too hard over here?"

Griffin blinked as if he'd been lost in thought, and shook his head before nodding.

Luc snorted. "Yeah, that answer made sense."

"Sorry, my brain was on this scene that's been giving me trouble."

"Aren't you on deadline?" Luc asked.

"Past it, actually," Griffin answered dryly.

"No shit? Isn't that a first?" Very unlike Griffin. Wes might be the highly organized brother, but Griffin, despite his lack of neatness at home, worked on schedule to a scary degree.

"Yep, which pisses me off. I should be home writing but..." He shrugged, and Luc nodded.

"It's your baby sister's wedding."

"Yep. She's only two down from me since Alex is between us in age, but she's still my baby sister. And she's married and looking into the future."

"Wedding bells ringing in your ears, Griff?" Luc didn't think the man had a steady girlfriend, but he didn't know everything about the Montgomerys. There were too many of them to know it all, though Maya tried.

"Nothing like that, not yet anyway. And speaking of wedding bells, looks like you and Meghan are pretty serious." He looked over Luc's shoulder, and Luc moved to see Meghan standing with her kids.

"I think we're getting serious," Luc said honestly. "But I don't want to spook her."

"Going to be hard not to with Richard lurking like he is."

"Fucking bastard," he grumbled.

"Amen."

"Talking about that piece of trash, Dick?" Alex slurred as he strolled up to them. There was an angry look in his eyes that set Luc on alert. Shit. This wasn't going to end well.

"Hey, man, let's get you a water," Luc said, trying to keep his tone low.

"Fuck off, Luc. I don't know what it is about this family and trying to get me water, but I'm tired of it. Plus, *bro*, you aren't family."

"Alex," Griffin snapped. "What the fuck is your problem?"

Well, shit. Luc put his hand on Griffin's arm, hoping he would get the hint. This was neither the time nor the place to do this. Miranda and Decker deserved a day filled with happy memories after the shit they'd been through. Confronting Alex right now wasn't the best option. Yeah, they needed to, but it could wait a couple hours.

Or so he thought.

From the manic look in Alex's eyes, perhaps they'd all waited too long.

"My problem? My fucking problem is that we're letting Miranda marry a man too old for her. Fuck, we're letting her get married at all. You've seen what happens when we Montgomerys get married. We fuck it up."

Luc stepped forward, but Alex raised his hand. The man's arm shook, so Luc didn't move any more than he had. Out of the corner of his eye, he saw Sierra and Meghan slowly back the children out of the room, but the rest of the Montgomerys and crew had their eyes on the show in front of them.

"Alex," Luc said calmly. "Let's talk about this outside. You can tell me everything, but let's do it somewhere else."

"Fuck you, Luc. You're not even family. Why are you here?"

The slurred words didn't hurt; they couldn't. Not when the agony in Alex's gaze was far worse than anything Luc could feel.

"Luc," Marie whispered, coming closer to her son. Alex raised his arm, and she froze.

Damn it.

"Jessica left me a long fucking time ago, but we stayed together. For what? For vows? They mean *nothing*. Mom and Dad are together, but for how long? Look at him! He's fucking *dying,* and we're not talking about it. Sure, Sierra and Austin are happy now, but she almost died giving him a kid, and now he wants more? Sooner or later it will be too much, and that's another marriage down the drain." Alex threw back the last of his drink and dropped the tumbler on the floor.

It bounced off the carpet, its muted thud echoing in Luc's ears.

"And Meghan, let's talk about that, shouldn't we?" Alex sneered. "Richard beat her down until she was just a fucking shadow of herself. Is that what *marriage* does? Makes us *nothing*? She's not even through with the bastard, and now she's leading you on a chain because she can't not be with a man. We're letting Miranda follow the same path because we're clueless. Marriage is for the weak. Marriage is a lie."

A slow rage built up in Luc's veins. He knew these weren't the words of a sane and healthy man. The drink had rotted the man's brains, the agony of whatever had caused Alex's divorce long since erasing the man the Montgomerys loved. Luc just hoped it wasn't too late because it took everything within him not to beat the shit out Alex for daring to speak like he did of Meghan and the rest of the Montgomerys.

"What?" Alex snapped, taking a look at the wide-eyed family around him. "Like you haven't thought it. I'm the only one brave enough to say it."

Before Luc could blink, Alex staggered toward him, his fist coming at Luc. He moved out of the way just as Alex powered forward. Only he hadn't thought about the glass table behind him. Someone screamed, and Alex crashed through the glass coffee table, shards of glass spraying across the room, embedding in Luc's skin.

"Alex!" Miranda screamed.

Luc knelt down, careful of the glass, and tried to help the man up, only he froze at the sight of a large piece sticking out of Alex's side.

"Call an ambulance," Luc barked.

"On it," Jake said from his side. "Fuck, we can't move him, not without making the glass go deeper."

"Fuck off," Alex slurred then passed out, either from pain or drink, Luc didn't know. But the anguish in the other man's eyes put away any anger on Luc's part. The man needed help, not his fists.

"Luc?" Meghan whispered from behind him.

"Get back, everyone," he bit out. "There's glass everywhere."

"You're bleeding," she said, and this time her voice was stronger.

He looked down at the patches of blood but shook his head. "They're superficial. Tiny cuts. We need to keep Alex still until the ambulance comes. Just make sure the kids stay out of here."

Meghan put her hand on his shoulder, even though he'd told her to go. "They are. Sierra is with them. I need to make sure you're okay." Her voice sounded hollow.

He stood up on shaky legs as Decker and Griffin came forward, keeping Alex still while doing what they could to stop the bleeding.

"Let me take care of you," Meghan said softly.

"Okay," he whispered back, following her, his body shaking.

Alex had fucked up, but so had the rest of them. They'd let him get this far, and they hadn't been able to do anything. They all said that Alex had to *want* to get help in order to find his way, and they tried to do what they could, but it hadn't been enough. Alex had officially hit rock bottom, and Luc had no idea what would come next.

The only thing he *did* know was that Meghan's hands were on him, stripping off his shirt in the kitchen while she looked for the small cuts.

"The ambulance is coming," Marie said from the doorway. Luc met her eyes, and his heart broke for her. "We'll make sure they look at you too, Luc." She thinned her lips then turned back to where her son lay bleeding and broken on her white carpet.

His gaze landed on the wedding cake, uncut and pristine. It seemed Miranda and Decker would always remember this day, only Luc knew it wouldn't be for the way it should have been. He met Meghan's eyes and sighed.

"I'm okay."

Meghan swallowed hard. "I'm not," she whispered.

She didn't lean closer, as if afraid of the glass in his skin, and he didn't blame her. He just rested his forehead on hers and let out a breath. He had her by his side, no matter what Alex said. That had to count for something.

It had to.

CHAPTER FIFTEEN

Meghan's hands shook. It wasn't shock. She knew that much. It had to be nerves or maybe pure exhaustion. The sun's rays shone in her bathroom, and she let out a breath. Exhaustion might be the answer.

She hadn't slept all night, and now the sun rose, signaling a morning she knew she wasn't ready for. She ran a hand through her hair. Talk about a lost cause. She needed a shower and a truck full of coffee so she could make it through the day. In fact, she might need two trucks' worth.

Today's plan entailed dinner with Luc's family, and Luc's mother had invited Cliff and Sasha as well. Only Meghan didn't feel up to meeting his parents again after so long and dealing with anyone other than her family after yesterday's debacle. She still couldn't believe Alex's words—let alone his actions.

She knew he drank too much, but like the rest of her family, she'd been so focused on her own life she'd missed the signs that things had turned dangerous. The fault rested on her shoulders as much as it did

Alex's. He'd been in pain and had turned to the bottle rather than his family.

Of course, Meghan had turned inward and focused on becoming independent and raising her children rather than drinking, but she couldn't blame Alex for his decisions. At least not on such a short amount of sleep. He'd hurt himself far worse physically than he had anyone else, but she'd never forget the blood on Luc's arms and chest. She could forgive her brother for his words over time, but hurting Luc and himself would be something that would take time to forgive.

At least she still had a brother to forgive.

If the glass had been slightly to the right, she'd have lost him then and there. Her knees went weak, and she had to grip the sink to keep from falling. She licked her lips, the taste of bile on her tongue acidic.

Griffin had jumped in the ambulance with Alex, with Maya and Jake following in Jake's SUV. Dad had nixed the idea of all of them going in support. It had been a blow to hear the words, but she understood. They needed to get the kids home, he needed rest, and Decker and Miranda needed to enjoy what was left of their wedding night. Decker had lived with a drunk, abusive father for most of his life. He didn't need to see more of that on the day that should have been the happiest of his life.

All of that merely veiled the real reason—Alex needed help, and he wouldn't get it if they attacked him or overcrowded him. She knew only second-hand what had happened in the hospital, and it hadn't been pretty.

Griffin had done his best to keep their brother safe and still so he could get stitched up. Then when Alex had thrown him out, he let Maya and Jake take over. Meghan didn't know what had been said, but whatever they'd done, it worked.

The two of them got Alex into a local rehab program that would take him in as soon as he was medically discharged.

Their brother was an alcoholic.

An alcoholic that had hurt himself and almost hurt so many more.

Things could have been far worse, but that didn't matter. Her baby brother's pain had been too great, and now she didn't know how to help him. She'd heard the words he'd said about her, had let each blow sink in because he'd spoken a version of the truth. She wasn't that woman anymore. She wasn't the shadow Richard had made her. Yet, sometimes, when she wasn't cognizant of it, she knew she let the shadow creep in.

She couldn't do that anymore. Not when she needed to be the self she'd created on her own in the past year...and with Luc in these last weeks.

She turned from the mirror at a soft knock on the door. Luc walked in, sweats riding low on his hips. Her gaze followed the strong lines of his chest and stomach, pausing on the small cuts on his skin. Nothing had been too deep, and the paramedic hadn't even brought Luc to the hospital, instead saying he'd be fine but they should watch for signs of infection. Nothing had needed stiches; nothing would leave permanent scars.

And yet she couldn't get the sight of blood on flesh out of her mind.

"Meghan?"

"You were bleeding," she whispered.

His eyes filled with pity, and he moved forward, his arms out. She leaned into his hold, pressing her nose to his skin, inhaling his scent, making sure he was real. He wrapped his arms around her and nuzzled the top of her head with his cheek.

"I was. But I'm not anymore. I'm okay, Meghan." He pulled back and studied her face. She wanted to duck under his scrutiny but didn't. "I wish we could have slept, but we were waiting on that phone call."

The phone call from Jake that hadn't come until an hour ago. She and Luc had stayed up all night talking and just holding one another until they'd heard about Alex.

"I feel like I need to sleep, but the kids will be up soon, and then we need to get ready for the day."

He trailed his hand down her back and cupped her ass. It was more of a casual grab, as if he just liked resting it there. She didn't push him away. In fact, she liked it.

"We can cancel on my family. They'll understand."

She held back a wince. As much as she wanted to do just that, she couldn't. "No, we can't. We can get the kids up, feed them, and then maybe take a nap before we go. I know your mom will understand, but Tessa never liked me, and not showing up will just make it harder."

Luc had been honest and told her exactly what Tessa had been saying. It cut deep, but at least he didn't keep things from her. She needed to prove to the other woman, as well as herself, that she was worth Luc's attentions and care.

"I hate that you feel you need to do that, sugar. They'll understand," he repeated.

"And maybe I could use a distraction from what's going on."

He met her gaze and nodded. "Okay, then." His mouth tilted up. "I have an idea of another distraction if you want. Plus, it will save water."

She shook her head. "That's a bad line."

"Let me take care of you," he whispered. "You took care of me yesterday. Now it's my turn."

"Won't you get tired of taking care of me?"

He cupped her face. "Never."

****

He got them both naked and into the shower, his movements slow, careful. He turned on the spray, careful to let his back take the brunt of it. Meghan's eyes closed as he massaged shampoo into her hair. She let him move her around like a puppet, groaning every so often when he dug his fingers into her scalp.

"Feel good, sugar?"

"You always feel good," she murmured. She opened her eyes and put her hands on his stomach. "Make love to me, Luc."

He swallowed hard. "I don't have a condom, baby."

"We don't need one. We're both clean, and I'm on the pill."

He nodded at his cock, standing at attention at the thought of being in her bare. "Okay, baby. You know I'll always want you." He cupped her face, knowing he might be making a mistake, but he couldn't help it. "I love you, Meghan."

Her eyes widened, and he held back a curse. "Luc."

"No, don't say anything. It's too soon for you, and you have too much on your mind, but I needed to say it. Now let me love you, let me make love to you." He kissed her before she could respond, knowing he'd taken the coward's way out. He hadn't been able to hold back his feelings any longer, not when things were so raw with Alex's words and actions.

He had no regrets, but damn. They might have taken a turn that he couldn't find a way back from.

She gripped his cock, her eyes narrow. "Make love to me," she repeated.

He licked his lips then leaned down to do the same to hers. Careful of the slippery floor, he turned her around so her hands rested on the wall. He moved her feet apart.

"I'm a little too tall for this, but we can make it work," he said, his cock pressing between her ass cheeks.

"I trust you," she said softly, and he almost cracked.

He bent at the knees, gripped her hips, and slid into her in small strokes. They both moaned, breathing heavily. He fucked her slowly, taking the time for them to come over the crest together, their bodies slick and pressed against one another. He cupped one breast, holding her close, and came when she did. When she turned her head, he took her mouth, putting every emotion he could into the kiss.

He fucking loved this woman and knew, one day, she'd love him too. Right then though, it wasn't about that, wasn't about the fear of the unknown. It was about him and her, Luc and Meghan.

Now. Then. And every moment in between.

****

"Will Mrs. Dodd like me?" Sasha asked from the backseat.

Luc pulled Sasha out of the truck and set her down on her feet as Meghan came around with Cliff. "My mother will love you," he said then leaned down and kissed Sasha's cheek.

Another part of Meghan's heart ached hearing his words, seeing the way he cared for her baby.

The man loved her.

Loved. Her.

And yet she hadn't said it back. Why hadn't she?

Oh, yes, that's right. I'm a coward.

She pushed that out of her mind, though, because she needed every ounce of strength she could get. Her body ached, her mind whirled, and exhaustion threatened to take over, but she couldn't back down. Makeup covered the dark circles under her eyes while caffeine and determination kept her moving. She'd do this dinner, show Luc she cared for him, even if she hadn't been able to say the words he needed to hear, and then go home.

Did she love his man? Did she even know what love was?

She'd fucked up before, and now fear that she'd do it again took away her ability to make a clear decision and listen to her heart. Luc hadn't said a word about her lack of a response, nor had he seemed surprised that she hadn't said it back.

That, above all else, told her how much she'd screwed up.

That this man would love her, not knowing whether she would ever be able to say it back—or perhaps couldn't—spoke of the strength of his character and heart.

Meghan didn't deserve Luc Dodd, but she'd be damned if she'd let him go. She was so fucking selfish. She couldn't say those three words that meant the world to him. Meant the world to her. She wasn't ready and that killed her.

The front door opened, and thoughts of love and Luc were pushed away because now she needed to steel herself for what might happen at this dinner. Cliff slipped his hand in hers, and she looked away from the incredibly gorgeous older woman on the front porch and down at her son.

"Ready?" she whispered.

"I guess."

She used her other hand to fix his hair. "I'm here no matter what, Cliff. Remember that."

He let out a sigh and nodded. Damn, she missed her baby boy. He still refused to tell her what was wrong, but at least he'd started to warm up to Luc. That had to mean something.

"There you are!" Maggie Dodd smiled at them and moved forward, her arms outstretched. She hugged Luc close, kissing him on the cheek. "There's my baby."

"How can Luc be a baby? He's big."

Sasha blinked up at Maggie, and Meghan held back a smile. She remembered Maggie from when she and Luc had hung out years ago. The woman's fierceness shone through in her protectiveness of her children, but she'd always had a kind word for Meghan.

Maggie laughed and shook her head. "He might be a big boy now, but he'll always be my baby. Much like you and your brother will always be your mom's babies."

"I'm not a baby. I'm a big girl." Sasha smiled as she said it, the gap slowly closing as her permanent tooth grew in. Had it really been that long since Luc had helped her with the tooth fairy? It seemed like a blink of an eye.

"You can be both to moms," Maggie said then knelt down. "I'm Luc's mom, Ms. Maggie. You must be Sasha."

"Uh-huh." Sasha peeked over at Luc, who have her a small nod. Meghan's heart clutched at the sight. "It's nice to meet you and thank you for having all of us over."

Maggie grinned. "You are very welcome, Sasha." She stood up with Luc's hand on her arm. She turned, and Meghan sucked in a breath. This was it. *Meeting the parents.* "Meghan."

"It's good to see you, Ms. Maggie." She'd called Luc's mother that years ago, and it seemed natural to do it again.

Maggie came over and patted Meghan's cheek. "You can call me Maggie now, you know. You have babies of your own."

Meghan leaned into Maggie's touch, the maternal vibe she carried soothing some of the worries she'd felt coming that day. "This is my son, Cliff."

Maggie winked and looked down at Meghan's son. "Nice to meet you, Cliff."

"Nice to meet you too, Ms. Maggie," Cliff mumbled.

Meghan squeezed her son's shoulder in assurance. He wasn't being rude, but he wasn't the happy boy he'd once been. Meghan hoped this wasn't permanent.

"Well, I think we should go inside so you can see my other babies, as well as my husband," Maggie started up the walk. "I didn't mean to monopolize you all in the front lawn. It's not exactly the warmest weather out here."

Luc shook his head. "You couldn't wait for us to knock on the door. We get it."

"Shush, you," she said with a laugh.

They walked into the comfortable ranch-style home and took off their coats. Luc's father, Marcus, looked just like a slightly older version of his son. In fact, if this was what Meghan had to look forward to in the future, she'd be one lucky woman. That stray thought didn't scare her as much as it should have.

Still a coward, though.

Luc's sisters, Tessa, Jillian, and Christina were much like Meghan remembered. They were each older than she and Luc but had aged well. Like when they were younger, Jillian and Christina warmed right up to Meghan. They smiled, hugged her, and the children, and made Meghan feel at home.

Tessa, however, was just like her old self.

Meghan hadn't needed Luc's warning when it came to his eldest sister's feelings, considering the cold shoulder and even colder looks Tessa gave her, even with Maggie and the rest looking on.

Ouch.

She still wasn't sure what she'd done to Tessa in this life, or even a past one, but whatever it was, Meghan knew she'd need to get past it. Luc loved her. *Loved* her. And if she could get her head out of her ass, she could have a future with him.

Any future with him would have to include Tessa—cold glares and all.

"We're eating in the dining room today since there are so many of us," Maggie said as she put her arm around Cliff's shoulders. Cliff didn't pull away. Instead, he smiled at her.

Meghan held back a relieved breath, and from the look in Luc's eyes, he hadn't missed the action either. Progress, she thought, progress. Maggie pulled Cliff toward the table and sat him right beside her. Meghan ended up sitting between Sasha and Luc with Tessa directly in front of her. She didn't think it was an accident the other woman had chosen to sit there.

Oh boy, this was going to be fun.

They ate a feast of fried chicken, beef roast, two different kinds of potatoes, and three different kinds of vegetables. She ate well at Montgomery dinners, but Maggie Dodd knew how to cook. When she told her that, Maggie beamed with pleasure.

Luc leaned over and kissed Meghan's temple. Warmth spread through her, and she turned her head to smile at him. It wasn't as weird as she thought it would be, joining his family for dinner as if they were a couple with a bright future.

Because, if she let herself be happy, let herself be loved, they *did* have a bright future.

Luc had spent countless dinners with her family already. He'd spent many nights at her house eating with her kids as well. She knew part of the reason he felt so at home with the Montgomerys was because of her brothers and the fact that he'd done it so many times before she and Luc even thought of being a couple.

"So, is this serious?"

Meghan blinked and turned toward Tessa, though not so fast that she missed the tightening around Luc's eyes.

"Huh?" She hadn't been quite prepared for Tessa's question. Sasha leaned into her, and Meghan slid her arm around her daughter.

"Is this serious?" Tessa asked again, a spark of anger in her eyes. "I mean you're here with your children, parading around like you're a married couple and whatnot. Is this serious?"

"Tessa. Stop it."

Meghan cleared her throat and put her hand on Luc's knee. "No, Luc. Let's just get this out of the way." She leaned down and kissed Sasha's hair. "Can you and Cliff go watch TV in the living room for a minute? As long as it's okay with Ms. Maggie."

Maggie narrowed her eyes at her eldest daughter then nodded. "Go ahead, babies. This won't take long."

Cliff and Sasha left, allowing Meghan to rein in her emotions. She wasn't the Meghan she'd been even six months ago. She'd grown, found the confidence she never thought she had, and wouldn't sit back and let this woman's attitude ruin anything she had with Luc. Whatever else was going on with Tessa, this wasn't truly about Meghan. She understood that. However, she needed to stand up for herself.

"Now that my children are out of the room, I can answer your highly inappropriate question."

Tessa cocked her head, her eyebrows raised. "How is it inappropriate? You're dating my brother and now parading your family around here like you're part of us. That's fine, I guess, if you're going to be here for longer than a weekend of fun. But how do we know that? You were friends with him for years without ever being with him, and now you're all over him. It makes me suspicious. I mean I know you have issues with your ex, but how is that Luc's problem? He's spending more and more time with you helping deal with your kids and your ex that he's not focusing on himself. Do you even know he's had problems at work because he's with you? Do you even care?"

Meghan took a deep breath, squeezing Luc's knee so he would let her speak first.

"Wow, that is a lot of hate in one diatribe. I'm sorry you feel that way about me, that you have so little trust in a relationship that has nothing to do with you, that you feel it's okay to lash out like that. However, you are not part of this relationship. You weren't when we were younger and only friends, and you aren't now."

"You broke my brother's heart and made him leave Denver," Tessa snapped.

"Tessa. You know better than that," Luc cut in, his voice low, angry.

"I've got this, Luc." She let her gaze leave Tessa's so she could meet Luc's. She patted his cheek and smiled. "I've got this," she repeated.

From the look in his eyes, she knew she'd annoyed him, perhaps even hurt him in that she wouldn't let him take care of her, but she needed to do this. If she didn't, Tessa would never back down. Of course, she might not ever back down anyway, but that wasn't going to be Meghan's issue after this.

"I didn't know Luc's feelings then." Meghan surprised herself at how calm she sounded. It hurt like hell that she'd broken his heart when they were younger, but she hadn't known. Hadn't seen. He hadn't told her. This was now, and they were all grown up and different people. "However, whatever happened back then, I did not force him to move away. Not in the way you're thinking. Now I might have missed out on him in my life for ten years, and I will always regret that, but I got my children in the middle of it all. I can't forget that fact either. I don't know what your problem with me is. It could be that you knew Luc's feelings for me back then, but I didn't know."

"It doesn't make it better," Tessa snapped.

"It makes it mine. This is not your relationship. What happened in the past is over and is between Luc and me. However, you said something about my children, and that is something I cannot ignore. You can hate me and not want me for Luc, but you will *never* say anything negative about my children or the situation they are in. What happens in their lives and what my ex wants to do is none of your concern. Luc is amazing and standing by my side because he wants to, because he cares about me. I will *never* take advantage of that."

Meghan raised her chin, her hand firmly in Luc's. "If you're going to act like this every time I'm around, then I'm going to ask you not to be near my children. I can take a lot, but you will not say anything negative around my children. Do you understand me?"

Tessa looked away, her chest heaving. "I want what is best for my brother."

"So do I, Tessa."

Tessa stood up and strode out of the room. None of Luc's family followed her, instead looking as lost as Meghan had once felt.

"I need to apologize for my daughter," Marcus said softly.

Meghan shook her head. "No, you really don't." She met his gaze then Maggie's and their other daughters'. "I care about your son. He's important in my life, in my children's lives. And that's all I want to say about that if it's okay with you."

Luc leaned over and kissed her cheek before pulling her into his arms. "It's more than enough."

She sighed, knowing it wasn't quite enough. She'd stood up for herself and Luc, and for her children, and she admitted what was going on with Richard, but it wasn't enough. She'd told Tessa her feelings but not all of them. How could she do that if she hadn't told Luc she loved him?

Because she did. Loved him with all of her heart.

And she'd tell him.

Soon.

CHAPTER SIXTEEN

She didn't love him.

Or at least she hadn't told him.

Luc tried to not let that bother him, but he couldn't help it. He'd bared his soul, and she'd held him close, not saying a thing back. Yet, he couldn't be hurt by it. Saying "I love you" to someone declared his feelings. That didn't mean he should expect a response. That wasn't what it was all about.

If anything, he'd grown past what had held him back all those years ago. When they were only friends, and he was forced to watch her marry that bastard, he hadn't spoken up. That had been on him, and he knew that.

Now he'd spoken from the heart and would need to deal with the consequences. He knew she cared for him and wanted him in her life. She also leaned on him and opened up for him more than she ever had before. They'd made progress, and he hoped over time she'd come to love him.

That didn't mean it didn't hurt like hell.

He pinched the bridge of his nose and took a deep breath. He was at work, for God's sake, mooning over the woman in his life rather than doing the last few checks before they could punch out on the project site and move on to the next step.

"Hey, you ready to go through the checklist?" Wes said as he came up to Luc's side. He had his tablet in his hand and a pencil in his mouth. Since the guy currently didn't *need* the pencil because he had the tablet, it had to be a nervous tic of Wes's.

"Just about." Luc pulled out his notes, Meghan almost completely out of his mind until she came up to them.

"Hey, boys. We talking punching out?" She smiled at him, and he couldn't help but smile back. He didn't lean down and kiss her, but damn, he wanted to. Instead, he moved a fraction closer so he could feel her heat.

Wes looked up long enough from his tablet to snort then went back to work. "Yeah, just waiting on Decker, and then we can go through the list one more time so we can move on."

Luc rolled back on his heels and smiled. "I love this part. Everyone's moving around doing a hundred different things at once yet working like a team that's been together for years. By the end of the day, we'll be ready to move in the custom pieces and furniture for showing while Meghan can do the final touches she needs to on the landscaping." He met Meghan's eyes, and she winked. "Pretty cool if you step back and think about it."

"Well, we don't have that kind of time since we're right on schedule," Decker said as he walked up, rubbing between his shoulder blades as he did so.

Luc hadn't spoken much to Decker beyond work issues since his wedding, but he knew he was living in his own dream world with Miranda. From the look on his face, the man was fucking happy as hell—even with how the wedding had ended.

"Stop being so gloomy," Meghan remarked as she leaned into Decker for a quick hug. "Is my sister not treating you right?"

Decker rolled his eyes. "Miranda is doing fucking amazing, thank you very much. I'm just tired."

Luc ran his tongue over his teeth. "Not sleeping much?"

Decker barked out a laugh as Wes groaned. "You could say that."

"Oh, for the love of God, please don't tell me any more about my baby sister than I need to know." Wes glared at Luc. "You started it, and now you're done." He waved his hand between Meghan and Luc. "It's bad enough I get to see you both stealing little glances here and there at work, now I get this from Decker. I swear our family business is becoming a little too chummy."

Luc just shook his head and wrapped an arm around Meghan's shoulders. She let out a little gasp then hugged his waist. Since they were trying to make Wes uncomfortable, he might as well have her in his arms while they did it.

"I know for a fact your parents kissed on the job site, and Harry even played grab-ass with his wife when he thought no one was looking," Luc said. "He couldn't help it. He loves his wife."

Luc froze for a second at the word love but then let out a breath.

"Yeah, well, we're running a tighter ship around here now," Wes said, holding back a smile. "You guys don't do too badly with working together while you're seeing each other, so I really can't complain."

"Thanks, boss," Meghan said dryly. "So, how about we get back to work?"

Luc rubbed her shoulder then pulled away; the time for play had passed. They went through the rest of their list for the day, and Luc nodded along, answering when he needed to.

"I cleaned up the mess Steve left me," Luc said a few minutes in. "He fucked up my boxes and cut wires. I had to go through the whole fucking house to make sure there wasn't something missing." He shook his head, anger radiating through his veins again at what the bastard had done. "It pisses me off that he thought he'd get away with it. And what's worse, if I hadn't noticed in time, someone could have gotten hurt just by turning on the power to the wrong outlet."

Decker lifted his lip in a snarl. "I'm glad we booted his ass. The drywallers are pissed they had to redo part of the house, but it's not my problem. Some of them just blindly followed Steve." The man raised his chin. "That will not be happening again."

Luc let out a sigh. "Good, because it's fucking annoying working with a man like that."

Meghan rubbed his arm, and he sent her a small smile. He knew she didn't feel great about what had happened, but it wasn't her fault that some wingnut had an issue with him.

"Our new supplier came in on time, and that helped." Wes frowned at his notes but didn't seem worried. "We're going to be using them on the next project, too. Stan's out of luck with this, and we're done with him for good."

"Good," Decker, Meghan, and Luc said at the same time, pulling a laugh out of each of them.

"On that note, I've got to go back to work and get ready to punch out," Luc said as he squeezed Meghan's hand. "We got all we need?"

"Yep," Decker said. "You let me know if you need another man. I know you're short-handed today since

Tommy called in sick, and you had to take extra time on Steve's mistakes."

"Will do," Luc said then headed on into the project house.

He winked at Meghan on his way in, pleased when she winked back. Yeah, she hadn't told him her feelings yet, but things were going well. It wasn't awkward working together, and now that Steve had been fired, no one on the job site had an issue with Luc and Meghan being together. At least they hadn't overtly shown their displeasure.

He nodded at a few of the guys inside and went back to checking boxes and voltage. Since the house wasn't one they'd built from scratch, his job had been harder than usual. Add into that the fact that Steve and Stan had fucked him over and Luc was glad this job was almost at an end. Soon they'd be able to start on the next one and move on.

An hour later, Luc rolled back to his heels and studied the house from the outside. "I think we're ready to turn on the full breakers for the punch out."

Decker punched his shoulder, a grin on his face. "I know this is your favorite part."

Luc shook his head. "No, my favorite part is the beginning when it's a blank canvas. But now? Now ranks pretty up high up there."

He went back inside and turned on the main breaker, pleased when the overhead light fixture turned on. A job well done.

The loud explosion outside rocked him to the bones.

The scream that followed shook him to his core. "Meghan!"

He snapped off the power, just in case, and then ran outside. Out of the corner of his eye, he saw smoke and fire billowing from the meter on the side of the house. However, his attention was for the woman on the ground in front of him.

"Baby?" He skidded across the newly planted grass and gripped her shoulders. "Are you hurt?" He looked over his shoulder. "Call an ambulance."

"I'm fine, Luc." She latched onto his arms, her face pale and a bit dirty, but he couldn't see any blood. "The force of the explosion knocked me down. I screamed because it surprised me. But I'm not hurt." She moved to cup his face. "Really. I'm fine."

"Luc! Is Meghan okay?" Wes ran over to them, panic on his normally calm face. "Shit, little sister, let me call an ambulance."

Meghan shook them off and stood up. Or at least tried to. He gripped her waist and held her against him. He didn't trust himself to allow her to walk on her own right then. His pulse thudded in his ears, and his body shook.

"I'm fine. Unless someone else is actually hurt, I don't need an ambulance. Now did you take care of the fire?"

Wes nodded, and Luc turned to look at what had caused the problem in the first place. "Fuck. Is that the meter?"

"Yeah, it looks like it overloaded and blew. Decker has the fire out, and we're going to go take a look." Wes met Luc's eyes. "I know you checked all the breakers and boxes beforehand, but how the hell did it overload like that?"

Luc raised his chin, his heart not slowing. Meghan squeezed his hip, centering him. "It shouldn't have. Fuck. Let me go take a look."

He kissed the top of Meghan's head, not caring who saw, then stomped over to the meter on the side of the house. Someone had used a fire extinguisher on the damn thing, but the side of the house didn't look damaged. If anything, they'd gotten to it quickly enough that only the meter would need to be replaced. Unless, of course, he'd fucked up the wiring of the entire house, causing the meter to overheat and explode like it had.

Luc knew for a fact he hadn't done that. The hairs on the back of his neck stood on end, and he cursed. Fuck, if someone had tampered with the wiring, or anything else, they could have killed someone.

He narrowed his eyes at the partially melted meter, his gaze zeroing on a piece of copper tubing that sure has fuck shouldn't have been there.

"Holy hell."

"What?" Decker bit out.

Luc shook his head and pointed. "It's too hot for me to touch, and frankly, you're going to want to leave it here and call the cops so they have evidence. Someone stuck a fucking piece of copper tubing across the lugs on the meter. It's phase to phase so the damn thing short-circuited. When I turned on the power to the whole house, it was too much, and the meter exploded. It made more of a sound than is normally warranted, but that is why it did what it did." Luc fisted his hands on his side. "Someone did this on propose."

Decker let out a string of obscenities that would make a sailor proud. "Steve."

"Steve's my best bet unless there's someone else out there with a vendetta against me."

"You didn't get him fired. He did that himself," Wes bit out beside him.

Small hands pressed against his back, and Luc leaned against Meghan ever so slightly. She could have been *killed* because of that fucking bastard. He struggled to rein in his temper. He'd scared Meghan the last time this had happened, and though they'd made progress, he wasn't about to do it again.

"Fuck," Luc muttered.

"I'm calling the cops," Wes said as he pulled away. "Keep people out of the area. This shit is messed up."

"If it's any consolation, I don't think I'm going to need to replace anything except the meter on this," Luc said, his voice subdued. "It shouldn't set us back too much unless the authorities need us to."

Wes shook his head. "I built in time for emergencies. We'll be *fine*."

Luc hoped he was right because, fuck, this sucked. By the time the cops left, their day had been wasted, and Luc just wanted to go home and drink a beer. The whole thing nagged at him, and he wanted to shower and try to get smell of bitter defeat out of his skin.

"I called Maya, and she has the kids for the night," Meghan said softly. "I'm coming home with you."

He raised a brow at her tone. Gone was the timid Meghan who'd backed away when he got angry at someone else. This was the Meghan that sniped at him when her truck wouldn't start and he got too close. He fucking loved this Meghan. Of course, he loved all shades of her.

"You sure you just don't want to go home and sleep off the day? It's been a hell of a day."

She rolled her eyes and stood on her tiptoes in front of him. "Yeah, it's been a suck-ass day. Hence why I'm coming home with you. Someone tried to sabotage my family's project house and zeroed in on your work. It pissed me the hell off, and now I want to go home with you and make sure you know it's not your fault. If I have to get naked and sweaty to do it, well..." She let out a dramatic sigh and fluttered her eyelashes. "Well, I guess that's just something I'll have to do."

His cock went rock hard, and he snorted at the innocent look on her face. "I think the naked and sweaty can be arranged."

She smiled full-out then reached around and slapped his ass. "Now get into your truck and get home. I'll follow you."

He leaned down and captured her lips in a kiss. "Thank you," he whispered.

Her head tilted, and she scrunched her brows. "For what? I haven't even done anything yet."

"But you're going to, and you're here. It's all I can ask for." Oh, he could ask for a hell of a lot more, but he wouldn't quite then. Not yet.

She kissed his chin then pulled away. "I'll see you soon. Drive safe."

He watched her go and shook his head. She might not have said the words yet, but he damn sure felt them in each move, each caress. He'd wait for however long it took for her to find it in her heart to see what they had. He only hoped it wouldn't take too long.

By the time he pulled up to his place, Meghan had already parked and gone inside. He'd given her a key the week before, and he had one for her place. It only made sense considering they'd been dating for long enough and had been friends for far longer. It was just one step closer to him having everything he wanted.

When he walked in, he swallowed his tongue.

Meghan wore his leather jacket.

Only his leather jacket.

The damn thing covered her breasts and reached the top of her legs, but fuck, she looked so edible. When she moved toward him, the flashes of skin between the slightly open folds of the coat made him groan.

"You were fast," he croaked.

"You drove slow. Gave me enough time to pull this off." She reached up and cupped his face. "I want you to push work from your mind. Steve will be taken care of, and the project house is in great shape. You're not in trouble, and we're moving on. Tonight is just about you and me."

He traced the soft skin between her breasts, his gaze on hers. "You sure do know how to take care of me."

She licked her lips. "It's easy to do." She blinked up at him, and he let out a breath. "I love you, Luc. I'm so sorry I didn't say it before. I've felt it, but I was too scared to do anything about it. I'm sorry I hurt you when I didn't say it back, but I'm saying it now. I love you with all of my heart, all of my soul. You're my future, my past, and my present. I'll never forget the feeling of knowing you love me, and I never want to."

Luc swallowed hard, not believing the words coming from her mouth. Holy hell. He hadn't expected this, hadn't expected *her*.

"You're everything, Meghan," he whispered. "I fucking love you so much. When you were on the ground today?" He swallowed hard. "It was like part of my heart had been pulled out and I was left a shadow of a man. Even if only for a moment."

She shook her head. "I was fine. I *am* fine. I want a future with you, Luc. I don't know what that means in every detail, but I'm done being afraid of what I feel, of what could happen. I know I can get through anything because you're on my side. You always have been, and it took me far too long to realize that."

He cupped her face, his hands shaking. "I love you, Meghan Montgomery."

"I love you too, Luc Dodd." She reached up and kissed his chin. "Now fuck me, make love to me, show me everything you have because I can't wait to find out everything I can about you, soul and all."

"Anything you want, Meghan. Anything." He crushed his mouth to hers, his body shaking. "The leather jacket on you is fucking hot, sugar."

"It's yours." She laughed as he slid his hands under the leather to cup her ass, spreading her cheeks.

"You can wear my clothes any time you want." He latched onto her neck, sucking, biting, savoring.

He walked toward the hallway then groaned. "I don't think I can wait." He undid his jeans and shook them off his hips. "Hop on, sugar."

"Hop on? Seriously?" She opened her mouth to laugh then groaned when he slammed into her in one thrust.

He fucked her hard against the wall, his body shaking and holding hers up. He had one of her knees practically up at her shoulders and the other leg wrapped around his waist. He pistoned in and out of her sweet cunt as he bit and sucked on her lips.

"I fucking love you, Meghan."

"Love you more," she panted.

She winked at him then slid one hand between them. He thought at first she was going for her clit, but then he sucked in a breath as she squeezed the base of his cock, moving her hand with each of his thrusts.

"Come, Luc. Fuck me harder and make me come with you."

He licked his lips and moved faster. "As you wish." Her eyes rolled as he slammed into her one more time, and they came together. His knees shook, and he slowly lowered them both to the floor. "Holy fuck, woman, I can't move."

She patted his shoulder lazily. "You better get moving soon. I want to suck your cock in the living room, and then I want you to eat me out on the table. We have a lot of space to cover and not a lot of time."

He groaned at the images those words brought to mind and cupped her ass, his finger playing with her hole. "I'm going to fuck you here one day."

"Good."

"How did I become so lucky?" he asked, holding her close.

"You waited for me to see," she whispered. "You waited."

He'd have waited a hell of a lot longer, but he didn't say anything. Instead, he rolled her over and slid into her from behind on the floor. They made love slowly then moved to each room of the house until they were both spent, out of breath, and in need of nourishment.

He fucking loved his Meghan and would always crave her. The fact that she loved him too? Icing on the best cake ever. Fucking icing.

CARRIE ANN RYAN

CHAPTER SEVENTEEN

Meghan gripped Luc's hand, sweat rolling down her back. She could do this. She could do anything with Luc by her side. In fact, she could do anything on her own as well. Having him there made her only that much more sure.

Of course, today wasn't a normal day.

No, today they were meeting in chambers with her lawyer, Richard, his lawyer, and the judge who would hear their case. If things went well for Richard, they'd go to the next step in the proceedings. If they went well for her, she'd go home to her babies and have Richard out of her life for good this time.

Of course, there were countless possibilities, and she had dwelled on each and every one of them. She honestly had no idea how today was going to go considering Richard had the money to back his plans, and she had only her honesty and evidence she'd been the sole caregiver for her children long before Richard had walked out that front door, bags in hand and a sneer on his face.

Luc squeezed her hand again, and leaned toward her. He brushed his lips over her temple, and she let out a breath. Tension still radiated through her, but his presence made it bearable.

"I'm still not sure why Richard asked me, no, demanded I come," Luc said softly.

She turned toward him and fixed his tie. "Because he knows you're in my life now, and he's going to try to use that against us. What he doesn't know is that you're much more than just a part of my life. You're also a part of Cliff's and Sasha's."

Luc smiled down at her but didn't kiss her. Considering where they were, she didn't blame him.

He stiffened and looked behind her when the elevator dinged. She turned around, her chin high, knowing who would be there.

Richard looked the same as always, his hair smoothed back, his jaw set. On his arm, a tall blonde looked down at Meghan and Luc, her eyes narrowing.

So this was Ambrosia. Her children's stepmother. She and Richard had married the previous month without letting Meghan or the children know. It had hurt her babies, she was sure of it, but they'd shrugged it off. The fact that Cliff and Sasha had to shrug off anything made her angry. However, this wasn't the time for anger. This was the time for cool and collected facts that would show her to be the mother her babies needed and kick Richard to the curb for good. There was no way this woman would get her paws on Meghan's children. If Ambrosia truly wanted children, it didn't matter what childbirth would do to her body. Meghan's stretch marks were a badge of honor, and Luc kissed them nightly.

She'd gain more stretch marks to have Luc's children, but that was a subject for another day.

"Meghan, Luc." Richard's voice slid right over her. The sneering tone didn't make her feel worthless this time. Instead, it made her feel only a little pity for the man who'd done his best to break her and failed.

Richard might have thought she was broken, but she'd only bent.

She wouldn't bend anymore.

"Warren vs. Montgomery-Warren?" a clerk said from an open doorway.

Meghan would have to get rid of the Warren part at some point. Her children might be forced to have the name, but she hated it. Though having the same last name as Cliff and Sasha helped out in legal things and traveling. She let out a sigh. Great, now her mind was going off on tangents.

Time to get a move on and protect her children.

Meghan rolled her shoulders and turned away from Richard, not bothering to be civil and acknowledge his presence. They were here today because Richard felt the need to try and destroy her life. She'd fight with everything she had and more.

Fuck him and the blonde bitch he rode in on.

She held back a wince at that mental image. So not the time.

The two parties sat on opposite sides of a long table. Meghan pulled at the bottom of her dress, her hands shaking. Luc, who sat on her right, tugged at her hand, and she stopped fidgeting. She met his gaze, and the strength she'd worked so hard to resurrect slid over her. Yes, she could do this.

Her lawyer—a shark who had once worked with Griffin on a novel—cleared her throat and nodded at the opposing party. Meghan honestly didn't want to do this. If things went sour, then she'd be forced to bring Sasha and Cliff in. She wouldn't be able to protect them as much as she had so far.

"We're here in the custody matter of Cliff and Sasha Warren," the judge, an older black woman, said slowly. She put on her reading glasses and nodded over the papers in front of her. The lines at the edges of her mouth deepened as her lips thinned.

"I'm not quite sure how this case ended up on my docket," she said, her voice strong.

"Judge Hastings—" the opposing council began.

"No, it's my turn to speak," Judge Hastings cut in. "I understand you asked for Judge Bower for this case, but he was unavailable."

Meghan blinked, her back going ramrod straight. What did this mean? Had Richard wanted Bower because he had the man in his pocket? She risked a glance at her ex-husband and held back any visible emotional reaction. Richard looked downright pissed.

What was going on?

"I am not quite sure how this case has gone as far as it has, but now that I have it, I'm making the final decision," Hastings continued. "Richard Warren has no case. He signed off full custodial rights during the divorce proceedings and now is coming in with a change of heart. Instead of clearly stating why he wanted the children in his care, he sent out page after page of why the current custodial parent was not good enough. Not once did he mention that he wanted the children at all."

Anger burned through Meghan's veins. How dare that bastard paint her as an unfit mother? He wasn't a father. He'd never been a father. It took more than a sperm donation to be part of that. He'd done his best to discredit her and add in drama and fear she didn't need. She hoped to God the judge saw that fully.

"Like I said before, this case should never have been brought before me." She held up her hand as Richard's lawyer tried to speak. "You're lucky I don't look back into the divorce proceedings and previous custodial rights agreements too hard. I'm not going back and changing what was already written and agreed upon. Mrs. Montgomery-Warren will retain full custodial rights. Mr. Warren had the previously agreed upon visitation. However, in light of the fact that he hasn't visited the children once in the past year this has been in place, I'm adding that his visitations will be supervised visitation only." The judge turned and addressed Richard directly. "Mr. Warren, you've not once visited your children in all this time. If you had, perhaps things would have gone differently for you. I am dismissing this case with prejudice. Should you attempt another end-run, Mr. Warren, I assure you it will go hard on you. Court is adjourned." The judge got up and left without so much as a glance at those in the room.

Meghan blinked, unsure of what she'd just witnessed. She'd won? She could keep her babies?

How...how had that happened so quickly? Her lawyer came up to her and said congratulations. Meghan could only nod, not able to comprehend much of anything else at the moment.

Luc pulled her up, and she walked on shaky legs out of the room, leaning heavily on his large body.

"What just happened?" she whispered.

"I think you won," Luc whispered back, his body shaking much like hers.

It didn't make sense. Everything had happened so fast she wasn't sure what she was doing. She sucked in a breath, knowing she needed to leave the building before she did something stupid like throw herself at the judge and thank her.

Instead, she wrapped her arms around Luc's middle and beamed up at him. "I can't believe it."

"It hasn't settled in yet."

She shook her head and rested her cheek on his chest. His heart beat against her ear, and she smiled.

Of course, her smile only lasted a moment when she caught the look in Richard's eye. The bastard didn't sneer like usual. No, this was something far more dangerous.

The man seethed.

Ambrosia flounced by him, and he snarled something before turning away from Meghan and Luc. She let out a sigh then sucked in a breath as Luc's arms tightened around her.

"I don't like that man."

"I don't either," she whispered, knowing the walls had ears. "Let's go home to the kids."

Home.

It didn't escape either of them that she'd said it as if they were a family in more ways than one. One thing at a time, but damn if it didn't sound right to say home with Luc in the same sentence.

He kissed her head, and she smiled.

Yes, things would be all right.

Finally.

****

Luc ran a hand over Meghan's shoulder as they sat on the couch, watching Cliff and Sasha play knight and dragon on the living room floor with Boomer playing guard. The sound of children's laughter and the sweet tinkle of Meghan joining in calmed him. He hadn't had any idea of what to expect walking into those chambers that morning, but now that it was over, all he could do was breathe out in relief. He had the woman he loved in his arms and the children he loved as his own playing in front of him. He couldn't ask for more.

Of course, he could ask for a lot more, and he knew that would come. Meghan loved him, and the kids looked to him for advice and genuinely liked him being around. That was a hell of a lot more progress than he'd ever thought possible when he gave Meghan a ride to the project site all those months ago.

There was only one thing left that needed to be taken care of, though, before they could take the next step.

"Hey, Cliff, can you come here a minute."

Meghan leaned up and gave him a questioning look, but he shook his head.

Cliff frowned but came toward them until he stood in front of the couch. Sasha, curious as ever, bounced until she sat next to Luc, leaning on him and smelling like little girl and jam. Seriously, the kid was always sticky and tended to have damn jam hands, but he loved her.

"What is it?" Cliff asked, his voice low and a little scared.

"You know your mom and I had a meeting with the judge today, right?" Luc asked.

Meghan sat up straight and put her hand on his knee. After they got home, they'd told the kids some of what had happened. They explained that they wouldn't have to leave and that Meghan would always be there. Both kids had looked relieved, but there was still something off with Cliff.

It was far past time for them to deal with that.

"Yeah," Cliff said softly.

"Now that you know you're here with us always, why don't you tell your mom and me what's been bothering you?" He had a feeling he knew, but Cliff had to be the one to say it. It had gone on for far too long, and Meghan hurt every day because of it.

"I..." The little boy shuffled from foot to foot.

239

Damn it. Well, maybe Luc had to be the one to say it after all. Or at least get the ball going.

He leaned forward, moving so both of his arms rested on his thighs. This put him at Cliff's eye level. "You know your dad left because that was his problem, right?"

Meghan sucked in a breath, and Sasha burrowed into his side. "Luc," Meghan whispered.

He didn't respond to her, his eyes on Cliff's alone. "He left because he had problems of his own. He did *not* leave because of you. He did *not* leave because of something you did. Or because of something Sasha did. Or because of something your mom did." He swallowed hard, Meghan's fingernails digging into his side. "What happened was not your fault. Not. Your. Fault."

Cliff's eyes filled with tears, and he shook his head. "Dad said I was bad. He said I was too loud and not nice to Sasha. That's why he left."

"Oh, baby," Meghan said, pulling her son into her arms. She soothed his back as he cried and she murmured to him.

Luc turned and brought a crying Sasha into his arms. She curled up, and he leaned into Meghan, knowing all four of them needed each other now more than ever. Boomer jumped onto the couch, though he wasn't supposed to, and leaned on Meghan's other side.

"Your dad left because of his own issues," he repeated once Cliff and Sasha settled down. He cleared his throat. "Your mom is never going to leave you. *I* am never going to leave you."

Meghan met his gaze, her eyes wide, and she nodded. "We're here to stay, Cliff. Your dad said things that hurt all of us, but no matter what, he can't hurt us again. The four of us are here together, and we're going to stay that way." She cupped Cliff's face and kissed his forehead. "I'm sorry I didn't know what was wrong before. I'm sorry I couldn't make it better."

"I'm sorry I was a brat."

Meghan hiccupped a laugh, and Luc shook his head. "You weren't a brat."

"You might have been a little bit of a brat," Luc deadpanned, and Meghan shushed him. "I know what your dad did sucked, and he was wrong. But you don't have to keep it all inside, Cliff. We're here, and we're not leaving. Okay?"

Cliff nodded, his tears finally subsiding. "Okay," he whispered.

Sasha patted Luc on the chest, and he looked down at the little bundle in his arms. "I love you, Luc."

His throat caught, and he swore his eyes filled with tears. "I love you too, Sasha baby."

He kissed her on the cheek, and she snuggled close. He turned to Cliff and patted him on the knee. "Love you too, kiddo."

Cliff smiled every so slightly, and it was as if a weight had been lifted off his chest. "Love you, Luc."

Meghan hiccupped a sob and waved her hand. "Don't mind me. I'm just crying because I'm happy."

Cliff leaned forward and whispered loudly to Luc, "She does that a lot, but that's because she loves us."

Luc threw his head back and laughed then wrapped his arm around Meghan, pulling her and Cliff close. "That she does, Cliff, that she does." They were a family right then. Maybe not something legal on paper, but that would come.

He wanted to marry Meghan and adopt her children. That was something he couldn't deny, and he didn't want to wait much longer.

Soon, he told himself. Soon.

They leaned on each other a bit more before the doorbell rang. He frowned at Meghan then stood up, setting Sasha on the couch in his vacant space.

"You expecting anybody?"

She shook her head. "No, the family usually texts before they stop by."

Something off settled over him, and he ran a hand over the back of his head. "I'll get it then. Maybe it's just a salesmen."

"In this neighborhood?" she asked. She wiggled out from under Cliff but remained on the couch by the kids and Boomer.

Yeah, they'd have to talk about her neighborhood soon. He had more than enough room for everyone at his place. That, however, would be something they discussed later—after he dealt with whoever had come to Meghan's house.

He looked through the peephole and cursed. "Meghan, get the kids and Boomer to the back."

She stood up, her eyes wide. "Who is it?"

He looked at the kids then back at her. "Who do you think?" He didn't want to alarm them any more than he already had, but he had a bad feeling about this.

Meghan closed her eyes for a moment then took the kids to the back of the house with Boomer.

Luc had his phone in one hand, ready to call the cops if needed, then opened the door. If he didn't, then Richard would stand out there all night making a scene. That was the kind of bastard Meghan's ex-husband was.

"What the fuck do you think you're doing answering Meghan's door?" Richard demanded.

This was going to shit fast.

What are you doing here?" he asked, not bothering to answer Richard's question.

"I'm here to talk to Meghan about what she has done."

"Excuse me?" Meghan asked, squeezing between Luc and the door.

Luc held back a curse and pushed her back so she could still see Richard but wouldn't get hurt if the other man lashed out.

"You heard me," Richard snarled, spittle forming at the corner of his mouth. "Ambrosia *left* me because you fucked everything up for me. I always knew you were a selfish bitch, but fuck you."

Luc took a deep breath. Killing this man on Meghan's front porch wouldn't help anyone, even if it would make him feel slightly better.

"You need to go," Luc said, his voice low.

"You don't own this property. You can't tell me to go."

"No, but I can tell you to go. I don't care if your wife left you. That's not my fault. Nothing you think I've ever done to you is my fault. You've deluded yourself into thinking that and emotionally bruised me until you got your way. But no more. Now go away."

Richard clenched his jaw and turned ever so slightly to face Meghan.

"It is your fault, Meghan. It is *always* your fault."

Richard moved so fast Luc almost missed the reflection of the streetlight off the barrel of the gun. He pushed Meghan back, knowing even the small glimpse Richard got of her would make her the target.

Only he wasn't fast enough to protect himself.

It didn't matter.

Only Meghan mattered.

The burn arced across the right side of his chest, and he let out a grunt. Time moved slowly at that point, his knees going out from under him, Meghan's screams piercing his ears.

Boomer barked from somewhere in the back, and he prayed the kids wouldn't see him bleed, wouldn't see him die.

He blinked up at the ceiling, knowing somehow he'd landed on his back, or maybe Meghan had pushed him there. Blood pooled in his mouth, and he tried to reach out, tried to force Meghan to duck.

He didn't know if Richard was still around, still aiming at her.

He had to protect her.

He had to save her

But he was too late.

The darkness came, and the pain went away.

His last thought was of Meghan and her touch. He loved her touch. Too bad he'd never feel it again.

CHAPTER EIGHTEEN

Death came in many shades, many scents, many dreams, but today was not the day she'd let the man she loved die. Meghan held a throw blanket to Luc's chest, her hands shaking. Blood seeped around the towel, her fingers looking as if she'd dipped them in rust. Only his chest moved—everything else was stock-still. But at least he breathed.

The kids had run out into the entryway, but she'd screamed at them to go up to their room. She'd heard them sob on their way back to the room, taking Boomer with them. They shouldn't have to see this. Shouldn't have to see the man who was more of a father to them than the man responsible for their blood look like this. She could focus only on Luc, and yet she knew she needed to worry about her children and Boomer, too. It was all too much. Richard had run away as soon as he'd fired the shot, but she couldn't tell what would happen next. What if he came back? What if she couldn't get Luc to safety? What if she wasn't enough?

Damn it. No. That was *not* who Meghan was anymore.

She kept one hand on the wound and reached out for the phone Luc dropped when he hit the ground.

"I'm on the phone with the ambulance now," a woman said, her voice oddly calm.

Where did she come from? "I...I can't stop the bleeding."

Meghan saw the woman nod out of the corner of her eye. She knew this woman. Crap. From where? Yes! She was the one who'd gotten a tattoo from her brother. Odd that these were the facts Meghan chose to focus on rather than the man she loved bleeding out under her hands.

"I'm Autumn. Your new neighbor. Weird coincidence." The other woman took a deep breath. "It'll be okay," she said softly.

"How can you know that?" Meghan snapped then immediately regretted it. "How...how are you here?"

Autumn put her hands over Meghan's, helping with more pressure. Meghan looked down at the blood coating her hands, and bile rose in her throat.

"I live next door, remember?" she replied, her voice calm, as if trying to talk to a child. "I heard the shot and came right over."

Meghan would wonder about that later—what kind of woman would run toward a gunshot rather than away. However, she couldn't think about any of that right then.

"You can't die, Luc Dodd. You can't leave us. I love you. Please. Please don't die."

She said that over and over again, her words blurring until someone pulled her off him. She fought to go back, but Autumn whispered in her ear that she had to let the paramedics take care of him.

"I'll take care of the children," she was saying once Meghan snapped out of it. "Let me wash my hands, and I'll take the kids. I'll call whoever you need me to. Go with your man in the ambulance and talk to the police when you can. I'll help your babies."

Meghan stood up on shaky legs. "I...I need to see them before I go."

Autumn shook her head. "You don't have time, and you have blood on your shirt and pants. You'll only scare them. I'll call your family. Promise."

Still numb, she nodded then followed the paramedic and got into the ambulance, answering questions when she could. Luc was not allowed to die today. He'd healed her in more ways than she thought possible. If only she could heal him too.

Three hours later, she couldn't think. The waiting room seemed impossibly small, and no one had told her anything. Autumn had come through, having called Meghan's parents from the number Meghan had on her fridge. From there, her parents had called all of her siblings, as well as Luc's family. Someone had brought her an extra set of clothes so she didn't have to see Luc's blood anymore.

Now everyone sat or paced in the small waiting room, eager for any news about Luc. Not everyone, she thought. Alex was still in rehab, and Austin and Sierra had stayed home with their children, as well as Sasha and Cliff. Autumn and Callie were with Sierra, helping keep everyone as calm as possible.

She owed Autumn more than she'd ever be able to repay.

Only she needed to know Luc was safe and *alive* before she could think too hard about that.

"Baby, sit down," Maggie said as she patted the seat beside her. "The doctors will come soon."

Meghan did as she was told and took Maggie's hand. Marie moved from where she sat next to Meghan's father and sat on the other side of Meghan. Placed between the two matriarchs of the families in the room, Meghan held on for dear life, praying and trying not to think too hard about what could happen.

"Are the police done questioning you?" Decker asked, his voice deep, solemn.

Meghan blinked then nodded, grateful to speak about anything other than her fear for Luc. "Yes. Richard dropped the gun before he fled, so they'll have that evidence, too. They said they'd find me once they caught him."

Miranda leaned into her husband, and he wrapped an arm around her shoulders. "I'm glad Austin and everyone are at his house with the children."

Meghan let out a shaky breath. "Me, too. The police don't think Richard would try to find..." She couldn't finish the words, not with her chest squeezing so tight.

"The children are safe," Storm whispered as he came to kneel before her. He held onto her knees, and she nodded. "Austin won't let any harm come to those in his care. If you want, Wes and I can head over there to help."

She blinked at her brother, her lower lip wobbling. She would *not* cry. Not until they knew Luc was safe. She was only barely keeping it together as it was.

"We can do that, Meghan," Wes said, his hands in his pockets. "Give us something to do. Tabby'll come with, right?"

The Montgomery Inc. admin nodded, her long red hair in a messy bun on her head. She'd come in with Wes and Storm. She wasn't family, but she was part of the crew and Luc's friend. "Of course. We'll check in with the children and the others, then bring food if you need it. How about that?"

Meghan just nodded, her throat tight. Her family ended up in this goddamn waiting room too many times. In the past two years, they had bled, been through treatments, and taken years off her life. This had to be the last one. She didn't know if she could handle it again.

As long as Luc was all right though, she knew she'd find the will to handle anything.

Another thirty minutes passed after the trio left, and Meghan found herself sitting by each family member, Luc's family, and even Jake. Jake just held her, knowing she needed it. He didn't give her a pitying look, though, only whispered she could do this, she could do anything.

Luc's sisters sat together, their hands clasped as they whispered in prayer. Tessa wouldn't look at her, but Meghan couldn't find the energy to care. She already blamed herself as it was. She didn't need Tessa to do it as well. Yes, Richard had pulled the trigger, but Luc had been the one to step in front of her, taking the bullet meant for her.

"Dodd family?" An older man in scrubs came through the door, and every single person stood up. The man's eyes widened at the sight of so many people—many of them large, bearded, and inked—in one spot.

Meghan couldn't speak. And as she wasn't married to Luc, Maggie and Marcus had to be the ones to do so. The law didn't care about love and promise, only paperwork and blood ties.

"That's us," Marcus answered, his voice firm, deep, so much like Luc's that Meghan wanted to cry. He looked over his shoulder at everyone and held out a hand. Meghan gripped it like a lifeline, coming to his side while Maggie stood on the other. "All of us."

The doctor nodded. "Luc is stable and out of surgery."

He continued on, explaining something about a punctured lung and other injuries that hadn't been as severe, but Meghan couldn't hear it all. She blinked, her vision blurring. Her ears hummed, a loud buzzing sound growing with each breath. Her knees shook, and suddenly she was in Griffin's arms, his hand on her face.

"Meghan?" Griffin asked, his hand cupping her cheek. "Meghan? Did you hear? He's okay. He's going to be fine. A hundred percent after he recuperates. Meghan?"

She tried to speak, but everything she'd been holding in threatened to burst.

Vaguely she heard the doctor come near her and check her pulse. "Has she eaten?" he asked.

Her family answered for her, and she struggled for breath. Damn it. She'd passed out, bringing the focus to herself rather than on Luc like it should have been. She waved everyone off and tried to stand. Griffin pulled her up to her feet, worry etched on his face.

"I'm fine," she said, her mouth so dry she felt as if she'd swallowed cotton. "I just got overwhelmed." She took a deep breath then stood without aid. "I'm fine," she repeated. "Sorry for scaring everyone. When can we see him? Or did you say that when I was out of it?"

The doctor leveled her a look. "Drink some fluid and get something in your stomach, young lady. Doctor's orders."

"We'll take care of her," Meghan's mother said from behind her.

The doctor nodded. "Good. See that you do. As for Mr. Dodd, he's in the ICU for the evening, and you will be able to go in two at a time tomorrow to see him."

Meghan shook her head. "Tomorrow?"

"Yes, tomorrow all of you can see him. As for tonight, I'll let two of you go now to see him for five minutes, but that's it. He's still under and will need time and rest in order to heal. We'll go over the technical aspects of his recovery soon."

Meghan's heart ached, but she didn't move forward when the doctor stepped back toward the door. Luc's parents deserved to see him. Meghan could see him in the morning. She could be that strong.

Marcus, evidently, had other plans. He kissed her temple and put Meghan's hand in his wife's. "Go see my boy and tell him we'll be here for him."

Her eyes widened. "But..."

"No buts, young lady. He's yours. I know that. Be strong for my son, Meghan."

"I'll try," she said softly, tears threatening again. She still hadn't cried, wasn't sure she could without breaking down completely.

She gripped Maggie's hand tightly and followed the doctor back through the long hallways as patients, nurses, staff, and other doctors went about their business around them.

By the time they made it to where Luc slept, her pulse was beating loudly in her ears.

"Sweet Jesus," Marie whispered beside her, and Meghan held the other woman's hand for dear life.

Tubes and wires seemed to connect to almost every part of his body, though she knew that wasn't the case. Someone had pulled a blanket up over his chest but under his arms so the darkness of his skin lay stark against it. The doctor had said he'd wake up soon and would be able to live a normal, healthy life. None of the damage was permanent; it had just scared her to death.

They weren't allowed to touch him, but Maggie leaned over her son, whispering a prayer. Meghan stood on the other side of him, resisting the urge to hold his hand. She didn't want to hurt him, didn't want to do anything to hamper his recovery.

"Come back to me, Luc. Come back to us. I...I love you, Luc Dodd. You don't get to leave me." The numbness that had allowed her to function started to wear off, and she knew she had to get out of there soon or she'd break down in front of the world.

A single tear fell down her cheek, but she didn't brush it away—nor would she let another tear fall. By the time they were forced to leave him alone, her body shook, but she still didn't break. Griffin drove her to Austin's after she said her goodbyes to the others. She knew her voice was wooden, her actions stiff, but she couldn't function until Luc woke up. They wouldn't let her sleep there, wouldn't let her hold him.

"The kids are asleep in Leif's room," Sierra said softly, reaching out once Meghan walked inside. "It took a while, but they finally passed out."

"Meghan," Austin said simply and held out his arms. Meghan let her big brother hold her, but she, again, didn't break. Instead, she pulled away after a moment and met her brother's eyes.

"Can I take a bath?" she asked, knowing she needed to be alone.

Austin gave her a weird look but nodded. "Of course. You can use Sierra's and mine. It's big and has jets."

"Anything will be fine," she whispered.

She followed him back to the master bath and watched as he pulled out a towel for her, his movements slow, as if he was afraid of scaring her away.

"I'm fine, Austin. I just need a moment or two alone and I'll be better." She raised her chin, her hands shaking. "He almost died," she whispered. "He almost died, and Richard was the one who did it."

Austin pinched her chin, the pain bringing her out of her head. "That bastard is on his way to jail as soon as he's caught. He won't hurt you and yours again. As for Luc? He's not dead. You know I went through hell with Sierra, and Decker did the same with Miranda. We all healed, and you will do the same. I know you love that man, and he's like a brother to me as well. He's safe, Meghan."

She licked her lips, her body trembling. "I...I know that. Our family though? I'm tired of doctors."

"I know, babe, I know. Now take a bath, cry, drink some water or wine or whatever you need Sierra and me to bring you, and know we're here for you when you get out. I know it would be weird if Griffin and I were in here, but you know Sierra would be here in a heartbeat if you need her."

She put her hand on Austin's broad chest. "I know. Thank you, Austin."

"You're a Montgomery, Meghan. Never forget that. We don't."

With that, he kissed her on the nose then left the bathroom, closing the door behind him. Meghan turned on the taps on the bath, letting the hot water steam in the room. She stripped down, remembering the last time she'd taken a bath when she felt like this.

The day Richard left her she'd put her babies to bed and had taken a bath so she could break down.

Now, she slid into the bath, the hot water burning but just enough that it made her *feel*.

Tears slid down her cheeks as she wept once again like she had before, but this time for a man she truly loved. A man who'd almost been taken away because he loved her so much he'd risked his life for her.

Her body shook in the hot water as she sobbed.

He was alive.

He breathed.

He'd be okay.

He was *hers*.

Meghan wouldn't wait any longer for him, wouldn't take the slow course when it came to having Luc in her life. She'd almost lost him once, twice if she counted his leaving town. She wouldn't lose him again.

Luc Dodd was hers, forever and after.

Hers.

****

One Month Later

Luc rolled his eyes as Sasha did a little dance in his living room. No, make that *their* living room. Meghan and the kids had moved into his place as soon as Luc was able to come home from the hospital. They hadn't slept another night in the home where Richard had destroyed the sense of peace they once had.

Luc's fist tightened at the thought of the bastard who now sat in prison, his court case coming up. There was no doubt the man was guilty, and they had sufficient evidence to prove it. Now all that was left was to see how long he would spend behind bars.

Well, that and get Richard to sign over all parental rights so Luc could adopt Sasha and Cliff as his own.

One thing at a time though. First, he had to marry their mother. He smiled at that thought. He still hadn't proposed, though he wanted to. Every time he got close, he'd stop, wondering if he was going too fast. Then he'd kick himself, considering he knew how short life could be, the bullet that had sliced into his lung being evidence for that.

Meghan walked into the living room, her smile bright and her arm around a laughing Cliff. "Pizza for dinner okay tonight?"

"Sounds good to me," Luc answered, kissing her when she sat down next to him on the couch. He still wasn't a hundred percent, but he was getting there. Having Meghan by his side helped.

"Good because I'm craving cheese," she said with a laugh.

"Weirdo," he whispered then let out a sigh when she leaned on his uninjured side. She'd been so careful not to touch him that these touches now meant the world to him.

"Your weirdo," she said back.

"True." He met Cliff's eyes, and the little boy gave Luc a quick nod. It wasn't the most romantic place, but damn if it wasn't perfect anyway

He pulled away from Meghan and smiled. "I love you."

She frowned at him. "I love you too. What's wrong?"

He snorted. "Why does anything have to be wrong?" He reached under the pillow on the couch and pulled out a jewelry box.

"Oh, my God," Meghan whispered, her eyes filling with tears. "Yes. You know the answer is yes."

"Seriously? You're not even going to let me ask the question? I've been waiting a decade to have you as mine, and you won't even let me ask?"

"She said yes, Luc!" Sasha squealed and danced again, bringing her brother into it. Cliff, with the reluctance of an older brother, let her twirl him around.

"Why don't you ask so I can say yes again?" Meghan whispered, tears streaming down her cheeks.

"We haven't been together that long, Meghan, but you're my everything. You're already in my home, my heart, and my life. Now, please, be my wife."

"You rhymed!" Sasha giggled, and Luc crossed his eyes at her.

"Did you mean to rhyme?" Meghan asked.

He let out a soft curse, and Meghan slapped his knee. "No, I didn't, but the message is the same. Love me, Meghan. Marry me."

"Yes," she said quickly then cupped his face, her lips soft, wanting.

He bit her lower lip then pulled back. "Damn it, Meghan, I love you. You realize that, right? I love you with everything I have and those kids too. I'm so glad I came back to Denver to see my best friend. So fucking glad."

She patted his cheek and smiled. "You're my best friend, Luc, then and now. It took me too long to realize that I had everything I wanted in my life without looking. I'm blessed with you, even if it took me too long to find the words to say it." She winked. "Though this means you have to get the Montgomery tattoo."

He snorted. "You're going to be a Dodd, sugar. Why should I get a tattoo?"

"I'll be Meghan Montgomery-Dodd because, *babe*, once a Montgomery, always a Montgomery."

He brought her closer, careful of his injury. "That I can live with, sugar. Montgomery ink and all." He had his best friend and lover in his arms, their children laughing beside them, and a life filled with more than he could have hoped for.

It had taken a decade of wandering for him to realize that life for him lived within Denver and within this woman's arms. Sometimes it took more than a word, more than hope and a prayer.

Sometimes it took ink, blood, and tears—a sacrifice worth that and more.

Coming Next in the Montgomery Ink Series:

Griffin gets a story of his own in WRITTEN IN INK

A Note from Carrie Ann

Thank you so much for reading **HARDER THAN WORDS**. I do hope if you liked this story, that you would please leave a review. Not only does a review spread the word to other readers, they let us authors know if you'd like to see more stories like this from us. I love hearing from readers and talking to them when I can. If you want to make sure you know what's coming next from me, you can sign up for my newsletter at www.CarrieAnnRyan.com; follow me on twitter at @CarrieAnnRyan, or like my Facebook page. I also have a Facebook Fan Club where we have trivia, chats, and other goodies. You guys are the reason I get to do what I do and I thank you.

Make sure you're signed up for my MAILING LIST so you can know when the next releases are available as well as find giveaways and FREE READS.

The Montgomery Ink series is an on going series. I hope you get a chance to catch up!

Montgomery Ink:
Book 0.5: Ink Inspired
Book 0.6: Ink Reunited
Book 1: Delicate Ink
Book 1.5 Forever Ink
Book 2: Tempting Boundaries
Book 3: Harder than Words
Book 4: Written in Ink (Coming Soon)

About Carrie Ann and her Books

New York Times and USA Today Bestselling Author Carrie Ann Ryan never thought she'd be a writer. Not really. No, she loved math and science and even went on to graduate school in chemistry. Yes, she read as a kid and devoured teen fiction and Harry Potter, but it wasn't until someone handed her a romance book in her late teens that she realized that there was something out there just for her. When another author suggested she use the voices in her head for good and not evil, The Redwood Pack and all her other stories were born.

Carrie Ann is a bestselling author of over twenty novels and novellas and has so much more on her mind (and on her spreadsheets *grins*) that she isn't planning on giving up her dream anytime soon.

www.CarrieAnnRyan.com

Redwood Pack Series:
Book 1: An Alpha's Path
Book 2: A Taste for a Mate
Book 3: Trinity Bound
Book 3.5: A Night Away
Book 4: Enforcer's Redemption
Book 4.5: Blurred Expectations
Book 4.7: Forgiveness
Book 5: Shattered Emotions
Book 6: Hidden Destiny
Book 6.5: A Beta's Haven
Book 7: Fighting Fate
Book 7.5 Loving the Omega

Book 7.7: The Hunted Heart
Book 8: Wicked Wolf

The Talon Pack (Following the Redwood Pack Series):
Book 1: Tattered Loyalties
Book 2: An Alpha's Choice (Coming Aug 2015)
Book 3: Mated in Mist (Coming Soon)

The Redwood Pack Volumes:
Redwood Pack Vol 1
Redwood Pack Vol 2
Redwood Pack Vol 3
Redwood Pack Vol 4
Redwood Pack Vol 5
Redwood Pack Vol 6

Dante's Circle Series:
Book 1: Dust of My Wings
Book 2: Her Warriors' Three Wishes
Book 3: An Unlucky Moon
The Dante's Circle Box Set (Contains Books 1-3)
Book 3.5: His Choice
Book 4: Tangled Innocence
Book 5: Fierce Enchantment
Book 5.5: Fallen for Alphas (Coming Soon)
Book 6: An Immortal's Song (Coming Soon)

Montgomery Ink:
Book 0.5: Ink Inspired
Book 0.6: Ink Reunited
Book 1: Delicate Ink
Book 1.5 Forever Ink
Book 2: Tempting Boundaries
Book 3: Harder than Words
Book 4: Written in Ink (Coming Soon)

The Branded Pack Series:
(Written with Alexandra Ivy)
Books 1 & 2: Stolen and Forgiven (Coming Aug 2015)
Books 3 & 4: Abandoned and Unseen (Coming Sept 2015)

Holiday, Montana Series:
Book 1: Charmed Spirits
Book 2: Santa's Executive
Book 3: Finding Abigail
The Holiday Montana Box Set (Contains Books 1-3)
Book 4: Her Lucky Love
Book 5: Dreams of Ivory

Excerpt: Alluring Ink

Ink is forever. So is love. Try Ranae Rose's Inked in the Steel City Series and get to know the staff of the Hot Ink Tattoo Studio as they find love in the Steel City.

ALLURING INK

Love is risk. Love is heartbreak. Love is an addiction a single mom like Crystal can't afford. And accomplished tattoo artist Dylan is a temptation she can't resist. He's only in town for a few weeks as a guest artist, but the attraction is instant. With her past shadowing everything she does, it feels good to have someone who doesn't judge ... and doesn't know.

Love is just the spark before the crash and burn, especially when your demons are something more than standard-issue. Dylan craves Crystal with everything he has, but their days together are supposed to be numbered.

Book 7 in the Inked in the Steel City Series

* * * * *

CHAPTER 1

Crystal sat on the edge of her seat in the café across from the Hot Ink Tattoo Studio, clutching her purse. As she stared through the glass panel windows, she scanned the foot traffic streaming by for any sign of her brother's blond hair. When he finally appeared, she stopped holding her breath.

She couldn't remember the last time she'd been so giddy. She tapped her toe against the tile as he caught her eye, nodded and entered the café.

"I already ordered for us," she said when he approached the little table she'd claimed. "Your usual. I know your schedule is tight lately."

"Thanks. How much was it?"

She shook her head as he pulled out his wallet.

"It's my treat." She waved a hand as a pang of guilt sailed through her. "Just sit down."

He tried to give her money but she refused. Their mini-argument was cut short when a barista called out the number on her receipt, and she went to get their food.

James seemed happy with his lunch, but Crystal had to force herself to take a bite of her turkey and pesto sandwich. She'd been waiting so long to have this conversation with her brother – she'd dreamed of it ever since she'd returned to Pittsburgh a year ago, straight out of rehab and deeply in his debt. Now, it was finally real.

It was the biggest step in the right direction she'd taken since making the decision to do rehab.

"I asked you to meet me because there's something I need to talk to you about," she said.

His expression changed just a little, his green eyes darkening and the muscles around his mouth tensing.

"It's good news," she hurried to say. "I'm moving out."

"You are?" He set down his sandwich and locked her in eye contact, as if looking for some sign of a joke.

"Yes. I signed the lease on an apartment yesterday."

"Where at?" He launched into a series of questions, grilling her on the neighborhood and amenities, the cost of rent and a dozen other things. She waved a hand. "It's only a few blocks from your place." She described the complex she'd be moving into.

Slowly, he nodded. "Neighborhood's okay, and you'll have me nearby, but... Can you afford it?" His gaze was deep and searching, almost sad. "I know they don't pay you a lot."

She couldn't hold back a smile, even though he was right – she wasn't exactly raking in the big bucks working in cosmetics at a department store. "You're right about that. But I have a secondary source of income."

Actually, her job at the make-up counter had more or less become her secondary source of income. She was making more money from her other work – a fact that had had butterflies whirling through her stomach for months now.

James raised his eyebrows. "You do?"

"Yes..." She took a deep breath and tried not to give away how excited she was about revealing her big secret. "You know how much I love make-up artistry."

He nodded, his gaze lingering on her face. She actually wasn't wearing much make-up today.

Okay ... so she'd gone a little buck wild with some new eye make-up samples she'd received from a start-up cosmetics company, but she'd taken it easy with everything else, brushing on just a hint of blush and gloss.

"Yeah," he said. "Judging by the number of boxes that've been delivered to our apartment over the past few months, I figured you'd invested most of your paychecks in lipstick."

She frowned. Had he really thought she'd been squandering her money in the name of vanity?

Maybe she should've told him what she'd been up to sooner. It was just that her success had seemed so unreal at first – still did, really – that she hadn't wanted to jinx it.

"I didn't pay a dime for most of that stuff," she said. "The manufacturers sent me the products to review. I've been making my own make-up how-to videos for the better part of a year now. I started just a couple months after I moved in, and I've built up quite a following. I even have my own website."

His brow creased. "How've you been making money from that?"

She grinned. "Advertisements. They play before my videos start and I run them on my site, too. It may not sound like much, but my web traffic and viewers have increased so much over the past few months that I'm earning pretty good money."

At least, the amount she was earning seemed phenomenal to her – all the jobs she'd ever held had been in food service and retail. Being able to make more than a pittance above minimum wage doing something she loved was a dream come true.

James sat frozen, his coffee cup in hand. "I had no idea you were doing any of that."

She brushed her long blonde hair away from her face. "I didn't want to tell you at first – I thought you might think it was a waste of time. I started out doing it for fun – to get back in touch with something I love. It'd been forever since I'd felt useful, or good at anything..."

He frowned.

"It was just my little hobby," she said, "but it's really taken off."

"I'm happy for you. But will it last?"

She shrugged. "I've been working hard at educating myself on how to make the most of it. Anyway, I've been saving my earnings. After getting my most recent check, I had enough to pay the deposit and first month's rent on my apartment, and to pay you back."

"Pay me back?"

"For all the money you spent on Emily while I was away. I have enough to reimburse you for what I figure you spent on daycare, formula, diapers and all that. If my math is wrong just—"

"No," he said. "Keep your money. You're probably going to need it."

She froze. Keep the money? There was no way she could do that.

She'd been living with James for about a year now and she'd spent every single day of it riddled with guilt over the burdens she'd imposed on him, financial and otherwise. She couldn't make up for the fact that she'd stuck him with caring for a newborn for several months, but she could at least compensate for the money she'd cost him.

It was the least she could do, and he wasn't going to talk her out of doing it.

"No way," she said. "When I moved in with you, I said I'd pay you back as soon as I could, and that's exactly what I'm going to do."

"I don't need your money. I have more clients than ever, and Arianna and I have been planning to move in together whenever you move out. So my cost of living will almost be cut in half."

Another twinge of guilt fired through her. She knew very well that her and Emily living with James had been holding him back from moving in with his girlfriend, Arianna. Getting the hell out of their way was probably the nicest thing she could do for them.

"Even so," she said. "I want to pay you back. I won't feel right until I do."

"Keep the money to fall back on. Or use it to start a college fund for Emily. I won't take it."

College. While Crystal was determined to give Emily a better life and the shot at success that she and James had never been provided, she wouldn't use the money she owed him to do it.

"C'mon," he said when she opened her mouth to protest. "I don't want your money. I don't want Emily to have to scrape and claw her way toward being able to support herself someday, either. Save it for her education."

Crystal frowned. The news she'd been so eager to share with James had turned into a battle of wills. She and James shared more than just their blond hair and green eyes – they were both equally stubborn.

"I appreciate your generosity," she eventually said, "but... The truth is, I need you to take the money so that I don't feel like such a loser. I've been looking forward to the day I'd finally be able to pay you back for an entire year. Until I do that, the weight of the world is going to stay on my shoulders."

He looked genuinely surprised. Putting down his sandwich, he met her eyes and pressed his hands against the table. "You're not a loser. You've turned your whole life around, and that's a hell of a lot more than most people could ever do."

Heat crept into her cheeks, and she stared into the depths of her coffee, embarrassed. Didn't he think of her as an annoyance sponging off of his generosity?

That was what she felt like.

He grabbed her hand and wouldn't let her pull away. "I'm proud of you. Don't ever think that I'm not."

She mumbled something about all that he and Arianna had done for her, her emotions swirling in a haze of reluctant pride and mortification.

She wished so badly that she'd never messed up her life in the first place, that she'd never had to put James in the position she had. Though she was proud of the progress she'd made, she was still deeply embarrassed by her past.

The idiotic things she'd done would shadow her forever, and she knew it. Knew people thought of them whenever they looked at her, and probably wondered if she'd slip up again.

She wouldn't. No matter what. But they didn't know that.

James eventually let go of her hand, and they ate in silence. She used the quiet time to scheme on ways to give him the money. If he wouldn't take it directly, what could she do?

Buy him lunch every day for a year? Get him the best birthday present of all time?

None of the ideas she came up with seemed good enough.

"So," he said when they finished their meals, "I've got a surprise for you too."

"What is it?" She stacked their trays, gathering up their empty plates and coffee cups.

"I finally came up with a design for your tattoo. You'll have to take a look, but I think you're going to like it."

She moved to the edge of her seat as a jolt of excitement hit her. "Really?"

She'd asked him to design a tattoo for her last month, and he'd agreed.

She wanted something to celebrate the transformation she'd been through during the past year – permanent ink to mark a permanent change.

Who better to tattoo her than her brother, who she couldn't have done it without?

He nodded toward the window and the street beyond, where the Hot Ink Tattoo Studio's blue neon sign glowed softly in the August sunlight. "Come on over and take a look."

Get the rest of the story in **Alluring Ink**. Out now.

Tattered Loyalties

**From New York Times Bestselling Author
Carrie Ann Ryan's Talon Pack Series**

Tattered Loyalties

When the great war between the Redwoods and
the Centrals occurred three decades ago, the Talon
Pack risked their lives for the side of good. After
tragedy struck, Gideon Brentwood became the Alpha
of the Talons. But the Pack's stability is threatened,
and he's forced to take mate—only the one fate puts in
his path is the woman he shouldn't want.

Though the daughter of the Redwood Pack's Beta,
Brie Jamenson has known peace for most of her life.
When she finds the man who could be her mate, she's
shocked to discover Gideon is the Alpha wolf of the
Talon Pack. As a submissive, her strength lies in her
heart, not her claws. But if her new Pack disagrees or
disapproves, the consequences could be fatal.

As the worlds Brie and Gideon have always known
begin to shift, they must face their challenges together
in order to help their Pack and seal their bond. But
when the Pack is threatened from the inside, Gideon
doesn't know who he can trust and Brie's life could be
forfeit in the crossfire. It will take the strength of an
Alpha and the courage of his mate to realize where
true loyalties lie.

Find out more in Tattered Loyalties. Out Now.

Delicate Ink

From New York Times Bestselling Author Carrie Ann Ryan's Montgomery Ink Series

Delicate Ink

On the wrong side of thirty, Austin Montgomery is ready to settle down. Unfortunately, his inked sleeves and scruffy beard isn't the suave business appearance some women crave. Only finding a woman who can deal with his job, as a tattoo artist and owner of Montgomery Ink, his seven meddling siblings, and his own gruff attitude won't be easy.

Finding a man is the last thing on Sierra Elder's mind. A recent transplant to Denver, her focus is on opening her own boutique. Wanting to cover up scars that run deeper than her flesh, she finds in Austin a man that truly gets to her—in more ways than one.

Although wary, they embark on a slow, tempestuous burn of a relationship. When blasts from both their pasts intrude on their present, however, it will take more than a promise of what could be to keep them together.

Find out more in Delicate Ink. Out Now.

Dust of My Wings

From New York Times Bestselling Author Carrie Ann Ryan's Dante's Circle Series

Dust of My Wings

Humans aren't as alone as they choose to believe. Every human possesses a trait of supernatural that lays dormant within their genetic make-up. Centuries of diluting and breeding have allowed humans to think they are alone and untouched by magic. But what happens when something changes?

Neat freak lab tech, Lily Banner lives her life as any ordinary human. She's dedicated to her work and loves to hang out with her friends at Dante's Circle, their local bar. When she discovers a strange blue dust at work she meets a handsome stranger holding secrets – and maybe her heart. But after a close call with a thunderstorm, she may not be as ordinary as she thinks.

Shade Griffin is a warrior angel sent to Earth to protect the supernaturals' secrets. One problem, he can't stop leaving dust in odd places around town. Now he has to find every ounce of his dust and keep the presence of the supernatural a secret. But after a close encounter with a sexy lab tech and a lightning quick connection, his millennia old loyalties may shift and he could lose more than just his wings in the chaos.

Warning: Contains a sexy angel with a choice to make and a green-eyed lab tech who dreams of a dark-winged stranger. Oh yeah, and a shocking spark that's sure to leave them begging for more.

Find out more in Dust of My Wings. Out Now.

CPSIA information can be obtained
at www.ICGtesting.com
Printed in the USA
LVOW07s1936111017
552035LV00013B/1361/P

9 781947 007345